GERALD MURNANE was born in Coburg, a northern suburb of Melbourne, in 1939. He spent some of his childhood in country Victoria before returning to Melbourne in 1949 where he lived for the next sixty years. He has left Victoria only a handful of times and has never been on an aeroplane.

In 1957 Murnane began training for the Catholic priesthood but soon abandoned this in favour of becoming a primary-school teacher. He also taught at the Apprentice Jockeys' School run by the Victoria Racing Club. In 1969 he graduated in arts from Melbourne University. He worked in education for a number of years and later became a teacher of creative writing.

In 1966 Murnane married Catherine Lancaster. They had three sons. His first novel, *Tamarisk Row*, was published in 1974, and was followed by eight other works of fiction. His most recent book is *A History of Books*. He has also published a collection of essays, *Invisible Yet Enduring Lilacs* (2005).

In 1999 Gerald Murnane won the Patrick White Award. In 2009 he won the Melbourne Prize for Literature. In the same year, after the death of his wife, Murnane moved to Goroke in the north-west of Victoria.

ANDY GRIFFITHS is one of Australia's most popular children's authors. He has written more than twenty books, including the much-loved 'Just!' and 'Treehouse' series (with the illustrator Terry Denton) and *The Day My Bum Went Psycho*, and has sold more than five million copies worldwide.

andygriffiths.com.au

ALSO BY GERALD MURNANE

Fiction

Tamarisk Row

The Plains

Landscape with Landscape

Inland

Velvet Waters

Emerald Blue

Barley Patch

A History of Books

Non-fiction

Invisible Yet Enduring Lilacs

A Lifetime on Clouds
Gerald Murnane

Text Publishing Melbourne Australia

textclassics.com.au
textpublishing.com.au

The Text Publishing Company
Swann House
22 William Street
Melbourne Victoria 3000
Australia

First published by William Heinemann, Australia 1976
This edition published by The Text Publishing Company 2013

Cover design by WH Chong
Page design by Text
Typeset by Midland Typesetters

Printed in Australia by Griffin Press, an Accredited ISO AS/NZS 14001:2004 Environmental Management System printer

Primary print ISBN: 9781922147455
Ebook ISBN: 9781922148506
Author: Murnane, Gerald, 1939- author.
Title: A lifetime on clouds / by Gerald Murnane; introduced by Andy Griffiths.
Series: Text classics.
Dewey Number: A823.3

CONTENTS

Going to America
by Andy Griffiths

GERALD Murnane is the author of some of the most original books ever written by an Australian. His first novel, *Tamarisk Row*, is an obsessive exploration of the imaginative terrain of childhood. His third novel, *The Plains*, is a meditation on love, landscape and creativity that has an hallucinatory power. The novel that came between these two extraordinary books, *A Lifetime on Clouds*, has long been out of print. And yet it is, for my money, the funniest and most accessible of all his works. It is also a moving and fearless account of adolescent angst. Murnane's frank treatment of sexuality, longing, adult hypocrisy, and the guilt and confusion created by a sexually repressive 1950s Catholic boys' school is as engaging now as when it was first published, in 1976.

The protagonist of *A Lifetime on Clouds* is the fifteen-year-old schoolboy—and self-confessed sex maniac—

Adrian Sherd, who lives in the south-eastern suburbs of Melbourne. By coincidence, in 1976 I was a fifteen-year-old schoolboy living in the south-eastern suburbs of Melbourne and, although I don't think I qualified as a sex maniac (not compared to Adrian Sherd, at least), I did have a strong interest in the subject.

On my bedroom wall I had a poster of Suzi Quatro wearing a partially unzipped white leather jumpsuit, and I was convinced that if I could find just the right angle I would surely be rewarded with a glimpse of her left breast. I spent a lot of time that year with my cheek pressed against the wall, desperately trying—and failing—to penetrate the mysteries of that jumpsuit.

Fortunately, other sources of raw material for my burgeoning interest in the female form were provided by the lurid covers of my horror comic collection, which often featured partially clothed damsels in distress. And I participated in Church of England Boys' Society paper drives that exposed me to such racy publications as the ironically named *Truth* and its steamy Heart Balm letters page, as well as the *Sunday Observer*, which could be relied on to contain pictures of streakers running across sporting fields or down busy city streets. And if all else failed there was always the bra section of Kmart catalogues, although these were only to be called on in emergencies.

But, despite my considerable efforts, I was a rank amateur when measured against Adrian Sherd, who takes a far more systematic approach to his fantasy life. Every afternoon Adrian sets his model train running across a large, crudely drawn map of the United States. Whichever state it stops in will be the setting for one of his vividly imagined nightly escapades with scores of willing and scantily clad starlets, the inspiration for which he gathers from glimpses of the Hollywood movies his mother does not allow him to watch, the pages of the *Argus* newspaper, and coveted and difficult-to-obtain magazines such as *Man Junior* and *Health and Sunshine*.

Adrian brings an admirable rigour to his trips to America and maintains a strict policy not to allow any of the women he sees in real life into his fantasies. On the one occasion he breaks this self-imposed rule, and issues an imaginary invitation to the 'piney woods of Georgia' to a young, 'carefully groomed' married woman he sees on the train, he finds he can't relax.

> Whenever he met her eyes he remembered he would have to face her on the train next morning... It would be hard pretending that nothing had happened between them on the previous night.
>
> There was another difficulty. Jayne and Marilyn and Susan and their many friends always had the same look about them—a wide-eyed half-smile with lips slightly parted. The new woman had an irritating way of changing her expression. She seemed to be thinking too much.

One of the many delights of the novel is the contrast between the debauchery of Adrian's imagined life and the humdrum reality of postwar Melbourne suburbia:

> One very hot Saturday morning Adrian Sherd was staring at a picture of the Pacific coast near Big

Sur. He hadn't been to America for several days, and he was planning a sensational extravaganza for that very night with four or perhaps even five women against a backdrop of mighty cliffs and redwood forests.

His mother came into the room and said she had been down to the phone box talking to his Aunt Francie and now Adrian and his brothers and mother and Aunt Francie and her four kids were going on the bus to Mordialloc beach for a picnic.

The pleasures of America pose a dilemma for our insatiable hero who, increasingly terrified and burdened with guilt, attempts to reform himself—Adrian is Catholic, after all, and has been taught that masturbation is a mortal sin. He does this not by abandoning his fantasies but by redoubling his efforts to create an even more elaborate one, in which he courts, marries and raises a family with a good Catholic girl whom he has seen taking communion in church. This fantasy is so gloriously and painstakingly realised that it occupies most of the last half of the novel. Not only does it weaken the starlets' hold on Adrian's mind, but it makes the second half of the book possibly even more entertaining—and certainly more earnest and affecting—than the first.

There is much to love in this novel and many passages that are profoundly funny—laugh-out-loud moments which, at the same time, evoke strongly felt and often deeply painful emotions. Throughout, Murnane masterfully maintains a deadpan tone.

For instance, Adrian is angry and disappointed that he and his friends have been cheated by Father Dreyfus's much-anticipated sex-education film, which the brother promised would show them 'the moment of fertilisation'. Adrian imagines that, at the very least, this means the film will present them with 'a statue or a painting of a man and woman doing it', but instead they are shown a picture of the female reproductive system and an animated image of an 'army of little sperm men invading the diagram'. 'The commentator got excited. He thought there was nothing so marvellous as the long journey of these tiny creatures. Adrian didn't care what happened to the little bastards now that the film had turned out to be a fraud.'

What follows is one of the most shockingly funny images of the entire book and a great example of how Murnane isn't afraid to go where angels fear to tread. (Okay, it's on page 130 if you can't wait.)

Or consider Father Lacey's speech to Adrian's class, urging them to avoid non-Catholic newspapers:

'There's one Melbourne newspaper in particular that regularly prints suggestive pictures which are quite unnecessary and don't have anything to do with the news of the day. I won't name the paper, but some of you have probably noticed what I'm talking about. I hope your parents have, anyway.

'This very morning for example I happened to notice a picture on one of their inside front pages. It was what they call a sweater girl...

'I'll speak quite frankly now. There are many famous and wonderful pictures of the naked female body with the bosom exposed—some of them are priceless treasures in the Vatican itself. But you'll never find one of these masterpieces drawing attention to the bosom or making it appear larger than it really is.'

And then there are Adrian's delightfully pompous imaginary lectures to his imaginary wife on their imaginary honeymoon in Triabunna, Tasmania.

'I won't beat about the bush, Denise darling. In one sense, what I'm going to do to you tonight may seem no different from what a bull does to his cows or a Hollywood film director does to one of his starlets. (Denise looked startled and puzzled. He would have to explain this point to her later.) It's not a pretty thing to watch, I'm afraid, but it's the only way our poor fallen human natures can reproduce themselves. If it seems dirty or even ridiculous to you, I can only ask you to pray that you'll understand it better as time goes by.'

So fervid is Adrian's imagination that in the course of *A Lifetime on Clouds* he provides nothing less than an alternative history of the world—from the Garden of Eden through to 1950s Melbourne—focusing on the role that masturbation has played in shaping civilisation. We are all familiar with Adam and Eve's crime of eating the fruit of the tree of knowledge, and Cain's slaying of his brother, but, according to the gospel of Adrian Sherd, what Cain did after spying on his mother and sisters as they bathed in the Tigris was even worse.

When he was alone again, he formed his hand into the shape of the thing he had seen between their legs and became the first in human history to commit the solitary sin.

Although it was not recorded in the Bible, that was a black day for mankind. On that day God thought seriously of wiping out the little tribe of Man. Even in His infinite wisdom He hadn't foreseen that a human would learn such an unnatural trick—enjoying by himself, when he was hardly more than a child, the pleasure that was intended for married men only…

Lucifer himself was delighted that Man had invented a new kind of sin—and one that was so easy to commit.

If you only read one Gerald Murnane novel in your life, make it this one. There is so much pleasure to be had from reading this book that it's surely a new kind of sin—and one that is so easy to commit.

A Lifetime on Clouds

PART ONE

He was driving a station wagon towards a lonely beach in Florida—an immense arc of untrodden white sand sloping down to the warm, sapphire-blue waters of the Gulf of Mexico. His name was Adrian Sherd. His friends in the car with him were Jayne and Marilyn and Susan. They were going on a picnic together.

They were almost at the beach when Jayne said, 'O damn! I've left my bathers behind. Has anyone got a spare pair?'

No one had. Jayne was very disappointed.

The sea came into view. The women gasped at the beauty of it under the cloudless sky. Jayne said, 'I can't resist that glorious water. I'm going to have my swim anyway.'

'Will you swim in your scanties and brassiere?' asked Marilyn.

'No. The salt-water would ruin them.'

Sherd pretended not to be listening. But his stomach was weak with excitement.

'You mean you'll swim in the—?' Susan began.

Jayne tossed back her long dark hair and glanced at Sherd. 'Why not? Adrian won't be shocked—will you, Adrian?'

'Of course not. I've always believed the human body is nothing to be ashamed of.'

The grass above the sand was lush and green like a lawn. Sherd and Jayne spread out the picnic lunch. The other two hung back and whispered together.

Susan came over and spoke. 'It won't be fair for Jayne if she goes swimming with nothing on and Adrian is allowed to peer at her all day. Adrian will have to strip off too. That's a fair exchange.'

They all looked at Sherd. He said, 'That wouldn't be fair either. Susan and Marilyn will see me in the raw without having to take their own bathers off.'

Jayne agreed with Sherd that the only fair thing would be for all four of them to leave their bathers off. But Susan and Marilyn refused.

After lunch Susan and Marilyn went into the trees and came back wearing their twopiece bathers. Jayne and Sherd waited until the others were in the water. Then they slipped out of their clothes with their backs turned to each other and ran down the sand staring straight ahead of them.

In the water Jayne dived and splashed so much that it was some time before Sherd saw even the tops of her breasts. At first he thought she was teasing him. Then he realised he was behaving so calmly and naturally himself that she didn't know how anxious he was to see her.

Jayne ran out of the water at last and Sherd followed her back to the car. She stood side-on to him and dried herself, bending and twisting her flawless body to meet the towel.

Sherd couldn't pretend any longer that he saw this sort of thing every day. He stood in front of her and admired her. Then, while she sat beside him with only a towel draped round her shoulders, he made a long speech praising every part of her body in turn. And when she still made no effort to cover herself, he was moved to confess the real reason why he had brought them to the lonely beach.

Jayne was not alarmed. She even smiled a little as though she might have suspected already what was in his mind.

Susan and Marilyn came out of the water and went behind the trees to change. They both stared hard at Sherd as they passed.

Jayne said, 'I still think it's unfair, those two seeing you in the nude and hiding their own bodies. I'm sure you'd like to look at them, wouldn't you?'

She bent her lovely compassionate face close to his and said, 'Listen, Adrian. I've got a plan.'

After this, events happened so fast that he barely had time to enjoy them properly. Jayne tiptoed up behind the other two women. Sherd followed, trembling. Jayne tore the towels away from their naked bodies, pushed Susan into the car and locked the door. Marilyn squealed and tried to cover herself with her hands, but Jayne grabbed her arms from behind and held her for Adrian to admire. Then, while Marilyn walked around swearing and looking for her clothes, Jayne dragged Susan out of the car and showed her to Adrian.

Adrian lost control of himself. He looked just once more at Jayne. Her eyes met his. She seemed to know what he was going to do. She couldn't help feeling a little disappointed that he preferred another's charms to her own. But she saw he was overcome by his passions.

Jayne leaned back resignedly against the car and watched. Even Susan forgot to cover herself, and watched too. And the two of them stood smiling provocatively while he grappled with Marilyn's naked body and finally subdued her and copulated with her.

Next morning Adrian Sherd was sitting in the Form Four classroom in St Carthage's College in Swindon, a south-eastern suburb of Melbourne.

The day started with forty minutes of Christian Doctrine. The brother in charge was taking them through one of the Gospels. A boy would read a few lines and then the brother would start a discussion. 'It will pay us to look very closely at this parable, boys. Robert Carmody, what do you think it means?'

Adrian Sherd had a sheet of paper hidden under his Gospel and a packet of coloured pencils on the seat beside him. He was looking for a way to make the Christian Doctrine period pass more quickly. Instead of drawing his usual map of America showing the main railways and places of interest, he decided to sketch a rough plan of his classroom. He drew twenty-nine rectangles for the desks and marked in each rectangle the initials of the two boys who sat there.

He thought of several ways of decorating his sketch. Because it was a Christian Doctrine period, he chose a spiritual colour scheme. He took a yellow pencil and drew little spears of light radiating outwards from the boys whose souls were in the state of grace.

Adrian awarded his golden rays to about twenty boys. These fellows spent all their lunch-hour bowling at the cricket nets or playing handball against the side of the school. Most of them were crazy about some hobby—stamp collecting or chemistry sets or model railways. They talked freely to the brothers out of the classroom. And they made a show of turning their backs and walking away from anyone who started to tell a dirty joke.

Next Adrian edged with black the initials of the boys who were in the state of mortal sin. He started with himself and his three friends, Michael Cornthwaite, Stan Seskis and Terry O'Mullane. The four of them admitted they were sex maniacs. Every day they met beside the handball courts. Someone would tell a new dirty joke or discuss the sex appeal of a film star or interpret an adult conversation he had overheard or simply report that he had done it the night before.

Adrian blackened the initials of other fellows who were not friends of his but had let slip something that betrayed them. Once, for instance, Adrian had overheard a quiet boy named Gourlay telling a joke to his friend.

GOURLAY: Every night after cricket practice I pull a muscle.

FRIEND: After practice? How come?

GOURLAY: Oh, it happens when I'm lying in bed with nothing to do before I go to sleep.

Adrian marked both Gourlay and his friend in black—the friend because of the guilty way he had laughed at Gourlay's joke.

He took only a few minutes to colour all the mortal sinners. There were about a dozen. This still left nearly thirty boys unmarked. Adrian puzzled over some of these. They were well grown with pimply faces and they shaved every second or third day. They had been seen to smile at dirty jokes and they always looked bored during Christian Doctrine periods. Adrian would have liked to colour them black to boost the numbers of his own group, but he had no definite evidence that they were habitual sinners.

In the end he put a pale grey shadow over the initials of all the remaining boys as a sign that their souls were discoloured by venial sins.

The Christian Doctrine period was still not finished. Adrian drew a yellow cloud above his chart to represent heaven. Down below he drew a black tunnel leading to hell. There was room at each side of his page for more of the universe, so he put a grey zone at one side for purgatory and a green zone opposite for limbo.

He sat back and admired his work. The colours around the initials indicated clearly where each boy's soul would go if the world ended suddenly that morning before any of them could get to confession or even murmur an act of perfect contrition.

None of them could go to limbo, of course, because that was a place of perfect natural happiness reserved for the souls of babies who had died before baptism or adult pagans who had never been baptised but had lived sinless lives according to their lights. But Adrian had included limbo in his chart because it had always attracted him. A brother had once said that some theologians believed limbo might be the earth itself after the General Judgement. They meant that, after the end of the world, God would remake the whole planet as a place of perfect natural happiness.

Sometimes when Adrian realised how unlikely it was that he would get to heaven, he would willingly have traded his right to heaven for safe conduct to limbo. But because he had been baptised he had to choose between heaven and hell.

He slipped his chart into his desk and looked around the room at the fellows he had marked with black. They were an odd assortment, with not much in common apart from the sin that enslaved them. They even differed in the way they committed their secret sin.

Cornthwaite only did it in total darkness—usually late at night with a pillow over his head. He claimed that the sight of it disgusted him. His inspiration was always the same—the memory of a few afternoons with his twelve-year-old cousin Patricia when her parents were out of the house. The girl's parents had told Cornthwaite afterwards that he needn't bother coming to the house again.

Adrian often asked Cornthwaite what he had done to the girl. But Cornthwaite would only say it was nothing like people imagined and he didn't want bastards like Sherd even thinking dirty thoughts about his young cousin.

O'Mullane preferred to do it in broad daylight. He swore he didn't need to think of women or girls. He got his excitement from the feel of whichever lubricant he was using. He was always experimenting with butter or hair oil or soap or his mother's cosmetics. Sometimes he stung or burnt himself and had to give up doing it for a few days.

Seskis only used film stars. He didn't care whether they wore bathing suits or street clothes so long as their lips were red and moist. He sometimes went to an afternoon show in a theatre in Melbourne where he could sit in an empty row and do it quietly through a hole in the lining of his trousers pocket while some woman parted her lips close to the camera.

Ullathorne looked at *National Geographic* magazines with pictures of bare-breasted women from remote parts of the world. He had once offered to lend Adrian one of his best magazines. Adrian admired some bare breasted girls from the island of Yap until he read in a caption under a photo that Yap women sometimes had spiders and scorpions living in their voluminous grass skirts.

Froude used a set of photographs. The man who came to his house to teach him violin used to slip a photo into Froude's pocket after each lesson. Each photo showed a different boy standing or sitting or lying down naked with his penis erect. The boys were all about thirteen or fourteen years old. Froude had no idea who they were. He had asked his music teacher and been told he would find out in good time.

Adrian had seen some of Froude's photos. They were so clear and well lit that he told Fronde to ask the music teacher if he had any similar pictures of girls or women.

Purcell used the nude scene from the film *Ecstasy* starring Hedy Lamarr when she was very young. He had read about the film in an old copy of *Pix* magazine and torn out the picture of Hedy Lamarr floating on her back in a murky river. He admitted it was hard to make out Hedy's breasts in the photo, and the rest of her body was out of sight under the water. But he said he got a colossal thrill just from having a picture of one of the only nude films ever made.

The other habitual sinners were mostly unimaginative fellows who simply made up adventures about themselves and some of the girls they knew. Adrian considered himself luckier than any of them, because he used the whole of the U.S.A. for his love-life.

The Christian Doctrine period ended at last and the class stood and recited the Prayer Between Lessons. The boys in mortal sin looked no less devout than the others. Perhaps they believed, like Adrian, that one day they would find a cure that really worked.

Adrian and his friends sometimes discussed cures for their habit. One day Seskis had turned up at school with the story of a novel cure.

SESKIS: I was reading this little booklet my father gave me. It was full of advice to young men and it said to avoid irritation and stimulation during the night you should wash and soap well around the genitals in the bath or shower.

CORNTHWAITE: Whoever wrote that must be crazy. Did you try it?

SESKIS: Two or three times in the bath. I soaped the thing until I couldn't see it for suds and bubbles. It stood up the whole time and nearly drove me mad. So I had to finish it off right there in the bath.

O'MULLANE: Like the time a priest told me in confession not to eat hot spicy foods for tea or supper. So I only had a slice of toast and a glass of milk for tea to see what happened. Next thing I woke up starving in the night and had to do it to put myself back to sleep.

SHERD: Sometimes I think the only cure is to get married as soon as you're old enough. But I reckon I could stop it now if I had to sleep in a room with someone else so they'd hear the mattress squeaking if I did anything at night.

O'MULLANE: Bullshit. When our parish tennis club went to Bendigo for the big Catholic Easter Tournament, Casamento and me and two big bastards were in bunks in this little room. One of the big bastards tried to get us all to throw two shillings on the floor and make it a race to do it over the edge of the bunks. Winner takes all.

CORNTHWAITE: Filthy bastards.

O'MULLANE: Of course the one who wanted the race was the bastard they call Horse from the size of his tool. He would have won by a mile.

SHERD: Tell the truth and say you were too embarrassed to do it with other people in the room. It proves what I said about my cure for it.

O'MULLANE: I would have backed myself with any money against bastards my own size.

CORNTHWAITE: The only cure is to get hold of a tart and do the real thing to her. O'Mullane will end up a homo the way he's going. And Sherd will still be looking for a cure when he's a dirty old bachelor.

After school each day Adrian Sherd walked from St Carthage's College half a mile along the Swindon Road tramline to Swindon railway station. Then he travelled five miles by electric train to his own suburb of Accrington.

From the Accrington station Adrian walked nearly a mile along a dirt track beside the main road. It was 1953, and outer suburbs like Accrington had few made roads or footpaths. He passed factories whose names were familiar—PLASDIP PRODUCTS, WOBURN COMPONENTS, AUSTRALIAN CARD CLOTHING, EZIFOLD FURNITURE—but whose products were a mystery to him.

Adrian's street, Riviera Grove, was a chain of waterholes between clumps of manuka and wattle scrub. Each winter, builders and delivery men drove their trucks over the low scrub, looking for a safe route, but the only people in the street who owned a car left it parked each night on the main road, two hundred yards from their house.

On one side of the Sherds' house was a dense stand of tea-tree scrub thirty feet tall with only one narrow track winding into it. On the other side was the wooden frame of a house and behind it the fibro-cement bungalow, twenty feet by ten, where the New Australian Andy Horvath lived with his wife and small son and mother-in-law.

The Sherds' house was a two-year-old double-fronted weatherboard, painted cream with dark green trimmings. It had a lawn with borders of geraniums and pelargoniums at the front, but the backyard was nearly all native grass and watsonia lilies. Along the back fence was a fowl-run with a shed of palings at one end. Near one of the side fences was a weatherboard lavatory (cream with a dark green door) with a trapdoor at the back where the night-man dragged out the pan each week and shoved an empty pan in. Sometimes the pan filled up a few days before the night-man's visit. Then Adrian's father would dig a deep hole in the fowl-run and empty half the pan into it. He did it furtively after dark while Adrian held a torch for him.

On the opposite side of the yard was a fibro-cement shed with a cement floor and a small louvre window at one end. One half of the shed was filled with bags of fowl-feed, garden tools and odd pieces of broken furniture. The other half was left clear. Leaning against one wall of the shed was a plywood door left over after the Sherds' house had been built. A model railway layout was screwed onto one side of the door. It was a Hornby clockwork layout—a main track with a loop and two sidings.

The Sherds' house had three bedrooms, a lounge, a kitchen, a bathroom and a laundry. The kitchen floor was covered with linoleum. All the other floors were polished boards. The lounge-room had an open fireplace, two armchairs and a couch of faded floral-patterned velvet, and a small bookcase. The kitchen had a wood stove and a small electric cooker with a hotplate and a griller. There was an ice-chest in a corner and a mantel radio over the fireplace. The table and chairs were wooden.

The only other pieces of furniture were the beds and wardrobes and dressing-tables—a walnut veneer suite in the front bedroom and oddments in the boys' rooms. Adrian's two younger brothers slept in the middle bedroom. Adrian had the back bedroom, which was called the sleepout because it had louvre windows.

As soon as Adrian got home from school he had to take off his school suit to save it from wear. Then he put on the only other clothes he had—the shirt and trousers and jumper that had been his previous school uniform but were now too patched for school.

Adrian's young brothers had been home from school for an hour already. (They travelled a mile and a half by bus to Our Lady of Good Counsel's parish school.) Adrian found and cleaned their school shoes as well as his own. He filled the wood-box in the kitchen with split logs that his father had left under a sheet of corrugated iron behind the lavatory. He filled a cardboard box in the laundry with briquettes for the hot-water system. Then he split kindling wood and stacked it on the kitchen hearth for his mother to use next morning. If his father was still not home, Adrian fed the fowls and collected the eggs.

Sometimes before tea Adrian climbed over the side fence and looked around in the tea-tree scrub. He visited a bull-ants' nest and tapped a stick near the entrance. The ants came storming out to look for the enemy. Adrian dropped leaves and twigs on them to tease them.

There were possums' nests high up in the branches of the tea-tree. Adrian knew the possums were hiding inside, but he had never been able to scare them out. The tea-tree had no branches strong enough for climbing, and the sticks that he threw got tangled in the twigs and foliage.

When Adrian had first discovered the ants and possums he decided to observe their habits like a scientist. For a few days he kept a diary describing the ants' habits and drew maps to show how far they travelled from their nest. He thought of becoming a famous naturalist and talking on the radio like Crosbie Morrison with his program, *Wild Life*. He even planned to dig away the side of the ants' nest and put a sheet of glass inside so he could study them in their tunnels. But he didn't know where to buy glass and he found he couldn't dig a hole with straight sides anyway.

If he walked on through the scrub he came to the Gaffneys' side fence. The Sherds knew very little about

19

the few other households in Riviera Grove. They were all what Adrian's parents called young couples, with two or three small children. Adrian sometimes saw a mother in gumboots pushing a load of kids in a pram through the muddy street or chasing a child that had waded too far into a puddle. One day he had spied on Mrs Gaffney through a hole in her fence. She was wearing something that he knew was called a playsuit and hanging out nappies on the line. He had a good view of her face and legs but he decided it was useless to compare her with any film star or pin-up girl.

After he had set the table for tea, Adrian read the sporting pages of the *Argus* and then glanced through the front pages for the cheesecake picture that was always somewhere among the important news. It was usually a photograph of a young woman in bathers leaning far forward and smiling at the camera.

If the woman was an American film star he studied her carefully. He was always looking for photogenic starlets to play small roles in his American adventures.

If she was only a young Australian woman he read the caption ('Attractive Julie Starr found Melbourne's autumn sunshine yesterday too tempting to resist. The breeze was chilly but Julie, a telephonist aged 18, braved the shallows at Elwood in her lunch hour and brought back memories of summer.') and spent a few minutes trying to work out the size and shape of her breasts. Then he folded up the paper and forgot about her. He wanted no Melbourne typists and telephonists on his American journeys. He would feel uncomfortable if he saw on the train one morning some woman who had shared his American secrets only the night before.

When tea was over Adrian stacked up the dishes and washed them for his brothers to dry and put away. At six-thirty he turned on the wireless to 3KZ. For half an hour while he finished the dishes or played Ludo or Snakes and Ladders with his brothers, he heard the latest hit tunes, interrupted only by brief advertisements for films showing at Hoyts Suburban Theatres.

Adrian always made a show of being busy at something else while hit tunes were playing. If his parents had thought he was listening to the words they might have switched the wireless off or even banned him from hearing the program again. Too many of the hit tunes were love songs about kisses like wine or memories of charms or touches that thrilled.

But Adrian was not really interested in the words. Nearly every night on 3KZ he heard a few short passages of music that seemed to describe the landscape of America. The opening notes of a romantic ballad might have just the right blend of vagueness and loneliness to suggest the Great Plains States. Or the last hectic chorus of a Mitch Miller record might put him in mind of the sensual Deep South where it was always summer.

The wireless was switched off again at seven. No one wanted to hear the news or the serials and musical programmes that followed it. Mr Sherd went to bed early to finish one of the stack of books that his wife borrowed each week from the library behind the children's-wear shop in Accrington (Romance, Crime, Historical Romance, New Titles). Mrs Sherd sat by the kitchen stove knitting. Adrian's brothers played with their Meccano set or traced through lunch-wrap paper some pictures from the small stack of old *National Geographic* magazines in the lounge-room. Adrian began his homework.

The house was quiet. There was rarely the sound of a car or truck in Riviera Grove or the streets around it. Every half-hour an electric train passed along the line between Melbourne and Coroke. It was nearly a mile from the Sherds' house, but on windless nights they heard clearly the rattling of the bogeys and the whining of the motor. As the noise died away, Adrian's brothers called out 'Up!' or 'Down!' and argued over which way the train had been heading.

Adrian worked at his homework until nearly ten o'clock. Every day at school three or four boys were strapped for not doing their homework. Their excuses astonished Adrian. They had gone out, or started listening to the wireless and forgotten the time, or been told by their parents to sit up and talk to the visitors. Or they had been sent to bed because there was a party going on at their house.

In the two years since the Sherds had moved to Accrington, they had almost never gone out after dark.

And Adrian could not remember anyone visiting them at night. The boys who had other things to do instead of homework came from the suburbs close to Swindon—places with made roads and footpaths and front gardens full of shrubs. The suburbs had dignified names such as Luton and Glen Iris and Woodstock. Adrian imagined the houses in these suburbs full of merry laughter every night of the week.

When his homework was finished Adrian went out for a few minutes to the back shed. He switched on the light and lowered his model railway track to the floor. On the wood beneath the tracks was a faint pencilled outline of the United States of America. Adrian wound up his clockwork engine. He lowered it onto the rails near New York City and hooked two passenger coaches behind it. The train sped south-west towards Texas then around past California to Idaho and on across the prairies to the Great Lakes. At Chicago there was a set of points. Adrian switched them so that the train travelled first around the perimeter of the country (Pennsylvania, New York State, New England and back to New York City) and then, on each alternate lap, down through the Midwest and the Ozarks to rejoin the main line near Florida.

After four or five laps of the track the train slowed down and came to a stop. Adrian noted carefully the exact place where its journey ended. Then he put the engine and coaches away and went back to the house and got ready for bed.

The map in Adrian's shed was crudely drawn. The proportions of America were all wrong. The country had been twisted out of shape to make its most beautiful landscapes no more than stages in an endless journey. But Adrian knew his map by heart. Each few inches of railway track gave access to some picturesque scene from American films or magazines. No matter where the train might stop, it brought him to familiar country.

Nearly every night Adrian made an American journey and found himself in some pleasant part of the American outdoors. Sometimes he was content to wander there alone. But usually he went in search of American women. There were dozens to choose from. He had seen their pictures in Australian newspapers and magazines. Some of them he had even watched in films. And all of them were just as beautiful as he had imagined them.

In the weeks before the coronation of the new Queen, Adrian and his mother made a scrapbook out of cuttings from the *Argus* and the *Australian Women's Weekly*. On the night when the coronation was broadcast direct from London, the Sherds sat round the wireless with the scrapbook open on the kitchen table. They followed the exact route of the procession on a large map of London. When the commentator described the scene in Westminster Abbey they tried to find each of the places mentioned on a labelled diagram, although some of the Protestant terms like transept and nave confused them a little.

When nothing much was happening in the Abbey, Adrian feasted on the choicest items in the scrapbook—the coloured illustrations of the crown jewels and Her Majesty's robes and regalia. They were the most beautiful things he had ever seen. He delighted in every sumptuous fold of the robes and every winking highlight of the jewels. Then, to appreciate their splendour still more, he compared them with other things he had once thought beautiful.

A few years before, when he was an altar boy, he used to stare each morning at the patterns on the back of the priest's chasuble. There was one with the shape of a lamb outlined in amber-coloured stones on a background of white. The lamb held in its upraised foreleg a silver staff with a golden scroll unfurled at the top. The whole design was topped by the disc of an enormous Host with rays beaming from it and the letters I.H.S. across it in beads the colour of blood.

Adrian had once asked the priest after mass whether the stones and beads on the chasuble were proper jewels. The priest had looked a little apologetic and said no, the parish wasn't wealthy enough for that. They were (he paused) semi-precious stones. Adrian was not at all disappointed. Any sort of precious stones appealed to him.

On coronation night Adrian studied the picture in the *Argus* of Her Majesty's robe and saw that no chasuble could rival it.

The solemn ceremony of the coronation itself was too much for Adrian to visualise with only the wireless broadcast to help him. But two days later when the *Argus* published its full-colour souvenir supplement, he saw the scene in the Abbey in all its splendour. He compared all that magnificence with two scenes that he had once thought would never be surpassed for beauty.

Years before, he had watched a film about the *Arabian Nights*. It was the first technicolor film he had seen. Evelyn Keyes was a princess guarded by black slaves in her father's palace. Cornel Wilde was the man who fell in love with her and tried to elope with her. At one point in the film, the slaves were carrying Evelyn Keyes through the streets of Baghdad in a sedan chair. She was inside her private compartment, concealed by thick purple and gold drapery. Cornel Wilde stopped the slaves and tried to fight them. Evelyn Keyes peeped out for a few seconds and smiled shyly at him.

Adrian never forgot that brief glimpse of her. She was dressed in pastel-coloured satins. A white silk veil covered part of her face, but anyone could see she was breathtakingly beautiful. Her complexion was a radiant pinkish-gold, and the gorgeously coloured fabrics around her set it off to perfection.

In one of his adventures, Mandrake the Magician

(in the comic strip at the back of the *Women's Weekly*) found a race of people like Ancient Romans living on the far side of the moon. When they were ready for sleep at night, the Moonlings climbed onto filmy envelopes inflated with a special light gas. All night long the handsome moon-dwellers, in long white robes, sprawled on their transparent cushions and wafted from room to room of their spacious houses.

But the glamour of Evelyn Keyes could not match the simple beauty of the young Queen, and the Moonlings on their floating beds were not half so graceful and dignified as the lords and ladies of England in Westminster Abbey.

For a few days after the coronation, Adrian was restless and agitated. Picking his way through the puddles in his street or carving railway sidings and points into his wooden ruler in school, he thought how little pageantry there was in his life. At night he stared at the coloured souvenir pictures and wondered how to bring the splendour of the coronation to Accrington.

One night when he arrived with Lauren and Rita and Linda in the Bluegrass Country of Kentucky, the women started to whisper and smile together. He realised they were planning a little surprise for him.

They told him to wait while they went behind some bushes. Lauren and Linda came back first. They wore brief twopiece bathing suits that dazzled him. The fabric was cloth-of-gold studded with semi-precious copies of all the emeralds and rubies and diamonds in the crown jewels.

Behind them came Rita, draped in a replica of the coronation robe itself. And when the other two lifted her train he saw just enough to tell him that under the extravagant ermine-tipped robe she was stark naked.

Some mornings when Adrian Sherd stood in the bathroom waiting for the hot water to come through the pipes and fingering the latest pimples on his face, he remembered his American journey of the previous night and wondered if he was going mad.

Each night his adventures became a little more outrageous. On his first trips to America he had walked for hours hand in hand with film stars through scenic landscapes. He had undressed them and gone the whole way with them afterwards but always politely and considerately. But as the American countryside became more familiar he found he needed more than one woman to excite him. Instead of admiring the scenery he had begun to spend his time talking coarsely to the women and encouraging them to join in all kinds of obscene games.

Some of these games seemed so absurd afterwards that Adrian decided only a lunatic could have invented them. He could not imagine any men or women in real life doing such things together.

He thought of his own parents. Every night they

left their bedroom door ajar to prove they had nothing to hide. And Mrs Sherd always bolted the bathroom door when she went to have a bath so that not even her husband could look in at her.

In all the backyards around Riviera Grove there was no place where a couple could even sunbathe together unobserved. And in most of the houses there were young children running round all day. Perhaps the parents waited for the children to go to sleep and then frolicked together late at night. But from what Adrian heard of their conversations in the local bus, it seemed they had no time for fun.

The men worked on their houses and gardens. 'I stayed up till all hours last night trying to put up an extra cupboard in the laundry,' a man would say.

The women were often sick. 'Bev's still in hospital. Her mother's stopping with us to mind the nippers.'

Even their annual holidays were innocent. 'Our in-laws lent us their caravan at Safety Beach. It's a bit of a madhouse with the two of us and the three littlies all in bunks, but it's worth it for their sakes.'

Adrian divided Melbourne into three regions— slums, garden suburbs and outer suburbs. The slums were all the inner suburbs where the houses were joined together and had no front gardens. East Melbourne, Richmond, Carlton—Adrian was not at all curious about the people who lived in these slums. They were criminals or dirty and poor, and he couldn't bear to think of their pale grubby skin naked or sticking out of bathing suits.

The garden suburbs formed a great arc around the east and southeast of Melbourne. Swindon, where Adrian went to school, was in the heart of them, and most of the boys at his school lived in leafy streets. The people of the garden suburbs had full-grown trees brushing against their windows. They spread a table-cloth before every meal and poured their tomato sauce from little glass jugs. The women always wore stockings when they went shopping.

Most of the houses and gardens in these suburbs were ideal for sexual games, but Adrian doubted if they were ever used for that purpose. The people of the garden suburbs were too dignified and serious. The men sat with suits on all day in offices or banks and brought home important papers to work on after tea. The women looked so sternly at schoolboys and schoolgirls giggling together on the Swindon Road trams that Adrian thought they would have slapped their husbands' faces at the very mention of lewd games.

The outer suburbs were the ones that Adrian knew best. Whenever he tried to imagine the city of Melbourne as a whole, he saw it shaped like a great star with the outer suburbs its distinctive arms. Their miles of pinkish-brown tiled roofs reached far out into the farmlands and market gardens and bush or scrub as a sign that the modern age had come to Australia.

When Adrian read in the newspaper about a typical Melbourne family, he saw their white or cream weatherboard house in a treeless yard surrounded by fences of neatly sawn palings. From articles and cartoons in the *Argus* he had learned a lot about these people, but nothing to suggest they did the things he was interested in.

The women of the outer suburbs were not beautiful (although occasionally one was described as attractive or vivacious). They wore dressing gowns all morning, and frilly aprons over their clothes for the rest of the day. They wore their hair in curlers under scarves knotted above the forehead. When they talked over their back fences it was mostly about their husbands' stupid habits.

The husbands still had sexual thoughts occasionally. They liked to stare at pictures of film stars or beauty contestants. But the wives apparently were sick of sex (perhaps because they had too many children or because they had run out of ideas to make it interesting). They were always snatching the pictures from their husbands' hands. On the beach in summer a wife would bury her husband's head in the sand or chain his feet to an umbrella to keep him from following some beautiful young woman.

Adrian was reassured to learn that some husbands dreamed (like himself) of doing things with film stars and bathing beauties. But he would have liked to know that someone in Melbourne was actually making his dreams come true.

The little that Adrian learned from the radio was more confusing than helpful. Sometimes he heard in a radio play a conversation like this.

YOUNG WIFE: I saw the doctor today.

HUSBAND (only half-listening): Oh?

YOUNG WIFE: He told me...(a pause)...I'm going to have a baby.

HUSBAND (amazed): What? You're joking! It can't be!

Adrian had even watched a scene like this in an American film. He could only conclude that many husbands fathered their children while they were dozing off late at night, or even in their sleep. Or perhaps what they did with their wives was so dull and perfunctory that they forgot about it soon afterwards. Either way it was more evidence that the kind of sexual activity Adrian preferred was not common in real life.

Even after watching an American film, Adrian still thought he might have been a very rare kind of sex maniac. The men and women in films seemed to want nothing more than to fall in love. They struggled against misfortunes and risked their lives only for the joy of holding each other and declaring their love. At the end of each film Adrian stared at the heroine. She closed her eyes and leaned back in a kind of swoon. All that her lover could do was to support her in his arms and kiss her tenderly. She was in no condition to play American sex games.

Adrian read books by R. L. Stevenson, D. K.

Broster, Sir Walter Scott, Charles Kingsley, Alexandre Dumas and Ion L. Idriess. But he never expected to find in literature any proof that grown men and women behaved as he and his women friends did in America. Somewhere in the Vatican was an Index of Banned Books. Some of these books might have told him what he wanted to know. But it was impossible that any of them would ever fall into his hands. And even if they did, he would probably not dare to read them, since the penalty was automatic excommunication.

But an innocent-looking library book eventually proved to Adrian that at least some adults enjoyed the pleasures that he devised on his American journeys.

Adrian borrowed books from a children's library run by a women's committee of the Liberal Party over a shop in Swindon Road. (There was no library at St Carthage's College.) One afternoon he was looking through the books on the few shelves marked Australia.

In a book by Ion L. Idriess Adrian found a picture of a naked man lolling on the ground against a back-drop of tropical vegetation while his eight wives (naked except for tiny skirts between their legs) waited to do his bidding. The man was Parajoulta, King of the Blue Mud Bay tribe in the Northern Territory. Although he and his wives were Aborigines, there was a look in his eye that cheered Adrian.

The people of Accrington and the outer suburbs might have thought Adrian was crazy if they could have seen him with his women beside some beach or trout stream in America. But King Parajoulta would probably have understood. He sometimes played the very same games in the lush groves around Blue Mud Bay.

On the first Thursday of every month Adrian's form walked by twos from St Carthage's College to the Swindon parish church. First Thursday was confession day for the hundreds of boys at the college. The four confessionals built into the walls of the church were not enough. Extra priests sat in comfortable chairs just inside the altar rails and heard confessions with their heads bowed and their eyes averted from the boys kneeling at their elbows.

Adrian always chose the longest queue and knelt down to wait with his face in his hands as though he was examining his conscience.

The examination of conscience was supposed to be a long careful search for all the sins committed since your last confession. Adrian's *Sunday Missal* had a list of questions to assist the penitent in his examination. Adrian often read the questions to cheer himself up. He might have been a great sinner but at least he had never believed in fortune-tellers or consulted them; gone to places of worship belonging to other denominations; sworn oaths in slight or trivial matters; talked, gazed or laughed in church; oppressed anyone; been guilty of lascivious dressing or painting.

34

Adrian had no need to examine his conscience. There was only one kind of mortal sin that he committed. All he had to do before confession was to work out his total for the month. For this he had a simple formula. 'Let x be the number of days since my last confession.

'Then the total of sins $= \frac{2x}{5} + 4$ (for weekends, public holidays or days of unusual excitement).'

Yet he could never bring himself to confess this total. He could have admitted easily that he had lied twenty times or lost his temper fifty times or disobeyed his parents a hundred times. But he had never been brave enough to walk into confession and say, 'It is one month since my last confession, Father, and I accuse myself of committing an impure action by myself sixteen times.'

To reduce his total to a more respectable size Adrian used his knowledge of moral theology. The three conditions necessary for mortal sin were grave matter, full knowledge and full consent. In his case the matter was certainly grave. And he could hardly deny that he knew exactly what he was doing when he sinned. (Some of his American adventures lasted for nearly half an hour.) But did he always consent fully to what took place?

Any act of consent must be performed by the Will. Sometimes just before a trip to America, Adrian caught sight of his Will. It appeared as a crusader in armour with his sword upraised—the same crusader that Adrian had seen as a child in advertisements for *Hearns Bronchitis Mixture*. The Will was struggling against a pack of little imps with bald grinning heads and spidery limbs. These were the Passions. (In the old advertisements the crusader had worn the word *Hearns* on his breast and the imps had been labelled *Catarrh*, *Influenza*, *Tonsilitis*, *Sore Throat* and *Cough*.) The battle took place in some vague arena in the region of Adrian Sherd's soul. The Passions were always too many and too strong for the Will, and the last thing that Adrian saw before he arrived in America was the crusader going down beneath the exultant imps.

But the important thing was that he had gone down fighting. The Will had offered some resistance to the Passions. Adrian had not gone to America with the full consent of his Will.

In the last moments before entering the confessional Adrian tried to estimate how many times he had seen this vision of his Will. He arrived at a figure, subtracted it from his gross total and confessed to a net total of six or seven mortal sins of impurity.

Adrian often wondered how the other regular sinners got through their confessions. He questioned them discreetly whenever he could.

Cornthwaite never confessed impure actions—only impure thoughts. He tried to convince Adrian that the thought was the essential part of any sin, and therefore the only part that had to be confessed and forgiven.

Seskis had a trick of faltering in the middle of his confession as though he couldn't find the right words to describe his sin. The priest usually took him for a first offender and treated him lightly.

O'Mullane sometimes told the priest that his sins happened late at night when he didn't know whether he was asleep or awake. But one priest cross-examined him and got him confused and then refused him absolution for trying to tell a lie to the Holy Ghost. O'Mullane was so scared that he gave up the sin altogether for nearly a month.

Carolan used to confess just four sins each month, although he might have committed ten or twelve in that time. He kept a careful record of the unconfessed sins and swore he would confess every one of them before he died. He intended to wipe them out four at a time each month after he had finally given up the habit.

A fellow named Di Nuzzo boasted one day that a certain priest in his parish never asked any questions or made any comment no matter how many sins of impurity you confessed.

Di Nuzzo said, 'I'll never go to any other priest again until I'm married. You just tell him your monthly total and he sighs a bit and gives you your penance.'

Adrian envied Di Nuzzo until the day when the priest was transferred to another parish. On the first Saturday of every month Di Nuzzo had to ride his bike nearly five miles to East St Kilda just to have an easy confession. Two years later, when Di Nuzzo had left

37

school, Adrian saw him one Saturday morning in the city waiting for a West Coburg tram.

Di Nuzzo grinned and said, 'It had to happen. They've posted him to a new parish on the far side of Melbourne. I have to take a bus for two miles from the tram terminus. But I'm saving up to buy a motor-bike.'

On the first Thursday of every month, when he came out of the confessional, Adrian knelt in front of Our Lady's altar and prayed for the gift of Holy Purity. Then he said a special prayer of thanksgiving to God for preserving his life during the past month while his soul had been in a state of mortal sin. (If he had died suddenly during that time he would have spent eternity in hell.)

For most of that day he told himself he had finished with impurity. He even kept away from Cornthwaite and his friends in the school-ground. But when he arrived home he saw his model railroad leaning against the wall in the shed. He whispered the names of landscapes he had still not explored—Great Smoky Mountains, Sun Valley, Grand Rapids—and he knew he would soon go back to America.

But he was not free to go back yet. On the following Sunday morning he would be at mass with his family. His parents would know that he had been to confession on the Thursday. They would expect him to go to communion with them. If he did not go, they would know for certain that some time between Thursday and

Sunday he had committed a mortal sin. His father would start asking questions. If Mr Sherd even suspected the truth about the American journey, Adrian would die of shame or run away from home.

For the sake of his future, Adrian had to avoid mortal sin from Thursday until Sunday morning. And it was not enough just to stay away from America. Any impure thought, if he wilfully entertained it, was a mortal sin. Such thoughts could appear in his mind at any hour of the day or night. It would be a desperate struggle.

The Thursday night was the easiest. Adrian needed a rest. The last few nights before his monthly confession usually wore him out. On those nights he knew he would not be visiting America again for some time, and he tried to enjoy every minute in the country as though it was his last.

On Friday at school he kept away again from Cornthwaite and the others. For as long as Adrian was in the state of grace, his former friends were what the Church called bad companions.

On Friday night he did all his weekend homework and stayed up as late as possible to tire himself. In bed he remembered the advice a priest had once given him in confession: 'Take your pleasure from good and holy things.'

He closed his eyes and thought of good and holy landscapes. He saw the vineyards on the hills of Italy, where ninety-nine per cent of the people were Catholics. He crossed the golden plateaus of Spain, the only country in the world where the Communists had been fought and beaten to a standstill. The whole of Latin America was safe to explore, but he usually fell asleep before he reached there.

On Saturday morning he read the sporting section of the *Argus* but was careful not to open the other pages. They were sure to have some picture that would torment him all day.

After lunch he went for a ride on his father's old bike to tire himself out. He chose a route with plenty of hills and made sure he would have to ride the last few miles into the wind. On the steepest climbs, when he could hardly keep the pedals moving, he hissed to the rhythm of his straining thighs, 'Chastise the body. Chastise the body.'

There were still temptations even in the bleakest suburbs. Sometimes he saw the backs of a woman's thighs as she bent forward in her garden, or the shapes of her breasts bouncing under her sweater as she pushed a mower. When this happened he slowed down and waited for a glimpse of the woman's face. It was nearly always so plain that he was glad to forget all about her.

He came home exhausted and had a shower before tea. (On other Saturdays he had a bath late at night. He lay back with his organ submerged and thought foul thoughts to make it break the surface like the periscope of a submarine.) The taps in the shower recess were so hard to regulate that he had no time to stand still. He came out shivering with cold. His organ was a wrinkled stub. He flicked the towel at it and whispered, 'Bring the body into subjection.'

After tea he listened to the *London Stores Show* on the wireless to hear the football results. Then he played a game of football he had invented. He arranged thirty-six coloured scraps of paper on the table for men and threw dice to decide the path of the ball. He played the game until nearly midnight. Then he went to bed and thought about football until he fell asleep.

On Sunday morning the Sherd family caught the bus to nine o'clock mass at Our Lady of Good Counsel's, Accrington. The people in the bus were nearly always the same from week to week. They even sat in the same seats. A young woman sat opposite the Sherds. Most Sundays Adrian took no notice of her. She had a pasty face and a dumpy figure. But on the first Sunday of each month the sight of her legs gave him no peace.

Adrian believed in the devil. It could only have been the devil who arranged for a pair of legs to lie in wait for him on the first Sunday of the month when he was within an hour of reaching the altar rails without sinning. To defeat this last temptation he recited over and over to himself from the Prayers after Mass, '... thrust Satan down into hell and with him the other wicked spirits who wander through the world seeking the ruin of souls.'

41

He never looked at the legs for more than a second at a time. And he never looked anywhere near them when his parents or the young woman's parents or the woman herself or any other passenger might have caught him at it. Sometimes he only saw the legs once or twice on the whole trip. But he knew by heart every curve and undulation on them, the freckles on the lower parts of the knee-caps, the mole on one shin, the tension of the stockings over the ankle bones.

The legs talked to him. They whispered that he still had to wait more than an hour until he was safe at the altar rails. They urged him to close his eyes during the sermon and visualise them in all their naked beauty and wilfully consent to enjoy the pleasure he got.

When he still resisted them they became more shameless. They kicked their heels high like dancers in an American musical. They even bared the first few inches of their thighs and reminded him that there was much more to see farther up in the shadows under their skirt. Or if he did not fancy them, they said, would he prefer some of the legs he would see during mass? The church would be full of legs. He would only have to drop his missal on the floor and bend his head down to retrieve it and there, under the seat in front of him, would be calves and ankles of all shapes to feast on.

Adrian never surrendered to the legs. Instead he made a pact with them. He promised that on that very Sunday night he would meet them in America and do whatever they asked of him. In return they were to leave him in peace until he had been to communion. The legs were always as good as their word. As soon as the pact was made they stopped bothering him and stroked and preened themselves discreetly out of his view.

During mass Adrian relaxed for the first time in days. He went to communion with his head high. On the bus trip home the legs caused no trouble. He found he could last for several minutes without looking at them. But before he left the bus he always nodded casually to them as a sign that he would observe the pact.

Only once had Adrian tried to break the terms of his agreement. He had made an unusually devout communion and on the bus after mass he was thinking what a pity it was that his soul would be soiled again so soon. He began to pray for the strength to resist the legs in future.

Across the narrow aisle of the bus the legs drew themselves up into a fighting posture. They warned him they would come to his bed that night and tempt him as he had never been tempted before. They would strip themselves and perform such tricks in front of his eyes that he would never sleep again until he had yielded to them.

Adrian knew they could do it. Already their anger had made them more attractive than ever. He apologised to them and hoped he hadn't made too big a fool of himself in front of them.

Whenever Adrian's friends started talking about sex, he had to use his wits to keep them from guessing his most embarrassing secret. This secret bothered him every day of his life. He was sure no other young man in Melbourne had such an absurd thing to hide.

Adrian didn't like to put his secret into simple words—it humiliated him so much. But it was simple nevertheless: he had never seen the external genital apparatus of a human female.

When Adrian was nine years old and a pupil of St Margaret Mary's School in a western suburb of Melbourne, some of the boys in his grade formed a secret society. They met among the oleanders in a little park near the school. Their aim was to persuade girls to visit the park and pull down their pants in full view of the society.

Adrian applied many times to join this society and was eventually admitted on probation. On the afternoon of his first meeting, the society was expecting six or seven girls but only two turned up. One of them refused even to lift her skirt—even after the boys of the society had all offered to take out their cocks and give her a good look. The other girl (Dorothy McEncroe—Adrian would always remember her, although she was a scrawny little thing) tucked her school tunic under her chin and lowered her pants for perhaps five seconds.

As a probationary member of the society Adrian

had been forced to stand at the back of the little group of boys. At the very moment, when McEncroe's pants were sliding down the last few inches of her belly, the boys in front of Adrian began to jostle each other for a better view. Adrian clawed at them like a madman. He was small and light for his age and he could not shift them. He got down on his hands and knees and wriggled between their legs. He pushed his head into the inner circle just as the dark blue pleats of the uniform of St Margaret Mary's School fell back into place over Dorothy McEncroe's thighs.

Adrian never had a second chance to inspect Dorothy McEncroe or any other girl at that school. A few days after the meeting, the parish priest visited all the upper grades to warn them against loitering in the park after school. The secret society was disbanded and Dorothy McEncroe walked home every night with a group of girls and pulled faces at any boy who tried to talk to her.

As he grew older, Adrian tried other ways of learning about women and girls.

One wet afternoon at St Margaret Mary's the children in Grade Seven were allowed to do free reading from the library—a glass-fronted cupboard in the corner. Adrian took down a volume of the encyclopedia from the top shelf. The book seemed mostly about art and sculpture, and many of the pictures and statues were naked. Adrian turned the pages rapidly. There were cocks and balls and breasts everywhere. He was sure he would find what he wanted among all that bare skin. His knees began to tremble. It was the afternoon under the oleanders again. But this time there was no one to block his view, and the woman he was about to see would have no pants or tunic within reach.

The girl behind him (Clare Buckley—he had cursed her a thousand times since) jumped to her feet.

'Please, Sister. Adrian Sherd's trying to read that book you told us not to borrow from the top shelf.'

The room was suddenly silent. Adrian heard the whistling of the nun's robes. She was beside him before he could even close the book. But she spared him.

'There is nothing either good or bad in art,' she said to the class. 'Adrian must have been away when I told you all not to bother yourselves about this book. We'll put it away for safe-keeping just the same.'

She carried the book back to her own desk. Adrian never saw it again in the library.

In later years Adrian sometimes came across other books about art with pictures of naked men and women. But whereas the men had neat little balls and stubby uncircumcised cocks resting comfortably and unashamed between their legs the women had nothing but smooth skin or marble fading away into the shadows where their thighs met. Adrian suspected a conspiracy among artists and sculptors to preserve the secrets of women from boys like himself.

46

He thought how unfair it was that girls could learn all about men from pictures and statues while boys could search for years in libraries or art galleries and still be ignorant about women. He almost wept for the injustice of it.

In his first months at St Carthage's College, Adrian learned a little more from an unexpected source. Every Wednesday the boys went for sport to some playing fields near the East Swindon tram terminus. Under the changing rooms was a lavatory with its walls covered in scribble. Some of the messages and stories were illustrated. Even here, most of the pictures were of men's and boys' organs, but Adrian sometimes found a sketch of a naked female.

From these crude drawings he pieced together an image of something that was oval in shape and bisected by a vertical line. He practised drawing this shape until it came easily to him, but he found it impossible to imagine such an odd thing between two smooth graceful thighs.

When Adrian first joined the little group around Cornthwaite, Seskis and O'Mullane, he listened to the names they used for the thing he was looking for. Cunt, twat, hole, ring, snatch, crack—when he heard these words he nodded or smiled like someone who had used them familiarly all his life. But long afterwards he brooded over them, hoping they might yield a clear image of the thing they named.

Adrian's friends knew there were certain magazines full of information and pictures about sex. They knew the names of some of them—*Man, Man Junior, Men Only, Lilliput* and *Health and Sunshine*. They believed that non-Catholic newsagents kept the magazines hidden under their counters or in back rooms.

Cornthwaite often boasted that he could get any of the filthy magazines. All he had to do was ask a big bastard in his parish tennis club to walk into his local newsagent and ask for one. Adrian begged him to buy a *Health and Sunshine*. He had heard this was the one with the most daring pictures. They were rumoured to show everything. But Cornthwaite never remembered to get him one.

One afternoon in a barber's shop in Swindon Road, Adrian found a *Man Junior* among the magazines lying about for customers to read. He was desperate to see inside it, but he was wearing his school uniform and he couldn't bring St Carthage's into disrepute by reading a smutty magazine in public.

He kept his eyes on the barber and his assistant and moved along the seat until he was sitting on the *Man Junior*. Then he bent forward and slipped the magazine down behind his legs and into his Gladstone bag. It was the first time he had ever stolen something of value, but he was sure the magazine was worth less than the amount necessary to make the theft a mortal sin.

Adrian looked through his *Man Junior* in one of the cubicles in the toilet on Swindon railway station. He saw plenty of naked women, but every one of them had something (a beach ball, a bucket and spade, a fluffy dog, a trailing vine, a leopard's skin or simply her own upraised leg) concealing the place he had waited so long to see. It all looked so casual—as though the big ball had just bounced past, or the dog had happened to stroll up and greet the woman an instant before the camera clicked. But Adrian was sure it was done deliberately. The smiles of the women angered him. They pretended to be brazen temptresses, but at the last moment they draped fronds of greenery across themselves or hid behind their pet dogs.

It was not safe to take the whole magazine home. Adrian tore out the three most attractive pictures and hid them in the lining of his bag. That evening he searched through his brother's *Boys' Wonder Book*. He had remembered an article entitled *An Easy-to-make Periscope*. He found the article and made a note of the materials needed for the periscope.

Next day at school he talked to a boy who was crazy about science. Adrian said he had just thought up a brilliant idea to help the Americans spy on the Russians but he wanted to be sure it would work. The idea was to take pictures of the walls around the Kremlin or any other place the Americans wanted to see into. Then American scientists could aim powerful periscopes at the photographs to see what was behind the walls.

The boy told Adrian it was the stupidest idea he had ever heard. He started to explain something about light rays but Adrian told him not to bother. Adrian was glad he hadn't hinted at what he really wanted to do with a periscope.

Adrian gave his three *Man Junior* pictures to Ullathorne, who collected bare-breasted women. He handed over the pictures in a back lane in Swindon, well away from St Carthage's. It was well known that a boy had been expelled from the college after a brother had found dirty magazines in his bag.

One Friday, a few weeks later, Cornthwaite told Adrian that if he liked to turn up at Caulfield Racecourse on the following Sunday, he might meet a certain fellow from Cornthwaite's parish who often sold second-hand copies of his big brother's dirty magazines.

Adrian said he would only come if the fellow was likely to have some copies of *Health and Sunshine*. It was too far to ride his bike five miles to Caulfield just to buy *Man* or *Man Junior*.

Cornthwaite said the fellow could sell you any magazine you liked to name.

Sunday afternoon was cold and windy but Adrian didn't want to miss the chance to get *Health and Sunshine*. He had the wind in his face all the way to Caulfield, and the trip took longer than he had expected.

The racecourse was a favourite meeting-place for the boys from Cornthwaite's suburb. Adrian found

Cornthwaite and a few others racing on their bikes in and out among the bookmakers' stands in the deserted betting ring. Cornthwaite said the fellow with the magazines had sold out and gone home long before. He offered Adrian a few pages torn from a magazine and said, 'I bought a *Health and Sunshine* myself. But then Laurie D'Arcy turned up and I sold it to him for a profit. But I saved you the best picture from it.'

Adrian took the ragged pages and offered to pay Cornthwaite for all his trouble. Cornthwaite said he wouldn't take any money but he hoped Adrian would stop bothering him about pictures for the rest of his life.

Adrian took his picture to a seat in the grandstand and sat down to examine it. It was a black-and-white photograph of a naked woman walking towards him under an archway of trees. And this time there was nothing between him and the thing that his parents and teachers, the men who painted the Old Masters, the women who posed for *Man Junior*, and even Dorothy McEncroe at St Margaret Mary's school years before had kept hidden from him.

The woman in *Health and Sunshine* strode boldly forward. Her hands swung by her sides. As calmly as he could, Adrian looked into the hollow between her thighs.

His first thought was that *Health and Sunshine* was a fraud like *Man junior*. The place was full of shadow. The woman had somehow managed to shield her secrets

51

from the light. Even without a beach ball or a leopard's skin she had still foiled him.

But then he realised it was an accident. The shadows came from the branch of a tree above the woman. The whole scene was mottled with shadows from the trees overhead. And there *was* something visible in the shadows between her legs. In the dull light under the roof of the grandstand he could not make it out clearly, but he was not beaten yet.

He took the picture out into the daylight and looked closely at it. He was even more convinced that a shape of some kind was concealed among the shadows, although it would take much longer to make out its finer details.

Adrian put the picture inside his shirt and stepped onto his bike. All the way home he was frightened of having an accident. He saw a crowd of doctors and nurses undoing his shirt on the operating table and discovering a page from *Health and Sunshine* over his heart. If they knew he was a Catholic they might tell the hospital chaplain who would discuss the whole matter with his parents around his bedside after he regained consciousness.

He arrived home safely and smuggled the picture into the bottom of his schoolbag. Next morning he took the last six shillings from his tin of pocket money. On the way to school he bought a reading glass in a newsagent's shop in Swindon Road. He told the man he looked for places where a man might take his lady-friends for a picnic. But all he saw were a few copses or spinneys so small or so close to roads and lanes that the picnickers could never have run naked or cried out obscene words without being seen or overheard.

If he had been awake he would have despised this landscape. But in his dream he longed to know it better. It seemed to promise a pleasure more satisfying than anything he had known in America.

The stone house was on a hill. He stood outside it searching for a door or a low window to look through. Behind him, he knew, was a view of miles of green fields dotted with darker-green trees and intersected by white lanes. If he could find a beautiful young woman, even an English woman, he would enjoy to the full whatever rare pleasures the landscape concealed.

Brother Cyprian said, 'The important thing to remember is this. We can't help what happens to us while we're asleep. We're fully responsible for what we do in the daytime, but in sleep there are chemicals and forces at work that we haven't the slightest control over.'

Somewhere inside the house was a woman or a girl of his own age with a face so full of expression that a man could stare at it for hours. She was wearing a turtle-necked Fair Isle sweater (so bulky that he saw no sign of her breasts), a skirt of Harris tweed and sensible shoes. As soon as Adrian found a window into her room they would exchange glances full of meaning. Hers robe from a girl's dusky limbs and display every one of her assets for close inspection.

Adrian knew exactly what this last sentence meant. The Yemen was not too far from Australia. When he left school and started work he would soon save up forty pounds plus his fares. As soon as he turned twenty-one he would travel to the Yemen and visit the slave market and buy one of the young women.

Or he need not even buy one. He could simply rattle some money in his pocket to look like a customer, and wait until a gaudy robe was flung back. And if one of the girl's thighs blocked his view or a shadow fell across her, he would pretend to be a very cautious customer who insisted on seeing every detail of the goods he was interested in.

One morning Brother Cyprian spent some of the Christian Doctrine period talking about dreams. The boys were unusually attentive. They could see he was nervous and embarrassed. While he talked he adjusted the pile of books on his desk, trying to make it symmetrical.

Brother Cyprian said: 'At this time of your lives you might find yourself feeling a little sad and strange because you seem to be leaving behind a part of your life that was happy and simple. The reason for this is that you're all growing from boys into young men. There are new mysteries to puzzle and bother you—things you never thought about a few years ago. And many

would tell him she was willing to agree to whatever he asked. And his would tell her he wanted no more than to walk beside her all afternoon through the English landscape. And even if they found themselves alone in some green field screened on all sides by tall hedgerows, he would ask no more than to clasp her fingertips or lightly touch her wrist where it gleamed like the finest English porcelain.

Brother Cyprian said, 'So you see, we can't commit a sin in our sleep. No matter what strange things we dream about, there's no chance of us sinning.'

Adrian groped through thickets of ivy. Even the walls of the place were becoming harder to find. Inside somewhere, the woman was operating her expensive film projector. She was showing an audience of hundreds of well-dressed English gentlemen coloured films of all the landscapes she longed to wander through, and hinting to them what they must do to earn the right to escort her on summer afternoons.

Adrian stood on the beach below a towering cliff on the Atlantic coast of Cornwall. High above, on the Sussex Downs, a young couple promenaded on the smooth sward. He heard the intimate murmur of their voices but before he could make out their words he had to escape from the incoming tide. When he saw the vast green bulk of the whole Atlantic coming at him he woke in his sleepout at Accrington.

Brother Cyprian was near the end of his talk. 'One

of the most alarming things that might happen to us is to wake up in the middle of some strange dream. You might find your whole body disturbed and restless and all sorts of odd things happening. The only thing to do is to say a short prayer to Our Lady and ask her for the blessing of a dreamless sleep. Then close your eyes again and let things take their course.'

Adrian had been desperate to get back to sleep and try again to enjoy the pleasures of England. But of course had never seen anything like an English landscape again.

In the schoolyard at morning recess Cornthwaite said, 'Did you get what Cyprian was raving about this morning—all that about naughty dreams?'

O'Mullane and Seskis and Sherd were not sure.

Cornthwaite said, 'Wet dreams. That's what it was. You bastards have never had that sort of dream because you've flogged yourselves silly every night of your lives since you were in short pants. If you go without it for a couple of weeks, one night you'll dream the filthiest dream you've ever dreamed of. You'll even shoot your bolt in your sleep if you don't wake up in the middle of it.'

Adrian tried not to look surprised. It was the first time anyone had explained wet dreams to him. He had never had one—perhaps for the reason that Cornthwaite had suggested. He realised why the brother had been so embarrassed talking about dreams.

For nearly a week Adrian kept away from America. He was waiting for a filthy dream. If the dream was as good as Cornthwaite had claimed, Adrian might have to make an important decision. He would carefully compare the dream and the best of his American adventures. If the dream turned out to be more realistic and lifelike than his American journey, he might decide to get all his sexual pleasure in future from dreams.

But whenever he remembered the young woman and the innocent landscapes of England he wished for dreams that would never be contaminated by lust. He decided to resume his American journey. If he wore himself out in America night after night, there was always the chance that he might experience again the pure joy of a dream of England.

Some nights when Adrian was tired of visiting America he thought about the history of mankind.

While he lived in the Garden of Eden, Adam enjoyed perfect human happiness. If it occurred to him to look at a naked woman, he simply told Eve to stand still for a moment. And he never once suffered the misery of having an erection that he could not satisfy. Eve knew it was her duty to give in to him whenever he asked.

After he was driven out into the world, Adam still tried to live as he had in Eden. But now he suffered the trials of a human being. Eve wore clothes all day long and only let him near her when she wanted a child. Every day he had erections that came to nothing. Many a time he looked out across the plains of Mesopotamia and wished there was some other woman he could think about. But the world was still empty of people apart from himself and his family. Even in the vast continent of North America there was no human footprint from the green islands of Maine to the red-gold sandbanks of the Rio Grande.

But at least Adam could remember his pleasant life in Eden. His sons had no such consolation. They grew up in a world where the only females were their sisters and their mother—and *they* always kept their bodies carefully covered.

When the eldest son reached Adrian's age he still hadn't seen a naked female body. One hot afternoon he could stand it no longer. He hid among the bull-rushes while Eve and her daughters went swimming in the Tigris. He only glanced at Eve—her breasts were long and flabby and her legs had varicose veins. But he looked hard at his sisters, even the young ones with no breasts.

When he was alone again, he formed his hand into the shape of the thing he had seen between their legs and became the first in human history to commit the solitary sin.

Although it was not recorded in the Bible, that was a black day for mankind. On that day God thought seriously of wiping out the little tribe of Man. Even in His infinite wisdom He hadn't foreseen that a human would learn such an unnatural trick—enjoying by himself, when he was hardly more than a child, the pleasure that was intended for married men only.

The angels in heaven were revolted too. Lucifer's sin of pride seemed clean and brave compared with the sight of the shuddering boy squirting his precious stuff into the limpid Tigris. Lucifer himself was delighted that Man had invented a new kind of sin—and one that was so easy to commit.

Luckily for mankind it was the first of many occasions when God's mercy overcame His righteous anger. The son of Adam never knew how close he had come to being struck dead on the spot.

Perhaps God relented because He saw how little joy the poor fellow got out of it. There were no newspapers or magazines to excite his imagination. All he could think of was one of the same girls he saw every day in his ordinary household in dreary Mesopotamia.

Eventually the sons of Adam married their sisters, and their descendants spread through the Middle East and became the ancient Sumerians and Egyptians.

By now the young men were much better off than the sons of Adam. Few of them had to commit sins of impurity alone. People matured so early in the hot climate that a young fellow of Adrian's age would be already married to a shapely brown-skinned wife.

If a young man couldn't wait, even for the brief time between puberty and marriage, he still didn't have to touch himself. There were slavegirls in every city. If a young man fancied a certain slave-girl he could ask his father to buy her and employ her in the house. If the young fellow was daring enough he would have her assigned to bathroom duties. She would fill his tub and fetch his towels on bath nights. Then he could arrange for the room to become so hot that the girl had to strip to the waist while she worked.

When the Jews settled in the Promised Land they were no less lustful than other peoples. Time after time God had to send a prophet to persuade them to repent. Even when the Bible did not name the sins of the Jews, it was easy to guess what they were. The weather in Palestine was always hot and the people often slept on top of their houses. The excitement of lying on the roof with hardly any clothes on, and hearing your neighbour's wife just across the way tossing about under her sheet, would have kept a Jewish man awake half the night thinking of sex.

In Old Testament times the only young men who kept up the solitary habit were poor shepherd boys far from the cities and the slavegirls. When fire and brimstone rained on Sodom and Gomorrah, there were lonely herd-keepers who watched from the stony hills around and didn't know whether to be glad, because all the spoilt young bastards were being roasted alive with their wives and slave-girls, or sorry, because they could never again peer down on the cities at dusk to watch the sexy games on the rooftops and catch a glimpse of some young woman they could remember afterwards in the desert.

By the time of Jesus, the Jews had become very reticent about sex. It was hard to judge how common or rare the solitary sin might have been in New Testament days. Jesus Himself never referred to it, but Adrian always hoped an Apocryphal Gospel or a Dead Sea Scroll would be found one day with the story of the Boy Taken in Self-Abuse.

The Scribes and Pharisees dragged him to Jesus and announced that they were going to stone him. Jesus invited the one without sin to cast the first stone. Then He started writing in the sand. One by one the old men looked down and read the dates and places of their boyhood sins and the names of the women they had used for inspiration. The boy read them too. And for years afterwards, instead of hanging his head in shame because the whole town knew about his secret sin, he remembered the pious old men who had tried it themselves in their youth and he looked the whole world in the face.

Adrian hummed or whistled his favourite hit tunes whenever he was alone, and especially at night when his parents had gone to bed with their library books and his young brothers were asleep. Sometimes he got up from his homework at the kitchen table and went into his room without turning on the light. He stared out of his window, trying to imagine the shape of the North American continent beyond the darkness that had settled over the southeastern suburbs of Melbourne. He tried not to notice the lighted window in the house across the back fence where Mr and Mrs Lombard were still doing their tea dishes because it took them hours to scrub all their kids and put them to bed. He sang his favourite tunes softly until America appeared under its brilliant sunshine on the far side of the world.

The square-dancing craze was over. The women of America had stopped wearing shapeless checked blouses and cowboy hats that dangled behind their heads. They were crowded together on a riverbank listening to Johnny Ray sing *The Little White Cloud That Cried*. Johnny threw back his head in agony and gasped out the last long syllable of his smash hit. The women threw their arms round each other and sobbed. They would have done anything to make Johnny happy, but he only stood with his eyes closed and thought of the waters of the Potomac or the Shenandoah rushing past on their way to the sea, and of how lonely the American countryside seemed to someone with no sweetheart.

The women followed the river to the sea. By sundown they were all strolling along the boardwalk of a great city, dressed in off-the-shoulder evening frocks and white elbow-length gloves. From the farthest horizon, rosy with sunset, the sound of the fishing fleet, returning to port at last, reached the throng of women. Jo Stafford's rendition of *Shrimp Boats* came from loudspeakers all along the beach. When they knew their menfolk were coming, the women rushed into the lobby of the biggest luxury hotel in town. They pushed through the fronds of potted palms and crowded round the startled desk-clerks and sang into their faces, 'There's dancing tonight.'

Rosemary Clooney grabbed the nearest bellhop boy and waltzed round the room with him while she sang *Tell Us Where the Good Times Are*. Each time she shouted the chorus she held him so close to her plunging neckline that her big bouncing breasts almost rubbed against his nose. The shy young man didn't know where to look, and the crowd went wild.

By now the men had arrived and changed into their tuxedos. The happy couples crowded into an upstairs ballroom. Dean Martin sang *Kiss of Fire* and everyone started to tango. When the song reached its climax, some of the more red-blooded men even tried to kiss their partners. But the women turned their heads aside because they knew what a kiss could do.

The crowd round the stage drew back and made way for Patti Page the Singing Rage with her version of *Doggie in the Window*. As she moved among the dancers, the mystery of who made the dog noises was solved at last. It was Patti herself, and she looked so fetching when she yelped that some of the men tried to fondle her like a cuddlesome puppy.

The Weavers burst into the room singing *The Gandy Dancers' Ball*. Everyone started dancing like miners or lumberjacks in an old Western saloon. But some of the women looked nervous. They knew what wild things the gandy dancers did when they were excited by dancing and pretty faces.

When the dust had settled after the dance, Frankie Laine sang *Wild Goose*. A hush came over the room. Someone pulled back the velvet drapes to reveal a view of brightly lit skyscrapers. High up in the night sky, a flock of wild geese was passing over the city on their way to the Gulf of Mexico. The people listening to Frankie remembered the wide open spaces of America, far from the world of Show Business with its low-cut gowns and easy divorces. Between the big cities were rural landscapes where people were all in bed listening to the innocent music of wild geese honking in the night sky. When Frankie was finished, a few of the dancers were so moved that they walked out of their girlfriends' lives and went back to the dear hearts and gentle people in their home towns.

Jo Stafford grabbed the mike again and sang the first bars of *Jumbalaya*. The dancers leaped to their feet. The words were puzzling, but everyone knew the song was something about Louisiana and the steamy tropical swamps where people wore shorts or bathers all day. To set the right mood for the song, Jo Stafford was wearing a grass skirt and a floral brassiere.

The tropical rhythm affected everyone. The dancing grew furious. At the end of each chorus, some of the men sang words that were rather *risqué*. Instead of the correct words 'big fun', they sang 'big bums'. And a few of the more shameless women giggled behind their hands and waggled their own bottoms.

As the song neared its end, more people behaved suggestively or sniggered over *double entendres*. They forgot about the rest of America in the darkness all round them. They couldn't have cared less about the thousands of Catholic parents trying to shield their children from the dangers of blue songs and films. They forgot everything except the sight of Jo Stafford swishing her grass skirt higher and higher in time with the wild pagan music and the off-colour words.

But nothing really evil happened. After a few minutes the song that had seemed to promise a lustful orgy came suddenly to an end.

Someone pulled back the drapes again. The cold grey light of dawn was spreading over the sky. The couples clasped hands and gathered at the windows while Eddie Fisher sang *Turn Back the Hands of Time*.

The men were all vaguely dissatisfied (like Adrian Sherd after he had listened to three *Hit Parades* on Sunday evening). All night they had heard about kisses that thrilled, kisses of fire, lips of wine, and charms they would die for. But now it was time to go home and they had done no more than dance the night away.

While the men were stealing a goodnight kiss from their girlfriends in the lobbies of their apartment buildings or on the porches of their frame houses, some of them might have found themselves humming a different kind of music.

It was not really hit music, although it often made the *Hit Parade* for a few weeks. When Adrian Sherd heard it he remembered that not everyone spent their evenings dancing in night clubs or folding charms in their arms. It was sad, lonely music—the theme from *Moulin Rouge*, or *The Story of Three Loves* or *Limelight*—and it seemed to come from countries very different from America.

When the people going home in America heard this music they wondered if there was some other kind of happiness that they had never found—and would never find as long as they spent their nights holding their loved ones dangerously near and tasting their lips.

One Monday morning Adrian's friends asked him what he had done over the weekend. All he could tell them was that he had listened to the *Hit Parades* on the wireless. Seskis and Cornthwaite laughed and said they were always too busy to sit and listen to music.

But O'Mullane said, 'The *Hit Parade* came in handy for me one night. I was lying out in my bungalow trying to think of an excuse to do it to myself and I heard this colossal song with Perry Como and a chorus of young tarts in the background. They were singing, "Play me a hurtin' tune" over and over again. I beat time to the music while I did it. The last few lines nearly made my head drop off. I'm going to buy the record and use it again some day.'

Every few months, on a Sunday afternoon, Mrs Sherd took her three sons to visit her sister, Miss Kathleen Bracken.

Adrian knew his aunt Kath would have entered a convent when she was young if one of her legs had not been shorter than the other. Adrian's mother called her a living saint because she went to daily mass in all weathers with her big boot clumping along the footpath.

Miss Bracken lived alone in a little single-fronted weatherboard house in Hawthorn. While his brothers ate green loquats or figs from the two trees in the back-yard, Adrian admired his aunt's front room.

Inside the door, near the light-switch, was a holy-water stoup in the shape of an angel holding a bowl against its breast. Whenever Aunt Kath walked past it she dipped her finger in the bowl and blessed herself. Adrian did the same.

There were three altars in the room: one each for the Sacred Heart, Our Lady of Perpetual Succour and St Joseph. Each altar had a statue of coloured plaster with a fairy-light burning in front of it (red for the Sacred Heart, blue for Our Lady and orange for St Joseph) and a vase of flowers. On certain feast days Aunt Kath burned a candle in front of the appropriate altar—a blessed candle obtained from the church on the feast of the Purification of Our Lady.

On a cabinet beneath a picture of Our Lady appearing to St Bernadette Soubirous was a flask of Lourdes water. Aunt Kath sprinkled a few drops on her wrists and temples when she felt off-colour. One day when Adrian's youngest brother ran a long splinter under his fingernail, she dipped the finger in the flask before she poked at it with a needle.

Adrian liked to ask his aunt about little-known religious orders or puzzling rituals and ceremonies or obscure points of Catholic doctrine. It was his aunt who told him always to burn old broken rosary beads rather than throw them away (so they wouldn't end up lying next to some dirty piece of garbage or be picked up by non-Catholics who would only make a mockery of them). She showed him leaflets about an order of nuns who dedicated their lives to converting the Jews, and another order who worked exclusively with African lepers. She knew all about the ceremony of *tenebrae*, in which the lights in the church were put out one by one. And one Sunday afternoon she took Adrian and his mother to a churching for a woman who had recently had a baby.

Whenever his aunt was talking, Adrian thought of her mind as a huge volume, like the book that the priest used at mass, with ornate red binding and pages edged with thick gilt. Silk ribbons hung out of the pages to mark the important places.

'Why aren't Catholics allowed to be cremated?' he asked her.

She took hold of the dangling violet (or scarlet or green) ribbon and parted the gilt edging at the section containing the answer.

'At one time, certain heretics or atheists used to have themselves cremated to show that their bodies couldn't be resurrected after death. So the Holy Father issued a decree so that no Catholic would appear to be siding with the heretics.'

In a drawer in the front room Aunt Kath had a collection of relics of saints, each in a silk-lined box labelled CYMA or ROLEX or OMEGA. The relics were tiny chips of bone or fragments of cloth housed behind glass in silver or gilt lockets.

When Adrian had been younger he used to enjoy visiting his aunt. But after he had begun his visits to America he felt he was polluting her house, and especially the front room. He still read her magazines (*The Messenger of Our Lady*, *The Annals of The Sacred Heart*, *The Monstrance*, *The Far East*) but he kept away from her altars and relics. He was frightened of committing a sacrilege by touching them with his hands—the same hands that only a few hours before had been dabbling in filth.

One day when he had at least a dozen sins on his soul, his aunt showed him a new relic she had just received from Italy. She unpacked it from a box stuffed with tissue-paper.

'Actually there are two of them,' she said. 'And I want you to have one.'

Adrian knew she prayed every morning that he would become a priest. Fortunately God saw to it that no prayers ever went to waste. His aunt's prayers would probably be used to lead some other more worthy boy to the priesthood.

She lifted out two tiny envelopes and held one up to the light. Adrian saw a dark patch in one corner.

His aunt said, 'They're only third class relics—I've told you about the different classes of relics—but they were jolly hard to come by.'

She put one envelope in Adrian's hand. 'It's from his tomb,' she said. 'Dust from the tomb of St Gabriel of the Sorrowing Virgin. St Gabriel had an extraordinary love for Holy Purity. He's the ideal patron for young people to pray to today when there's so much temptation about.'

Adrian tried to look as though it had never occurred to him to pray to any saint for purity because it came naturally to him.

All the way home with the relic in his pocket,

Adrian wondered how much the saints in heaven knew about the sins of people on earth. Did God in his mercy keep all the holy virgins and the innocent saints like St Gabriel from knowing about the foul sins of impurity committed every day? Or was the news of each sin broadcast all over heaven as soon as it was committed? ('News Flash: Adrian Sherd, Catholic boy of Accrington, Melbourne, Australia, abused himself at 10.55 this evening.') There were people already in heaven who knew him. ('Yes, he was my grandson, I'm sorry to say,' says old Mr Bracken.) If Adrian managed to break the habit at last and get to heaven in the end, he would have to hide from his relatives.

But then there was the General Judgement. Even if no one in heaven had heard of his sins before then, every person who had lived on earth since Adam would learn about them on Judgement Day.

Adrian Sherd walked up to the platform between two stern angels. The crowd of spectators reached beyond the horizon in every direction. But even the farthest soul in the crowd heard his name when it was broadcast over the loudspeakers.

Towering above the platform was a huge indicator like the scoreboard at the Melbourne Cricket Ground. Beside each of the Ten Commandments was an instrument like the speedo in a car. The crowd gasped when the digits started tumbling over to show Sherd's score for the Sixth Commandment. The blurred numerals whirled into the hundreds. Somewhere in the crowd his Aunt Kathleen shrieked with horror. This was the boy she had wanted to be a priest, the boy she had once enrolled in the Archconfraternity of the Divine Child, the hypocrite whose filthy hands had touched the sacred dust from St Gabriel's tomb.

Brother Methodius told the Latin class one morning that the Romans in the great days of the Republic reached the highest level of culture and virtue that a pagan civilisation could possibly attain. Many of their greatest and wisest citizens were hardly distinguishable from Christian gentlemen.

Adrian Sherd did not believe the brother. He knew that one people did not conquer another just to give them paved roads or a new legal system. Adrian knew what power was for. If the citizens of Melbourne had made him their dictator he would have gone straight to a mannequins' school and ordered all the women to undress.

The Romans were no different from himself. Among the back pages of his Latin textbook was a story entitled *The Rape of the Sabine Women*. (Adrian had waited all year for his Latin class to reach this story. But they progressed so slowly through the textbook that he suspected Brother Methodius of deliberately holding them back to avoid the embarrassing story.) Adrian often studied the illustration above the story and even tried to translate the Latin text on his own. Of course it was all watered down to make it suitable for schoolboys. The Roman soldiers only led the women away by their wrists. And even the Latin word *rapio* was translated in the vocabulary at the back of the book as 'seize, snatch up, carry away.' But Adrian was not deceived.

Whenever he read the story of a battle, Adrian barracked for the enemies of Rome. He had no sympathy for Roman boys of his own age. As soon as they started wearing the toga of manhood they could do whatever they liked with their father's slaves. But the young men of Capua or Tarentum or Veii had troubles like his. When they crept out as scouts towards the suburbs of Rome they saw young Publius or Flaccus enjoying himself in his orchard or courtyard with some young woman captured from a tribe like their own. But of course their own people were not strong enough to capture slaves.

But when the Roman legions finally invested their city, the young fellows saw every night, from the tops of their threatened walls, the goings-on in the Romans' comfortable camp. How many of them must have abused themselves for the last time when they lay down briefly between turns on watch and then fallen in battle next morning—killed by the very fellows whose pleasures they had envied so often.

As city after city was conquered in Italy and Gaul and Germany, everyone had the chance to own slaves.

The only people who still kept up the habit of solitary sin were the slaves themselves. Some of them did it thinking of the flaxen-haired maidens they had once known on the banks of the Rhine and would never see again. Others did it peeping around the marble columns at the bare-armed Roman matrons teaching their daughters to spin and weave.

And then came Adrian's hero, a man sworn to destroy Rome and avenge the raped slavegirls and wretched self-abusers.

Hannibal himself came from a lustful land. (It was later to be the home of the Great St Augustine, a sex maniac in his youth, but destined to be the holy Bishop of Hippo and a worthy patron saint for boys struggling to break the habit of impurity.) But as a young man, the Carthaginian had turned his back on all the pagan delights of North Africa. He spent the rest of his life wandering round the countryside of Italy far from the luxuries of the cities.

It was probably a blessing that he was one-eyed. When he led his army to the gates of Rome he would have seen only dimly from his siege-towers the beauty of the women inside the walls that he would never breach. Not that anything would have tempted him to give up his ascetic way of life. It was clear from his superhuman courage and endurance that he was the absolute master of his passions.

After the defeat of Hannibal, the Romans did what

they liked all over the civilised world. The only citizens who refused to join in the orgies were the early Christians, huddled by candlelight in their catacombs deep under Rome. Sometimes they could hardly hear the priest's words during mass for the squeals and grunts coming from overhead as a burly patrician subdued a slavegirl in his *triclinium*, or chased her naked into the pool in his *atrium*. It was no wonder the Christians preached against slavery.

Outside the Pax Romana were the primitive tribes on the Baltic coast or in the darkest Balkans who could only afford one wife each. When Latin writers described these people as barbarians or hinted at their savage practices, they were probably referring to the habit of self-abuse, which the Romans themselves would have all but forgotten.

But the barbarians had their day at last. When the Goths and Vandals sacked Rome, the lucky ones who got there first leaped on the stately Roman matrons and even the trembling Christian virgins with all the ferocity of men who had been shut out for centuries from the delights of the Empire. Those who were still hurrying towards Rome saw the flames rising over the Seven Hills and sinned by themselves one last time at the thought of what must have been happening in the Eternal City (and what they would soon be enjoying themselves).

During the Dark Ages, bestial tribesmen from Central Asia roamed around Italy, grabbing the ex-slavegirls and orphaned patrician girls who were still wandering bewildered beneath the cypresses on the grass-grown Appian Way. Those who missed out on the women abused themselves in front of the shameless murals and mosaics in the crumbling villas or, if they could read, over the scandalous novels and poems of the corrupt last days of the Empire.

But as time passed, some people were sickened by the sexual excesses. Pious men and women went into the desert and lonely places to found monasteries and convents. The Christian way of life was gradually established in the lands once ruled by the Romans. And the sex maniacs, like the wolves and bears and wild boars of Europe, had to flee into the swamps of Lithuania and the glens of Albania and go back to their furtive habits of old.

Once a month the College Chaplain, Father Lacey, strolled down from the local presbytery to talk to Adrian's class.

The chaplain was a tired man with white hair. The only time Adrian had gone to him in confession, Father Lacey had said sadly, 'For the love of God, can't you use some self-control, son?' and then announced the penance and rested his head in his hands and closed his eyes.

One day Father Lacey said to the class, 'The other day I happened to read an Australian Catholic Truth

Society pamphlet. It was written by a famous American Jesuit for young people in America, and I couldn't help thinking how much better off we are in Australia than the Americans—morally I mean. No doubt there are many fine Catholics in America. There are wonderful men among the American clergy. Monsignor Fulton Sheen, Cardinal Cushing, Father Peyton the Rosary Priest—they're not afraid to denounce immorality or Communism. But decent Americans must be nearly swamped sometimes with temptations against purity.

'One of the things the pamphlet was discussing was what the Americans call petting. Now this word "petting" was something I'd never come across before. I still think it sounds more like something you do to your dog or cat. Anyway from what this priest was saying it seems that one of the gravest problems in America today is the petting that goes on amongst young people.

'It's hard to believe, but apparently American fathers and mothers allow their children to stay out half the night in cars and parks and on street corners. And these young flappers and hobbledehoys (because that's all they are at their age—they're still wet behind the ears, so to speak), well naturally they face enormous temptations when they're alone in these places together. And boys, it's all so wrong. You know as well as I do that these things are for married people exclusively.

'Go back for a moment to the Middle Ages, to the great days of the Church. In those days the whole of the civilised world observed the Commandments of God and his Church. There were no problems of court-ship and company-keeping then. This petting that's worrying the people of America hadn't been heard of. Of course the young people of both sexes had the chance to meet each other and look each other over before marriage. They had their dances and balls in those days too. But it was all good wholesome fun. The young ladies were all chaperoned and watched over by their Godfearing parents. And the parents in their wisdom saw to it that no two young people had the opportunity to be alone together where they might face temptations that were too strong for them.

'Those were the days when knights sang about pure love. And it *was* pure. If a young man fell in love with a young woman he might wear her colours into battle or write a poem to her, but he certainly didn't hang around with her in dark doorways on the way home from the pictures.

'Young fellows of your age would probably be off to fight the Turks under the banner of Our Lady. That's who your lady would be. It was the Age of Our Blessed Lady. It's no coincidence that the period of history when men were bravest and most chivalrous and most honourable in the way they behaved towards the fair sex—that age was also the greatest age in history for devotion to Our Lady.

'But to get back to America again. There's another

expression I've heard and I suppose some of you must have too. It's a cheap vulgar expression if ever there was one—sex appeal. The way some Americans behave, you'd think it was all that mattered when a man was thinking of marriage. As long as the woman has sex appeal, she's sure to make a good wife.

'Well, we can see the result of all this in the divorce courts. I suppose even at your age you've read about some of these Hollywood stars getting married—he for the fifth time and she for the third. Think of it. America has gone mad over this thing called sex appeal. But I shouldn't say that. We know there are thousands of good Catholics in America—people in the fine old Catholic cities like Boston and Chicago struggling to bring up their children away from all the madness in the pagan parts of the country. And I'm happy to say there are even a few good Catholics in Hollywood itself.

'I was reading the other day in a Catholic magazine about the film star Maureen O'Sullivan. You've probably watched her if you go to the pictures occasionally. Well, in the midst of all the temptations of Hollywood, that woman is still an outstanding Catholic mother. She's been married all her life to a good Catholic man and they've brought up six or seven fine young children. So it can be done. And don't forget Bing Crosby either—a decent Catholic father who's never had his head turned by Hollywood. But how rare these people are.

'Boys, whenever I think about Hollywood and what it's doing to the world I'm glad I'm an old man. I honestly don't know how I'd save my soul if I had to grow up with all the temptations facing you young fellows today. In my time we had nothing like the films and books and even the newspapers that you fellows have to fight against. Today I suppose there's not one of you who doesn't go to the pictures now and then and give the paganism of Hollywood a chance to infect you.

' "Ah, but I only watch harmless films for general exhibition," you're saying to yourselves. Well, I sometimes wonder if there's any such thing as a harmless film. Did you ever stop to think what sort of lives these actors and actresses lead outside their films? Did you know for instance that nearly every young woman film star has to surrender her body to the director or the producer or whoever he is before she gets the part of the leading lady? And these are the sort of people that the young men and women of today are supposed to have for their heroes and heroines.'

While the chaplain went on to talk about Our Lady again, Adrian thought hard about the film stars he met on his American journeys. If Father Lacey was right about Hollywood, some of these women might have been through unspeakable agonies when they were younger. For all Adrian knew, Jayne with her innocent smile or Marilyn with her serene gaze might have spent her younger days with her eyes shut tight and her mouth clamped to stop herself from screaming while some pot-bellied Cecil B. De Mille ran his sweaty hands over her naked skin.

The women had never mentioned those things to Adrian for fear of spoiling the fun of their outings together. They were generous courageous creatures. He should have spent more time getting to know their life-stories instead of treating them as beautiful playthings. In future he would encourage them to share their old painful secrets with him. They would soon realise that nothing they could tell him about Hollywood would shock him.

Adrian's teachers often said that the name 'Dark Ages' was misleading and unjust. Protestant historians used the name to imply that the centuries when the Church was at the height of its influence were a time of ignorance and misery. In fact, as all fair-minded historians agreed, Europe in the so-called Dark Ages was more peaceful and contented than it had ever been since. And the countryside was dotted with monasteries that were centres of learning. Catholics should get into the habit of using the term 'Middle Ages' to cover the whole period from the end of the Roman Empire to the Renaissance and the Protestant Revolt (or Reformation as it was sometimes called).

Adrian was certain he would never have become a slave to sins of impurity if he had lived in the Middle

Ages. A boy in those days grew up in a simple two-roomed cottage and slept in the same room as his parents and brothers and sisters. He fell asleep hearing the calm breathing of his family round him and the comfortable noises of the cows and horses in the byre through the wall. If his parents wanted to have another baby they waited until their children were all sound asleep before they did anything about it. In a home like this there was no opportunity for a boy to sin in his bed without being discovered.

The luckiest boys went off to monasteries as soon as they reached puberty. In a monastery a boy had so many beautiful things to inspire him that he soon forgot about women. Every day as he walked in procession along the cloisters, he glimpsed through the narrow gothic windows the rolling hillsides covered with fruitful vines or grazing cattle. Every morning he saw the ordained monks each bent over his private altar in the shadowy nooks behind the high altar of the monastery chapel. When the sunlight flashed from the bulky silver of the chalices, and the folds of the elaborate vestments hissed against each other, he knew he would never wish for a greater pleasure than to say mass alone like that each day.

If a boy stayed at home he still had fewer temptations than a modern boy, because he was hardly ever alone. The whole village worked together all day in the fields. And the itinerant Franciscan and Dominican friars wandering up and down the roads of Europe kept a sharp lookout for young fellows mooning around in copses or thickets.

For centuries, Europe was hardly troubled by sex. Her most imaginative young men devoted all their energy to making gold and silver ornaments or stained-glass windows or religious paintings or illuminated parchments.

Historians were right when they said the Modern Age began with the Renaissance. Nude paintings and statues began to appear, even in the most fervently Catholic countries. And many of the female nudes were almost as attractive as twentieth-century film stars.

A young man of the Renaissance would have had many of the sexual problems that bothered Adrian Sherd. Even in those days, artists and sculptors had discovered the tricks that were used by photographers for *Health and Sunshine* magazine. The female statues had smooth marble between their legs and the women in the paintings stood in tantalising poses that did not quite reveal all.

The generation that grew up during the sexual excitement of the Renaissance became more and more resentful of the Church's strict attitude to impurity. These were the people responsible for the Protestant Revolt.

The most important changes made by the Protestants were to remove two institutions which had been a nuisance to the sexually lax. They abolished the celibacy of the clergy and the sacrament of confession.

Martin Luther himself was a priest. Why was he so anxious to do away with the vow of celibacy? Because he himself wanted to marry. And why was he in such a hurry to get married? Adrian had heard many times from priests and brothers that Luther was an unhappy tormented man who should never have become a priest in the first place. It was common knowledge that he was a glutton and used foul language. It wasn't hard to imagine such a man having terrible battles against impure temptations. The woman he eventually married was an ex-nun. What if he had known her, or at least caught sight of her, while he was still a Catholic priest? Was it possible that all his troubles with the Church first started when he realised he couldn't stop thinking about a certain pretty woman?

Adrian had arrived at an explanation for the Protestant Revolt. He believed it was quite likely that the whole thing had been started by a priest who was tempted beyond his endurance to commit a sin of impurity by himself. Adrian found it almost too shocking to think about. He would never have repeated it to anyone, not even a Protestant, because it reflected on the sacred office of the priesthood.

It was a fateful day in the history of impurity when the Protestant leaders decided that it was no longer necessary to go to confession to have your sins forgiven.

In drab cities all over northern Germany young men suddenly realised that what they thought about in bed at night need never be revealed to another living soul. They could do what they liked all week and still stand up on Sunday and sing hymns at the tops of their voices and look the minister in the eye.

The doctrine of predestination was all that a young man could wish for. Once he knew he was one of the elect, he could sin every night of his life and still be saved. If Adrian Sherd could have been born in Geneva in the great days of Calvinism he would have found religion a pleasure instead of the worry it was to him in twentieth-century Australia.

In the Protestant half of Europe, the Middle Ages were swept away forever. In Italy, Spain, Poland and the other Catholic countries, things were much the same as before except that many a young man must have wanted to migrate to a Protestant land.

When the Catholics and Protestants reached the New World, it was easy to see which religion was easier to live under.

At the beginning of the Modern Age, a young Spaniard no older than Adrian stood beside the Rio Grande and looked north-east across unexplored territory. The plains before him stretched away through Texas and Kansas and on to Nebraska and far Iowa. It should have been a stirring sight, but the young Spaniard was deeply troubled. He foresaw all the afternoons when he would stand alone by clear streams among miles of waving grasses and remember girls and women he had seen in old Castile and feel the overpowering urge to commit a sin of impurity. By the time he had explored the American prairies he might have had a hundred sins on his soul. When he got back to a Spanish city he would have to go to confession. It was a terrifying prospect.

At the same time, a young English gentleman looked westwards from a hilltop in Virginia. He was eager to explore all he could of the great continent before him. He would be a long time alone in the forests and prairies, but he knew a trick to cheer himself up at night. While he did it he would remember the pretty young ladies he used to admire each Sunday in his little parish church in Devon. Or he could look forward to the day when he arrived back in England and shook hands with the minister and sat down in his old family pew and looked round to choose one of the young ladies for his wife.

Late one Sunday afternoon Adrian was lying on his bed in his room at the back of the house. The sky outside his window was full of high grey clouds. A strong wind thumped the outside of the house and rattled a piece of timber somewhere in the wall. Adrian's mother and his youngest brother were away visiting one of his aunts. His father was dragging a plank backwards and forwards across the backyard trying to level the sandy soil before he sowed it with lawn seed. Adrian's younger brother was on the path at the side of the house, bouncing a tennis-ball against the chimney.

Next door, Andy Horvath and his wife and two or three other couples were having some kind of party in the bungalow behind the Horvaths' half-built house. At about three o'clock they had started singing foreign songs and they were still going strong. There was one song they kept coming back to. Adrian had heard it three or four times already. The way they sang the chorus made the hair prickle on the back of his neck. It was sad and savage and hopeless.

Adrian thought of all the quiet backyards stretching away for miles in every direction. Then he thought of America.

He went outside to the shed and sent his passenger train around the track. It stopped in the Catskill Mountains. He went back inside to his bed and pulled a rug over himself and thought about the green mountains of New York State.

Sherd grabbed Gene and Ann and Kim firmly by their wrists and bundled them into his car. He told them they were going to the Catskills just for the hell of it. Soon they were among steep hillsides where shady forests alternated with lush green meadows. Sherd stopped the car beside a lofty waterfall that hung like a veil of silver over a secluded glade.

He didn't waste time with idle chatter or a picnic lunch. As soon as they reached the little glade he told the women to get undressed. For some reason Gene and Ann and Kim wanted to tease him. They ran a little way into the trees and stood laughing at him.

But Sherd had come to the Catskills to save himself from being bored to death. He was in no mood to be trifled with. He ran after them. As they ran and stumbled ahead of him he had glimpses of their pink thighs and white undies that made him crazy with desire.

He caught the three of them in a meadow where the grass was waist-high and thick with wildflowers. He behaved like the strong silent type. He stripped all three of them. Then he flung himself on the woman of his choice and took his pleasure roughly and without a word of thanks. Afterwards he lay where he was and watched the meadows in the Catskills turning slowly from green to grey.

Mr Sherd came in from the backyard and said he'd call it a day because the sand was blowing all over him. Then Adrian's brother came inside and asked Adrian to play miniature cricket on the path and guess which way his spinners would turn. Adrian agreed to play for ten minutes and no more.

He stood at one end of the path while his brother bowled underarm spinners with a tennis-ball. When his ten minutes of cricket were over he sat down and listened.

The Hungarians were still singing in their bungalow. They were starting again on their favourite song. Adrian guessed it was about far-off mountains and forests. He tried to memorise the tune. They started off shouting it, but something stopped them when they reached the chorus. Adrian ran over and pressed his ear against a hole in the fence. He could hear the separate voices of each man and woman trying to pick up the song again. They were making noises like sobs, as though they couldn't sing for crying.

At school next morning O'Mullane could hardly wait to tell his friends about his adventure on the Sunday afternoon. He said, 'I was watching the tennis on the courts near the racecourse and having dog-fights on my bike with Laurie D'Arcy when I saw one of the strappers from Neville Byrne's stables—the one they call Macka—standing behind the pine trees smoushing this tart. She had red hair. I kept my eye on them and I saw Macka trying to get her into one of those old sheds behind the six-furlongs barrier. Well, he got her there at last and I said to D'Arcy we'd better be in this.

'So we sneaked up and peeped into the shed. Macka had her in a corner leaning back over a rail. He was still smoushing her and getting a handful at the same time under her jumper.'

Adrian said, 'Was she putting up a fight against him?'

O'Mullane said, 'Search me. Old Macka put a half-Nelson on her. He's a tough little bastard. She could have stopped him easily enough if she'd really tried I suppose. She kept saying "Not here, Bernie! Not here, Bernie!" Anyway she got away from him in the end and ran down a little hill into that long grass near the big iron fence. But Macka caught up with her and pushed her over or she dragged him down or they both fell over but anyway they ended up on top of each other and the last thing we saw was old Macka going for all he was worth.'

Adrian said, 'You mean he was doing her? Out there in the grass beside the racecourse?'

O'Mullane said, 'What do you reckon? But listen to the end of the story. I was sure I'd seen the tart somewhere before and Laurie D'Arcy said the same. After tea that night D'Arcy came round to my place and said he could show her to me right then. So he took me over to the Yarram Road shops and there she was serving in the milk bar with an apron on over the same clothes she was wearing with Macka. She said, "Yes, boys. What'll you have?" I said half out loud, "The same as Macka got," and I reckon she almost heard me.'

For the rest of the day Adrian felt sorry for himself for having to spend his Sunday lying on his bed dreaming of the Catskills while O'Mullane was having a real adventure at Caulfield Racecourse.

That afternoon he left his train at Caulfield and walked across the racecourse to the paddock that O'Mullane had described. He walked quickly across it, looking for a place where the grass was flattened, but there was nothing to tell him where the strapper and the girl had been. He stood where the grass was tallest and looked all round. The place was really only a large yard. It was not even private—a footpath ran close by, and one end of the yard was the wire fence of the public tennis courts.

Adrian hurried out of the racecourse and down to the little shopping centre in Yarram Road. He went into the milk bar. A young woman with red hair came out through the curtained doorway and said, 'Yes please?' He looked down to avoid her eyes and asked for two packets of P.K. chewing gum. He stared at her furtively while she served him. She was nothing like a film star but she was pretty in her own way. What surprised him most was how ordinary she looked for a girl in a story. He could see the pores in her cheeks and the freckles on the backs of her hands. And when she handed him his change and he stared at her apron, he saw the vague shape of her breasts rise and fall as she breathed.

He got out of the shop as fast as he could. The story of Macka and the girl was preposterous. He could not believe that on an ordinary dull Sunday afternoon, while he was lying on his bed listening to the wind and the rowdy New Australians next door, a girl with freckles on her wrists and no make-up on her face walked out of her sleepy milk bar and rolled round in the grass on Caulfield Racecourse with some strapper.

O'Mullane must have made up the whole story—perhaps because he was bored too. And it was a pretty poor story compared with what happened in the Catskills.

When he was younger, Adrian Sherd used to wish he had been born the eldest son of an English country gentleman in the eighteenth or nineteenth century and gone to one of the great public schools.

At school he would have read the classics in his private study and played cricket or rugger every afternoon. In his holidays he would have ridden across the broad acres he was going to inherit from his father. The tenants would have tipped their caps to the young master and told him where to find birds' nests and badgers' sets.

But after he had gone to St Carthage's College and learned from Cornthwaite and his friends what women were for, he realised there was something missing from the life of the young English gentleman.

When the son of the manor visited his neighbours, he could never meet the daughter of the house alone. Her nanny or governess or music teacher was always with her. The young fellow stood beside the harpsichord and turned the pages of her music, but the neck of her dress was too high for him to see anything.

Sometimes in his own house he followed the maid into the pantry to look up under her dress when she climbed to the highest shelf. But he always heard a discreet cough behind him and turned round to see the butler looking at him severely.

On his rides across his father's estates he saw plenty of girls—the daughters of yeomen and labourers and gamekeepers. But the English climate was so bad that they were always rugged up in spencers and mufflers. He wasted a lot of time dreaming of the warm weather when he might surprise a young woman bathing in a stream after a hard day's work in the harvest. And he realised why so many English poets praised the springtime.

At school it was painful to read stories of the pagan Greeks and Romans and their sunny Mediterranean lands while snow covered the quadrangle, and the only female in the building was the elderly Matron with her mustard plasters and camphorated oil. He was reduced to dreaming of a day when one of his chums would receive a party of visitors. The chum might invite him to take his sister's arm and do a turn of the garden path.

In the nineteenth century, when things were worst for young Englishmen (the women with iron hoops in their clothes and long leather boots and collars up to their chins) they heard about a land where people dressed less formally because it was summer for six months of the year. It was no wonder that so many of them flocked to Australia.

But if the young Englishman had a hard time, it was harder still for the poor Irish lad. Adrian Sherd had no doubt that in all the history of the world the worst possible place for a young man was Ireland after St Patrick had converted it to the Catholic faith.

To begin with, the country was overcrowded. Watchful old men sat outside every cottage door and pious old women in black shawls passed to and fro along every country lane. A young man trying to spy on a girl or catch her alone in a quiet place was nearly always reported to the parish priest.

Even the landscape was against the young Irishman. There were no dells or dingles or forests or prairies in Ireland. The country was mostly bare stony fields and peat bogs. When a young fellow finally grew so desperate that he had to do it to himself, the only place he could go was behind the largest stone on some hillside. Many a time the stone was not even big enough to hide him properly and he had to lie with his legs drawn up or crouch like a hare against the grass while he relieved himself as best he could. If he forgot himself in his excitement and let his twitching legs protrude from behind the stone, he was sure to be observed by some gossiping jarvey on the nearest road.

It was almost certainly this problem that drove the early Irish explorers out into the Atlantic. They were looking for the Western Isles or O Brasil, Isle of the Blest—some uninhabited place where a young man and his girlfriend or a man and his wife or just a young man by himself could get away on their own whenever he felt like it. If the Irish had reached America, as Adrian Sherd's father claimed they had, it would have been the perfect land for them. They certainly deserved it, after all the misery they had put up with at home.

But there was one thing that helped the young Irishman in his trouble. The women of Ireland practised the virtues of modesty and chastity like no other women in history. Thousands of them spent their formative years as Children of Mary. They imitated Our Lady so faithfully that they ended up looking like Madonnas with their white complexions and their dark eyes demurely downcast. Thanks to the exemplary virtues of Irish womanhood, the young Irishman was never tormented by the sight of bare legs or daring swimsuits. In fact, Adrian suspected that with priests and parents watching them closely, and the women of Ireland so careful not to tempt them, many young Irishmen might have avoided sins of impurity altogether.

When Adrian was still at primary school he used to go every year to the St Patrick's Night concert in his local town hall. One of the items was always *Eileen Aroon* sung by a choir of girls from Star of the Sea Convent, North Essendon. When the girls came to the words, 'Truth is a fixed star,' Adrian was always so inspired by the unearthly beauty of the melody and the innocent upturned faces with their rounded pink lips where no foul young man had ever planted an impure kiss, that he looked up past the blazing chandeliers of the town hall, out over the north-western suburbs of Melbourne and across the thistles and basalt rocks of the plains beyond, towards the dark sky over Ireland. There were fixed stars shining over Ireland—the stars in the dark blue mantle of Our Lady, who was still guarding the daughters of that holy country as she had for centuries past.

The last time Adrian had seen the concert (in the year before he began at St Carthage's) he was so moved that he made a vow never to think an impure thought about any girl with an Irish-looking face or an Irish-sounding name.

Adrian had kept his vow faithfully. None of the hundreds of females he had used for his pleasure had been Irish types. But he often wondered how he would have survived in the Ireland of his ancestors, where the only girls he ever saw would have been Irish colleens. Probably he would have emigrated as his ancestors had done. He hoped he would have had the sense to head for America instead of Australia.

On some afternoons Adrian Sherd caught a tram instead of walking down Swindon Road from St Carthage's to the Swindon railway station. The tram was always crowded with boys from Eastern Hill Grammar School and Canterbury Ladies' College. Adrian knew that these schools were two of the oldest and wealthiest in Melbourne. He felt very ignorant not even knowing where they were among the miles of garden suburbs beyond Swindon.

Whenever he looked at the Eastern Hill boys Adrian felt awkward and grubby. He held his Gladstone bag in front of his knees to hide the shiny domes in his trouser legs. He remembered all the brothers' talk about St Carthage's being a fine old school with a reputation for turning out Catholic doctors and barristers and professional men. It was bullshit. The Eastern Hill boys never saw Adrian, even when he was crowded so close that his sweaty maroon cap was only inches from their faces. When the tram lurched and he fell among them, the superb voices kept up their banter while one of the fellows brushed Adrian away like some kind of insect.

After a few weeks on the trams Adrian learned to stand unobtrusively near these young gentlemen, keeping his back to them but listening carefully.

One Eastern Hill fellow went to a party every Saturday night. The parties were in strange places that Adrian had never heard of—Blairgowrie, Portsea, Mt Eliza. At Blairgowrie the fellow had met a girl called Sandy and taken her home and crashed on with her. He said he was going to ring her up and ask her out to a party at Judy's place in Beaumaris. Judy's parents were to be in Sydney for the weekend. The party would be a riot.

The fellow went on talking, but Adrian couldn't take any more. He wanted to sit down in a quiet place and try to comprehend the incredible story he had just heard. But then the fellow told his friends he must move along the tram and win Lois. Adrian had to watch.

The fellow walked purposefully up the tram and leaned over a group of Canterbury girls. A girl with shapely legs and large innocent eyes gazed up into his face. They talked. She nodded and smiled. The fellow said something funny. He let it slide out of the corner of his mouth. The girl leaned back and showed the full length of her white throat and laughed. The fellow stood back and admired his work. Then he said goodbye and walked back to his friends.

They took the whole thing quite calmly. One of them said, 'Are you going to ask her out?'

The party-goer said, 'I don't really know. She's a nice kid. She'd be lots of fun. I think her parents make her study most weekends. I might wait and take her out to some quiet party not too far from her home.' The others were gentlemen enough to drop the subject.

It was some weeks before Adrian dared to stand near the Canterbury girls. He didn't want to offend them with the sight of his pimply face and crumpled suit and the Catholic emblems on his pocket and cap.

There were four Canterbury girls who were always huddled at one end of the tram. Whenever Adrian sneaked a look at them they were chattering or smiling with their gloved hands pressed daintily to their lips. They spoke so confidentially to each other that he guessed they were talking about boys. Each day for a week he stood a little nearer to their seats, always keeping his back to the girls. He hoped to learn something that even the Eastern Hill boys didn't know.

When he finally stood within earshot of them he was shocked to hear them talking the whole time about clothes—the ones they wore last weekend, the shops where they bought them, the alterations they had to make before they could wear them, the way they creased or crumpled after wearing and what they were going to wear next weekend.

Adrian was disappointed at first, but he worked out later that the girls only worried about clothes because they wanted to look beautiful when they went to parties with the Eastern Hill fellows.

As Adrian got to know the Eastern Hill men better, he discovered that some of them weren't perfect. There was one chap who was on the training list for the first eighteen in the Public Schools football competition. One day on the tram he was limping. He told his friends the story of the torn ligaments in his knee. Each time he said the word 'torn' he winced ever so faintly. It was the first time that Adrian had caught an Eastern Hill fellow doing what the boys at St Carthage's did so often. It was called putting on an act.

But when an Eastern Hill man put on an act it really worked. The fellow with the injured knee limped up to a group of Canterbury girls and told his story again.

Each time he winced, the concern in the girls' faces made Adrian almost wince himself.

Sometimes a Canterbury girl put on an act too. One day Adrian heard some girls talking about a debate. They thought their own side should have won. The topic of the debate had been 'That the introduction of television will do more harm than good.' At St Carthage's any boy who tried to talk about schoolwork outside the classroom would have been howled down, but the girls in the tram chattered eagerly about the effect of television on family life and reading and juvenile delinquency.

Then a girl who was angry that her side had lost the debate said, 'Illogical. The opposition's case was utterly illogical.' The big words embarrassed Adrian. The girl was putting on an act.

Some Eastern Hill boys joined the girls. A tall fellow with a voice like a radio announcer's said, 'What are you so excited about, Carolyn?'

Adrian listened hard. The Eastern Hill boys never discussed schoolwork on the tram. What would the fellow say when he realised the girls were only talking about a debate?

Carolyn explained exactly why the opposition's case had been weak. When she was finished, the tall fellow said, 'I quite agree with you,' and looked genuinely troubled. Carolyn smiled. She was very grateful for the fellow's sympathy.

Late in the year the elms around the tram-stop at

the Swindon Town Hall were thick with green leaves. When Adrian boarded the tram after school the sun was still high in the sky. In the non-smoking compartment the wooden shutters covered the windows, and the Canterbury girls sat in a rich summery twilight. After Adrian left the tram it turned sharply in the direction of St Kilda and the sea. He always watched the tram out of sight and wondered whether the young men and women still on board could smell salt in the evening breeze.

The Eastern Hill fellows had begun to talk about the holidays. They were all going away somewhere. Some of them said they would try to catch up with each other on New Year's Eve, but God knew what they might be up to that night. The way they chuckled about New Year's Eve was not quite gentlemanly.

The girls were going away too. They were talking about beachwear and party frocks. Adrian wished he could warn them to be careful of their friends from Eastern Hill on New Year's Eve.

It was the athletics season at St Carthage's. On House Sports day the weather was as hot as summer. Adrian noticed a strange girl watching the races with O'Mullane and Cornthwaite. Nobody introduced her properly but Adrian worked out that she was O'Mullane's sister Monica from St Brigid's College, the girls' school along the street from St Carthage's.

The boys from St Carthage's rarely saw the girls from St Brigid's. But on St Carthage's sports day any

St Brigid's girl with a brother at St Carthage's was allowed to miss the last period and visit the sports. (The girls had their own sports afternoon on the lawn behind their tall timber fence. Boys walking past heard them cheering politely but saw nothing.)

Adrian wasn't brave enough to talk to O'Mullane's sister but he wanted to impress her. He developed a limp. He explained to O'Mullane that his ligaments were probably torn somewhere. He sat down and ran his fingers along his calf and thigh muscles. The girl took no notice, but O'Mullane glared at him when his fingers moved above his knee.

Adrian tried to amuse the girl. He called out, 'Come on, Tubby,' to a plump boy struggling in a race. He told O'Mullane he would love to see some events at the sports set aside for the brothers—speed strapping contests, or sprint races with all competitors wearing soutanes. Monica O'Mullane looked at him but didn't smile.

Cornthwaite went onto the arena and left his track-suit behind. Adrian tied the legs of the tracksuit together. When Cornthwaite came back and tried to pull the suit on he fell with all his weight against Adrian. Adrian lost his balance and knocked O'Mullane against his sister. The girl dropped her gloves and program and had to pick them up herself.

No one laughed. Cornthwaite said loudly, 'You pathetic idiot, Sherd.'

After the sports Adrian walked alone to the tram-stop. He caught a tram much later than usual. He saw none of the young men and women he knew, but in one corner a strange fellow from Eastern Hill was chatting with a Canterbury girl as though they had been friends since childhood. Adrian heard part of a story the fellow was telling—something about him and his friends greasing the horizontal bar in the gym just before someone called Mr Fancy Pants started his workout. The girl thought it was the funniest story she had ever heard. As she laughed she almost leaned her head on the fellow's shoulder.

Adrian Sherd knew very little about Australia. This might have been because he never saw any Australian films. As a child he had seen *The Overlanders*, but all he remembered about it was how strange the characters' accents sounded.

Australian history was much less colourful than British or European or Bible history. The only part of it that interested Adrian was the period before Australia was properly explored.

In those days there was no reason for a man to go on being bored or unhappy in a city. Just across the Great Dividing Range were thousands of miles of temperate grasslands and open forest country where he could live as he pleased out of reach of curious neighbours and disapproving relatives.

Adrian had an old school atlas with a page of maps showing how Australia had been explored. In one of the first maps, the continent was coloured black except for a few yellow indentations on the eastern coast where the first settlements were. Adrian drew a much larger map with the same colour scheme, except that the dark inland was broken by tracts of a sensuous orange colour. They looked small on the map, but some of them were fifty miles across. They were the lost kingdoms of Australia, established in the early days by men after his own heart.

One fellow had chosen the lush plains of the Mitchell River near the Gulf of Carpentaria. On a low hill he had built a replica of the Temple of Solomon. The walls were hung with purple tapestries and the servants beat the time of day on copper gongs. The women went bare-breasted because the weather was always pleasantly warm.

Another man had chosen the park-like forests of the Victorian Wimmera. On the shores of Lake Albacutya he had set up a township copied from Baghdad in the days of Haroun Al Rashid. Each house had a fountain and a pool in a walled courtyard where the women were free to remove their veils.

In a valley of the Otway Ranges one man had a palace in which the walls were covered with copies of every obscene picture ever painted. A large tract in the Ord River district of Western Australia had been turned into Peru, with its own Inca and Brides of the Sun. Somewhere in Bass Strait was an island exactly like Tahiti before the Europeans found it.

Adrian had never seen any of the places in Australia where these palaces and cities might have been built. He had only been outside Melbourne two or three times. Those were the few brief holidays he had spent on his uncle's farm at Orford, near Colac, in the Western District of Victoria.

The landscape at Orford was all low green hills. Every few hundred yards along the roads was a farmhouse of white weatherboards with a red roof. Near every farmhouse was a dairy and milking shed of creamy-grey stone, a stack of baled hay and a windbreak of huge old cypresses.

Adrian's uncle and aunt had seven children. They played Ludo and Happy Families and Cap the Dunce for hours on the back veranda. Sometimes they read *Captain Marvel* and *Cat-Man* and *Doll-Man* comics in the lowest branches of the cypresses or tried to act stories from their comics around the woodheap and the haystack. Adrian asked them whether any parts of their district were still unexplored. They said they weren't sure, but they climbed onto the cowyard fence with him to point out that their own farm was nothing but grass and barbed-wire fences.

Adrian stood on the highest rung of the fence and looked all round him. The only hopeful sign was the roof of a strange building behind a line of trees on a distant hill. The heat off the paddocks made ridges and shapes like battlements in the roof. If the right sort of men had been the first to find their way to the lonely parts of Australia, the building might have been a temple of the Sun-God or a palace of pleasure.

But on the following Sunday Adrian went with all his uncle's family to mass and found that the building on the hill was St Finbar's church.

Not just the things that might have happened, but many important events that actually happened were missing from Australian history books. Adrian often thought about the early settlers. What did a man think when he sat down at night and realised he was the only human being for fifty miles around? If he was an Irishman he probably remembered that God and his guardian angel were watching over him. But what if he was a convict shepherd who had never been to church, or an English farmer who didn't take his religion seriously?

Somewhere in Australia, in a warm sheltered valley overhung with wattles or in tall grass in the lee of an outcrop of boulders, there should have been a granite obelisk or a cairn of stones with an inscription such as:

NEAR THIS SPOT ON THE EVENING OF
27 DECEMBER 1791
ALFRED HENRY WAINWRIGHT AGED 19 YEARS

BECAME THE FIRST EUROPEAN TO COMMIT
AN ACT OF SELF-ABUSE
ON AUSTRALIAN SOIL

Of course the Aborigines had been in Australia for centuries before the white men, but no one would ever know their history. They had lived a carefree bestial existence. Some of them, like King Parajoulta of Blue Mud Bay with his eight wives, showed signs of imagination. But without books or films they had no inspiration to do unusual deeds.

Adrian knew he was right to complain about the dullness of Australian history when he found a certain illustrated article in *People* magazine. Far out beyond the prairies of America, in a place called Short Creek, Arizona, a reporter had discovered families of Mormons still practising polygamy. It seemed that when polygamy had been outlawed many years before, a few men who wanted to keep up the custom had found their way to a remote district and gone on living the life they wanted.

It was one more proof that Americans were more imaginative and adventurous than Australians. There were plains and mountain ranges in Australia where whole tribes of polygamists could have settled. But now there were churches like St Finbar's, Orford, on the hilltops and people like Adrian's cousins staring out across the plains.

Adrian studied the photos in *People*. The families of Short Creek were disappointing to look at. The women had plain, pinched faces with the rimless spectacles that so many Americans wore, and barefooted children hanging onto their cotton dresses. But behind the town of Short Creek, rising abruptly from where the dusty main street petered out, was an enormous mountain range—the sort of place where a tribe of pagans or a palace with a harem of a hundred rooms might be safe from discovery for many years yet.

One morning Father Lacey spoke to Adrian's class about the Catholic Press.

He said, 'I don't have to remind you that here in Melbourne we have two excellent weekly papers, the *Tribune* and the *Advocate*, to give us the Catholic interpretation of the news. One of these papers should be in every Catholic home every week of the year to give you the sort of news you won't read in the secular press. I know of several good Catholic families who read their *Advocate* or *Tribune* from cover to cover each week and don't buy any of the secular newspapers. I'm happy to say those families are better informed about current affairs and the moral issues of modern life than most people who can't do without their *Sun* and *Herald* and *Sporting Globe*.

'You boys are perhaps too young to realise it, but I'm simply amazed sometimes at the stories and pictures

110

they print in the daily newspapers. In my day it was unheard of, but nowadays you can visit nearly any Catholic home and see papers lying around in full view of the children with stories of hideous crimes and lurid pictures staring up at you. It's one more sign that we're slowly turning into a pagan society. And far too many Catholics take this sort of thing lying down.

'There's one Melbourne newspaper in particular that regularly prints suggestive pictures which are quite unnecessary and don't have anything to do with the news of the day. I won't name the paper, but some of you have probably noticed what I'm talking about. I hope your parents have, anyway.

'This very morning for example I happened to notice a picture on one of their inside front pages. It was what they call a sweater girl. That's something else by the way that's crept into our modern pagan attitudes. I'm talking about the emphasis that some people nowadays put on the female bosom.

'Now we all know the human body is one of the most marvellous things that God created. And great artists for centuries have praised its beauty by painting it and making statues of it. But a true artist will tell you that you can't make a great work of art if you emphasise one part of your subject matter out of all proportion to its importance. Any artist worth his salt knows that true beauty consists of fitting all the elements of a design into a harmonious whole.

111

'I'll speak quite frankly now. There are many famous and wonderful pictures of the naked female body with the bosom exposed—some of them are priceless treasures in the Vatican itself. But you'll never find one of these masterpieces drawing attention to the bosom or making it appear larger than it really is.

'But to get back to these newspaper pictures. I must say I find it very sad to see a young woman being persuaded to stand up and pose in an awkward way to draw attention to the bosom that Almighty God gave her for a holy purpose—and all for the amusement of a few perverted men.

'Now this particular newspaper has been doing this sort of thing so often that we can safely say it's all part of a deliberate plan to appeal to the lowest elements among its readers. The men who issue the instructions for these sort of pictures to be printed are sitting back smugly, imagining that all these sweater girls and bathing beauties are going to sell thousands of extra copies of their paper.

'But that's just where they're wrong. Boys, I'll let you into a little secret. There are large numbers of decent Catholic men right now who are working to make this paper clean up its pictures or else they'll put it out of business.

'Yes. That's what I said. There are some of them who've formed a little group in this very parish of Swindon. This is real Catholic Action at work. No doubt some of your fathers are forming groups in your own parishes. The way these men are working is to bring these pictures of bosoms and under-dressed women to the notice of their workmates and fellow parishioners and friends and point out how unnecessary they are in a daily newspaper. There's no doubt that every decent person, whether they're Catholics or non-Catholics, will object to these pictures leaping out at them over the breakfast table or on the tram to the office. And if every one of those people stops buying the paper concerned and writes a letter of complaint to the management we'll soon get results.

'Our men have a few other tricks up their sleeves too, only I'm not free to tell you about them at the moment. Let's just say I think you'll find these bare limbs and exaggerated bosoms will soon be disappearing from our streets and homes. And when they do we'll have the Catholic men of Melbourne to thank for it.'

Adrian Sherd was almost certain that the priest was talking about the *Argus*, which was delivered to the Sherds' house every morning because Mr Sherd said it was the best paper for racing and football. Most of the women that Adrian took with him on his American journey had first appeared to him in the pages of the *Argus*. The poses they struck to excite him (leaning back against a rock with hands on hips and legs wide apart, or bending forward to expose the deep cleavage at the top of their bathers) came straight from the films section of the Saturday *Argus*.

If the Catholic men persuaded Mr Sherd to stop buying the *Argus*, Adrian would have no chance to meet new women. It was different for Cornthwaite and his friends who were allowed out to films any night of the week. They had all the beautiful women in the world to choose from. But Adrian depended on the *Argus* to introduce him to new faces and breasts and legs. Without it he would have to live on his memories. Or he might even end up like those old perverts who got arrested for drilling holes in bathroom walls or women's changing sheds at the beach.

Adrian talked to his friends afterwards. Stan Seskis said, 'It's the *Argus* all right, and my old man's one of those that are going to clean it up. He buys it every day and draws big circles in red ink round all the pictures of the tarts. Then he cuts them all out and pastes them in a scrapbook and takes them to a meeting every week at Mr Moroney's house.

'And it's not just pictures he collects. Sometimes he cuts out a story about some court case. He puts a red line under certain words that shouldn't be seen in a family newspaper. I'll bet none of you bastards know what a criminal assault really means.'

No one knew. Seskis told them. 'It's the same thing as rape. And if you read the *Argus* carefully every day, in the end you'll find a story about a criminal assault.

And if you use your imagination you can work out just how the bastard raped the tart.'

Adrian decided to prepare for the day when the *Argus* had to stop printing the pictures he needed. Every morning in the train between Accrington and Swindon he looked around for young women who could eventually take over from his film stars and beauty queens. It was nearly a week before he found a face and figure to compare with the *Argus* women. He picked out a young married woman so carefully groomed that she must have worked in a chemist's shop or a hairdresser's salon. He studied her closely without anyone noticing him. That night he invited her to join him and two friends on a trip through the piney woods of Georgia. She came along cheerfully but Adrian soon wished she had stayed at home.

Adrian could not relax with her. Whenever he met her eyes he remembered he would have to face her on the train next morning. She would be dressed in her ordinary clothes again (in Georgia she wore candy-striped shorts and a polka-dot blouse) and he would be wearing the grey suit and maroon cap of St Carthage's College. It would be hard pretending that nothing had happened between them on the previous night.

There was another difficulty. Jayne and Marilyn and Susan and their many friends always had the same look about them—a wide-eyed half-smile with lips slightly parted. The new woman had an irritating way

115

of changing her expression. She seemed to be thinking too much.

Worse still, Adrian realised when he saw her in Georgia that her breasts had no fixed shape. Each of the other women had a pair as firm and inflexible as a statue's. But the new girl's lolled and bounced on her chest so that he could never be sure what size and shape they were.

When the afternoon reached its climax Adrian gave up trying to fit the new girl into Georgia and deserted her for his old favourites.

Next morning the young woman was in her usual place in the train. Her face was stern and haughty and her breasts had almost disappeared under the folds of her cardigan. When the train crossed the high viaducts approaching Swindon, the morning sunlight came through the windows. The carriage was suddenly bright and warm like a clearing in the piney woods. Adrian looked down from where he was standing and saw a picture in someone's *Argus*. It's title was 'Why Wait Till Summer?' and it showed a girl in twopiece bathers on the deck of a yacht. She had a smile that showed she was eager to please, and her breasts were a shape that could be memorised at a glance.

Adrian looked from the picture to the girl in the corner. Her seat was still in shadow. She looked grey and insubstantial.

In school that morning Adrian thought of writing an anonymous letter to the editor of the *Argus* praising

116

pictures like 'Why Wait Till Summer?' and wondered if it would help to save the pictures from the Catholic men.

One very hot Saturday morning Adrian Sherd was staring at a picture of the Pacific coast near Big Sur. He hadn't been to America for several days, and he was planning a sensational extravaganza for that very night with four or perhaps even five women against a backdrop of mighty cliffs and redwood forests.

His mother came into the room and said she had been down to the phone box talking to his Aunt Francie and now Adrian and his brothers and mother and Aunt Francie and her four kids were going on the bus to Mordialloc beach for a picnic.

The Sherds went to the beach only once or twice a year. Adrian had never learned to swim properly. He usually sat in the shallows and let the waves knock him around, or dug moats and canals at the water's edge while the sun burned his pale skin crimson. At mealtime he sat at a grimy picnic bench with a damp shirt sticking to his skin and his bathers full of grit. His young brothers and cousins jostled him to get at the food, and he shrank back from the tomato seeds dribbling down their chins or the orange pips they spat carelessly around them.

On the long bus trip to Mordialloc, Adrian decided to make the day pass more quickly by observing women on the beach. He might see something (a shoulder strap slipping, or a roll of flesh escaping from a tight bathing suit just below the buttocks) that could be fitted into his adventures at Big Sur to make them more realistic.

The two families reached Mordialloc in the hottest part of the afternoon. They were going to stay at the beach until dark. The women and the oldest children carried baskets and string-bags packed with cold corned beef, lettuce leaves, tomatoes, hard-boiled eggs, jars of fruit salad and slices of bread-and-butter, all wrapped in damp tea-towels.

Adrian put on his bathers in the changing shed. He looked into the toilet cubicles and shower room to read the writing on the walls. Most of it had been whitewashed only recently. The boldest inscription was in a toilet cubicle. It read simply: MISS KATHLEEN MAHONEY YOU BEAUT. There was no illustration.

Adrian pitied the young man who had written those words. He was some larrikin who knew nothing about life in America. All he could use to excite himself was some girl he had lusted after in his own suburb. And Kathleen Mahoney was a good Catholic name. The girl had probably never looked twice at the uncouth bastard who scrawled her name in toilets.

If Adrian had had the time, he would have scratched out the inscription. But just then he found something much more important to worry about.

Even though the day was hot, his cock had shrivelled up to the size of a boy's while he was undressing. It was too small to dangle properly. When he pulled on his bathers it made a tiny pathetic lump that was clearly visible in the cloth between his legs. He walked out of the changing shed with small careful steps so his miserable button wouldn't be too obvious.

He got back to his mother and aunt and saw a strange woman in onepiece tartan bathers standing between them. When she turned round it was only his cousin Bernadette, who was no older than he was. He had taken no notice of her in her ordinary clothes. Her face was nothing much to look at and she always had her young sisters hanging round her. Now he saw that her thighs were as big and heavy as her mother's, and her breasts were a much more interesting shape.

Mrs Sherd and her sister Francie told all their children to swim in the shallow water until they were sent for. Francie said, 'We're going to sit down and have a good rest and we don't want any kids hanging round us.'

Adrian walked down into the sea and sat down. He kept his bathers underwater to hide the stub between his legs and looked around for his cousin Bernadette. She was nowhere in the water, or on the sand. He looked back at the pavilion. She was sitting in her tartan bathers beside the two women. She must have decided she wasn't one of the children any more.

Adrian was angry. He had to splash around in the shallows with his brothers and young cousins while Bernadette sat gossiping with the women. Yet he had romped with film stars on scenic beaches in America while Bernadette looked as though she had never even had a boyfriend.

He spent his time in the water making elaborate plans for his trip to the coast of northern California that evening. Bernadette would have looked at him differently if she could have known his true strength—in a few hours he was going to wear out three film stars one after the other.

At teatime Bernadette made a point of helping the women serve the food. Adrian stayed where his mother had told him to wait with the other children. When Bernadette came near him he pulled his shoulders back and drew himself up to his full height. He wanted her to realise he was taller and more powerfully built than she was. But she kept her eyes lowered and he had to sit down and cross his legs in case she noticed the insignificant wrinkle in the front of his bathing trunks.

While his cousin served the food she had to stand very close to Adrian. Two or three times she leaned across him so that her breasts were almost under his nose. Adrian thought he might as well glance at her body. Perhaps some detail of it would come in handy in America when he couldn't visualise one of his film stars as accurately as he needed.

Adrian pretended to be busy with his bread and butter and hard-boiled egg while he inspected Bernadette at close range. It was the nearest he had ever been to a full-grown Australian female body in a bathing suit, but he was far from impressed.

The skin between her throat and breasts had been burnt a little by the sun. It was a raw flesh-pink colour instead of the uniform golden-cream he preferred in a beautiful woman. There was even a small brown mole on the very slope where one of her breasts began, which automatically disqualified her from perfection.

Whenever she walked, her thighs and calves turned out to be full of muscles. Even the slightest movement made one or other of the muscles tense or slacken. It was impossible for Adrian to tell whether the legs were shapely because she never once kept them in an artistic pose.

He risked a quick glance between her legs and saw something that shocked him. When she passed close by him again he looked a second time. He was not mistaken. High up inside her leg where the white of her thigh met the tartan fabric of her bathers, a single dark brown hair, perhaps an inch long, lay curled against her skin.

He could not tell whether the hair had sprouted from the thigh itself or whether he was looking at the end of it only, and its roots were somewhere in the mysterious territory beneath her bathers. But it didn't really matter. Either way, the coarse coiled hair made nonsense of any claim she had to beauty. He could call to mind a whole gallery of beautiful legs. They were all motionless and symmetrical and as smooth as the finest marble.

After tea Adrian had to go back to the changing shed to put his clothes on. On the way to the shed he tried to remind himself of the trip to Big Sur that would make up for his miserable day at Mordialloc. But all his staring at his cousin had made him restless and tense. He thought he would probably never make it to California.

In the changing shed he gave in quickly. He locked himself in one of the toilet cubicles and set to work. He did not even close his eyes—he was in Mordialloc, beside Port Phillip Bay, Victoria, Australia all the while. But he resisted with all his strength the images of blemished skin and bunched calf-muscles and hairy thighs that urged themselves on him. He would not betray all the beauty of America for the sake of his lumpish cousin.

He looked all round him, staring at the walls in the twilight. Something white caught his eye. Of all the women he knew, in America and Australia, only Miss Kathleen Mahoney was with him at the end. He leaned his head against the soothing shapes of the letters of her name.

One morning late in the year Brother Cyprian announced to the class, 'After your exams we'll be having a Father Dreyfus at the school one night to show a film and give a talk and answer any of your questions on the subject of sex education.'

The brother read from a paper on his desk: 'The film has been shown to Catholic boys in secondary forms all over Australia. It shows in a perfectly clear and simple fashion all those matters which boys are often anxious to know but unfortunately are sometimes unwilling to find out from parents and teachers.

'The film offers the whole wonderful story of human reproduction from the moment of fertilisation to the hour of birth and illustrates clearly the workings of the human body both male and female.'

Brother Cyprian looked over the boys' heads at the back wall and said, 'All boys are urged to come to this film but of course there's no compulsion. Father Dreyfus is a man worth coming miles to hear on any subject. He's led an extraordinary life. He was in a Nazi concentration camp during the war. He rides a motorbike. He's what you might call a man's man.'

Adrian Sherd thought this was the best news he had heard all year. He tried to catch the eye of Cornthwaite or Seskis or O'Mullane to share his excitement. But they were all staring ahead as though there was nothing they needed to learn from any travelling priest and his famous film.

Adrian remembered the brother's words, 'from the moment of fertilisation'. He was going to see the most daring film ever made. At the very least he expected a statue or a painting of a man and woman doing it—a famous work of art that had been kept out of sight for centuries in some gallery in Europe. Yet if such a statue or painting existed it would have been the work of a pagan artist, and this was to be a Catholic film.

Perhaps he would see a married couple making a lump under the blankets of their bed. But Brother Cyprian had said, 'a perfectly clear and simple fashion.' The blankets would have to be thrown back to show the organs at work. The couple, of course, would be hooded or masked to protect them from embarrassment.

But surely this was too much to hope for. No film in all history had ever shown the act itself. Anyone, even a priest, would be arrested just for having it in his possession, let alone showing it to an audience. Adrian could only wait and count the days until he actually saw the film.

On the night of the film every boy in the class turned up. When Brother Cyprian blew his whistle to call them inside, they loitered and went on talking as though they weren't at all anxious to see whatever the priest had to show.

Father Dreyfus had a thick black beard—an unheard-of thing for a priest. He was sitting on top of the front desk with his hands in his pockets and his legs crossed. On all the other desks there were pencils and pieces of paper. The priest invited the boys to write down any questions they had about sex and marriage and said he would try to answer them before he showed his film.

Not many boys wrote down questions. Adrian tried to think of something to oblige the priest but he heard a familiar cough from the back of the room and remembered that Brother Cyprian was somewhere behind him in the shadows fiddling with the projector. If the brother saw him writing out a question he might think Adrian was preoccupied with sexual matters.

The priest read out the questions from the slips of paper and answered each one briefly. Most of the questions seemed childish to Adrian. He could have answered them himself with all the information he had got from Cornthwaite and his friends during the past two years.

There was only one really interesting question. Someone had asked what advice he ought to give to his best friend who hadn't been to confession for nearly a year because he was too scared to confess all the sins of impurity he committed by himself.

This was the first time that Adrian had ever heard the sin of self-abuse discussed in public. Priests and brothers often made vague references to it, but no one had ever mentioned it so boldly as the anonymous author of the question.

Adrian didn't hear the first part of the priest's answer. He was too busy trying to work out who had asked the question. The story about the best friend sounded unlikely. The questioner himself was the fellow who had a year's worth of sins on his soul.

All over the room, other boys were puzzling over the same matter. Adrian studied the faint turnings of heads and the surreptitious glances. Suspicion seemed to fall on Noonan, a big dull fellow. Adrian remembered Noonan getting up from his seat outside the confessional one First Thursday and leaving the church as though he wanted to be sick. It was a good trick. He could have practised it month after month while his total of sins mounted up.

After answering Noonan's question the priest said, 'Only the other day I was reading an American book on psychology. Young people and their problems. That sort of thing. I was very surprised to see some figures relating to the sin we're talking about. According to the book, over ninety per cent of boys have experimented with masturbation before they're eighteen years old. Of course these figures wouldn't apply to Catholic boys but it certainly makes you stop and think.'

After he had got over the shock of hearing the word 'masturbation' spoken by a priest (and in his own classroom), Adrian wondered what the figures implied. Perhaps he and Cornthwaite and the others wouldn't have felt so unusual if they had been lucky enough to grow up in America. Ninety per cent seemed a high figure at first, but of course American boys were subject to much fiercer temptations than Australians. Many of them had probably seen in the flesh the women that Adrian only saw in pictures.

When the priest had answered all their questions he told a boy to turn out the lights. Then he said to Brother Cyprian, 'Let her roll,' and the projector started.

It was an old, worn film. The sound crackled and boomed, and every few minutes a cloud of grey blobs and streaks fell across the screen like a sudden squall of rain. An overgrown child with long trousers and a bow-tie was asking his parents how he had come into the world. The people were all Americans. It was obvious from the way they smiled and patted each other and held themselves stiffly that they weren't even proper actors. They belonged to the mysterious multitude that Adrian had never seen in films—the Catholic American families who lived in a pagan land but still kept up the struggle to save their souls.

The parents said the usual things about God's wonderful work, and then the real stars of the film appeared. A close-up of the male reproductive organs filled the screen. Adrian was sure they belonged to a real person. Whoever he was, he had exceptional self-control. He stayed completely relaxed while the camera was only inches away from his cock and balls.

A few more diagrams appeared. It rained hard all over the screen again. Adrian prayed for the rain to clear before the female organs and the moment of fertilisation came on the screen.

The rain died down, and she stood before them at last. Only it wasn't really a she. Adrian almost groaned aloud. The swindlers had made a sort of dressmaker's dummy and sliced it off just above the navel. The thing swung round noiselessly on a swivel to show its genital organs. Adrian half-expected it to topple forward like the corpses in films that were propped up in chairs until someone turned them round to see why they wouldn't talk.

The female thing stayed on the screen for perhaps ten seconds. Even while he was straining to fix it in his mind forever, Adrian was aware that all of the fifty and more heads around him were suddenly motionless—all except one. Just behind Adrian, at the back of the room, Brother Cyprian jerked his head around and stared into a dark corner when the thighs and belly started turning towards him. Adrian understood—the brother was under a vow of chastity, and for him the thing on the screen was an occasion of sin.

Between its legs the creature had a low bald mound with a suggestion of a cleft or fissure along its middle. Adrian cursed the people who made the dummy or statue or whatever it was for putting the mound or whatever it was so far down between the legs that its

128

finer details were hidden. He was trying to imagine how the legs and the object between them would look walking towards him or stepping out of a bathing suit or lying down in an attitude of surrender, when they faded from the screen.

A huge diagram appeared. Adrian knew it like the back of his hand. It was the female reproductive system. He hardly bothered to listen while the commentator's voice explained what happened in the ovaries and oviducts and Fallopian tubes. Over the years he had found many sketches and diagrams and charts and sectional reliefs of the inside of a female body—but not one lifelike illustration of the outside.

He was trying to imagine the whole diagram enclosed in skin and packed away between two thighs, when he noticed something odd in the lowest part of the screen. A swarm of bees or a flight of tiny arrows was drifting through the lowest tube. It could even have been the grey rain in the film suddenly reversing and going back up the screen. But then the commentator announced what was really happening.

They were watching the moment of fertilisation. This was what Adrian and all his class had come from miles around to see. But it was nothing like real life. An army of little sperm-men was invading the diagram. The commentator got excited. He thought there was nothing so marvellous as the long journey of these tiny creatures. Adrian didn't care what happened to the little bastards now that the film had turned out to be a fraud.

The sperm cells were thinning out and growing weaker. The boys of Form Four at St Carthage's were still staring at the screen. They didn't seem to realise they had been cheated. Adrian stretched himself in his seat and wondered how the scene had been filmed.

Was it just an animated diagram like a cartoon? Or did the filmmakers pay some lunatic to shoot his stuff into a hollow tube inside the dressmaker's dummy? Or did they put a tiny camera inside a female organ so that Adrian and his class and even Father Dreyfus and Brother Cyprian were all sitting in the dark inside a woman's body while some huge fellow outside was doing her for all he was worth but none of them knew what was going on?

One day in December Stan Seskis told his friends he had read somewhere that a normal man should be able to have relations with a woman once every twenty-four hours unless he was ill or abnormal or something. Seskis said he had proved the truth of this by doing it to himself for ten nights on end and he was glad to know he was as good as any normal man.

Adrian Sherd had always been content to visit America three or four times a week. When he had tried it more frequently, his female companions always seemed listless and unco-operative and even the landscape was uninspiring. But he had to see whether Seskis was talking sense.

He reached a score of five consecutive nights. On the sixth night it was like torture. He arrived at a desert playground in Arizona. He was so jaded that he had brought two carloads of women with him instead of his usual two or three favourites. Jayne, Marilyn, Kim, Susan, Debbi, Zsa-Zsa—anyone who might come in useful was there.

He had to order them around like an army sergeant. He told one squad to strip off at once. A second squad had to take their clothes off slowly, dawdling over each item. Another group had to hide among the rocks and be ready to give in to him if he stumbled on them during the afternoon.

The fun and games dragged on for hours. The women began to complain. Sherd tried to think of some mad perversion that would bring everything to an end. The thing that finally did the trick was so absurd that he almost apologised to the women when it was over. He told them he didn't want to see any of them for at least a week. Then he flung himself down in the shade of a giant cactus and fell asleep.

The next day was Sunday. Adrian rode his bike to seven o'clock mass instead of going with his family on the nine o'clock mass bus. He told his parents he preferred the early mass because it left him the rest of the day for mucking around. But in fact he was tired of staying in his seat while his parents and brothers looked curiously at him as they climbed past his knees on their way to communion. He thought his father would surely guess soon which sin it was that kept him away from communion for weeks on end.

It was the Third Sunday of Advent, the last Sunday before school broke up for the long summer holidays. Inside the church, Adrian joined his hands and bowed his head slightly and looked at the people around him. He knew it was no use trying to pray unless he had some intention of giving up his sin in future.

The sermon was about repentance in preparation for the great feast of Christmas. The priest said, 'This is the season when we ought to remember all the ways we've offended Our Blessed Saviour during the past year.'

Some of the people near Adrian lowered their eyes and tried to look sorry for their sins. Adrian wished he could shout, 'Hypocrites!' in their faces. What did they know about sins? God saw into their hearts. He knew the year's total of mortal sins for everyone in the church. According to the records kept in heaven, the worst sinner, by a margin of at least a hundred, was a young man in the back row. He was pale and weary, as well he might be. Young and slightly built though he was, he had outscored people twice his age. More remarkable still, he had restricted himself to breaking one commandment, whereas they had the whole ten to choose from.

At communion time Adrian sat up to let the sinless ones past. A young woman's stocking brushed against his knee. The taut golden fabric shrank back from the drab grey of his school trousers. Adrian kept his eyes down. The champion sinner of Our Lady of Good Counsel's parish for 1953 was not worthy to set eyes on a pure young woman approaching the communion rail.

While the long queues of communicants moved slowly towards the altar, Adrian opened his missal at the page headed *Making A Spiritual Communion* and tried to look as if he was making one. If a person was not in a state of sin, but could not go to communion because he had eaten a meal or drunk a glass of water that morning, that person could unite himself in spirit with Our Lord in the Blessed Sacrament. If the owner of the golden stockings noticed Adrian when she returned to her seat, she would probably see the heading on the page of his missal and think he hadn't gone to communion because of a mouthful of water he swallowed while he was cleaning his teeth that morning.

The owner of the stockings turned out to be a girl in a school uniform. The skirt and tunic were a rich beige colour. On the tunic pocket was a snow-covered mountain peak against a bright blue sky. A circle of gold stars and a gold motto hung in the sky. It was the uniform of the Academy of Mount Carmel, in the suburb of Richmond. The girl seemed no older than

133

Adrian, although he knew already that her legs were heavy and rounded like a woman's.

Coming back from communion, the girl kept her eyes lowered. Her lashes were long and dark. She must have felt Adrian staring at her as she settled herself in her seat. She looked at him for less than a second. Then she knelt down and covered her face with her hands like all good Catholics after communion.

Adrian thought about the glance she had given him. She was utterly indifferent to him. If he had somehow reminded her that a few minutes earlier their legs had brushed together, she would have slapped his face. And if she could have seen the filthy state of his soul she would have got up and moved to another seat.

Adrian looked at the girl again. Her face was angelic. She had the kind of beauty that could inspire a man to do the impossible. He turned towards the altar and put his head in his hands. Slowly and dramatically he whispered a vow that would change his life, 'For her sake I will leave America forever.'

Adrian had often knelt outside a confessional and prayed the words from the Act of Contrition, 'And I firmly resolve, by the help of Thy grace, never to offend Thee again.' He had always known (and God had known too) that before a week was over he would be back in America again with his film stars. But in the back seat of his parish church, within a few feet of the girl in the severely beautiful uniform of the

Academy of Mount Carmel, he felt strong enough to keep his promise.

He conducted an experiment to prove it. He looked the girl over, from her ankles to her bowed head. Then he closed his eyes and summoned Jayne and Marilyn. He ordered them to dance naked in front of him and to shake their hips as suggestively as they knew how.

The experiment was a complete success. With his beige-clad angel beside him, the naked film stars looked obscene and revolting. Their hold over him was broken at last.

He tried one more experiment. It was an unpleasant one, but he had to do it—the fate of his soul for all eternity might depend on it. He stared at the girl's jacket and tried to imagine himself taking it off. It would not budge. He looked at her skirt and thought of the white underwear just beneath it. His arms and hands were suddenly paralysed. The lust that had ruled over him night and day for more than a year, his mighty lust, had met its match.

Riding home on his bike after mass, Adrian sang a current hit song. It was called *Earth Angel*. He sang the words slowly and mournfully like a man pleading with a woman to end his long years of misery.

He made his plans for the future. That very night, and every night after that, he would fall asleep thinking of a girl in a beige school uniform with a pale haughty face and dark eyelashes. He would shelter in the aura of purity that surrounded her like an enormous halo. In that zone of sanctity no thought of sin would trouble him.

On the following Saturday he would go to confession and rid himself for the last time of the sin that had threatened to enslave him. Every afternoon until school broke up, he would catch a different train from Swindon to Accrington and try to meet up with his Earth Angel on her way home. When school started again in February he would catch her train and see her every day.

On the last Monday morning of the school year, the boys in Adrian's form were all talking about the holidays. Stan Seskis explained to his friends a competition he had worked out in case they got bored in the long weeks away from school. All of them, Seskis, Cornthwaite, O'Mullane and Sherd, would keep a careful count of how many times they did it. They would be on their honour not to cheat, since they all lived in different suburbs and had no way of checking on each other. When they came back to school in February they would compare totals.

No one could think of a suitable prize for the winner, but they agreed the competition was a good idea. Adrian said nothing. Seskis asked him to rule up cards for them to mark their scores on.

Adrian had no intention of telling the others how his life had changed. He ruled up the score-cards during a free period in school. There were fifty blank squares on his own score-card. When he returned to school there would still be no mark on them. He was sure of this. The women who had tempted him to sin in the past were only images in photographs. The woman who was going to save him now was a real flesh-and-blood creature. She lived in his own suburb. He had sat only a few feet from her in his parish church.

For too long he had been led astray by dreams of America. He was about to begin a new life in the real world of Australia.

PART TWO

Every afternoon in the last weeks of 1953, Adrian Sherd caught a different train home. At each station between Swindon and Accrington he changed from one carriage to another. He looked in every compartment for the girl in the Mount Carmel uniform but he could not find her.

Adrian realised he had to endure the seven weeks of the summer holidays with only the memory of their one meeting in Our Lady of Good Counsel's Church to sustain him. But he swore to look for her each Sunday at mass and to go on searching the trains in 1954.

He spent the first day of the holidays tearing all the unused pages out of his school exercise books. He planned to use them for working out statistics of Sheffield Shield cricket matches and drawing maps of foreign countries or sketches of model railway layouts or pedigrees of the white mice that his young brother was breeding in the old meat-safe in he shed. It would all help to bring February closer.

Adrian's soul was in the state of grace and he meant to keep it that way. He was ready for his passions if they tried to regain their old power over him. He was sitting alone in the shed with a pencil and paper in front of him when he found himself drawing the torso of a naked woman. As soon as he saw his danger he whispered the words 'Earth Angel'. Then he calmly turned the breasts of his sketch into eyes and the whole torso into a funny face, and crumpled the paper.

In bed that night he joined his hands on his chest and thought of himself kneeling in church beside the girl he loved, and fell asleep with his hands still clasped together.

On the second day of the holidays, Adrian's mother announced that none of the family would be going to her brother-in-law's farm at Orford in January because her sister had just brought home a new baby and the Sherd kids would only be in the way.

Adrian's brothers rolled around on the kitchen lino, howling and complaining, but Adrian took the news calmly. All year he had been looking forward to the bare paddocks and enormous sky of the Western District. But now he was secretly pleased to be spending January in the suburb where his Earth Angel lived.

That night Adrian thought of himself sitting beside the girl and listening to a sermon on purity. He felt so strong and pure himself that he let his hands rest far down in the bed, knowing they would not get into trouble.

He looked for his Earth Angel every Sunday at mass and rode his bike for hours around unfamiliar streets hoping to meet her. After Christmas when he still hadn't seen her, he decided she had gone away for the holidays. He wondered where a respectable Catholic family would take their daughter for the summer.

The wealthier boys at St Carthage's went to the Mornington Peninsula. Adrian had never been there, but every day in summer the *Argus* had pictures of holiday-makers at Rye or Rosebud or Sorrento. Mothers cooked dinner outside their tents and young women splashed water at the photographer and showed off their low necklines. Adrian began to worry about the dangers his Earth Angel would meet on the Peninsula. He hoped she didn't care for swimming and spent her days reading in the cool of her tent. But if she did go swimming he hoped the changing sheds were solid brick and not weatherboard. He lay awake for hours one night thinking of all the rotted nail-holes in wooden changing sheds where lustful teenage boys could peer through at her while she undressed.

All round her in the shed the non-Catholic girls were putting on their twopiece costumes. But what did

143

she wear? Adrian couldn't go to sleep until he had reassured himself that she chose her beachwear from the range of styles approved by the National Catholic Girls' Movement. (Sometimes the *Advocate*, the Catholic paper, showed pictures of N.C.G.M. girls modelling evening wear suitable for Catholic girls. The necklines showed only an inch or so of bare skin below the throat. There were never any pictures of bathers suitable for Catholics but girls were advised to inspect the approved range at N.C.G.M. headquarters.)

One morning the front-page headline in the *Argus* was HEAT WAVE. In the middle of the page was a picture of a young woman on a boat at Safety Beach. Her breasts were so close to the camera that Adrian could have counted the beads of water clinging to the places she had rubbed with suntan oil. All that afternoon he lay on the lino in the bathroom trying to keep cool and hoping his Earth Angel kept out of the way of men with cameras. He thought of some prowling photographer catching her as she stepped from the water with a strap of her bathers slipping down over her shoulder.

At night he had so many worries that he never thought of his old sin. On New Year's Eve he remembered the boys of Eastern Hill Grammar School. That was the night when they all went to parties in their fathers' cars and looked for girls to take home afterwards. One of the Eastern Hill fellows might have seen

144

Adrian's Earth Angel on the beach and tried to persuade her to go with him to a wild party. Adrian tried to remember some incident from the lives of saints when God had blinded a lustful fellow to the beauty of an innocent young woman to protect her virtue.

One day in January Adrian went to a barber's shop in Accrington. One of the magazines lying around for customers to read was a copy of *Man*. Adrian studied the pictures quite calmly. The naked women were trying to look attractive, but their faces were strained and hard and their breasts were flabby from being handled by all the photographers who worked for *Man*—and probably all the cartoonists and short story writers and the editor as well. One glimpse of his Earth Angel's hands and wrists stripped of the beige Mount Carmel gloves had more power over him than the sight of all the nude women in magazines.

Late in January Adrian felt strong enough to take out his model railway. He sent passenger trains round and round the main line and the loop, but he was careful to snatch up the engine each time it slowed down. He still remembered clearly all the landscapes around the track where the train used to stop in the old days. So long as the train ran express through the scenes of his impure adventures he felt no urge to enjoy America again.

But one hot afternoon he was staring through the shed door at the listless branches of the wattle scrub over the side fence when he realised the train had stopped. He stood very still. The only sounds around him were the clicking of insects and the crackling of seed-pods on the vacant block next door. He was almost afraid to turn and see what part of America he had come to.

He was far out on the plains of Nebraska. The long hot summer had ripened the miles of wheat and corn. For just one moment Adrian thought of grabbing the first American woman he could find and wandering off with her into the hazy distance to find some shady cottonwood tree beside a quiet stream.

The thought that saved him was a simple one, although it had never occurred to him in all the weeks since his Earth Angel had changed his life. It was this: the temptation that came to him on the prairies of Nebraska proved he could never do without romantic adventures in picturesque landscapes. The way to keep his adventures pure and sinless was to take his Earth Angel with him.

That night Adrian proposed marriage to the beautiful young woman who had been educated at the Academy of Mount Carmel. After they had set a date for the wedding they sat down over a huge map of Australia to decide which scenic spots they would visit on their honeymoon.

On the hottest night of January, Adrian lay in bed with only his pyjama trousers on. He fell asleep thinking of the cool valleys of Tasmania where he and his wife would probably spend the first weeks of their marriage.

Later that night he was struggling through a crowd of men and women. In the middle of the crowd someone was gloating over an indecent magazine. Somewhere else in the crowd the girl from Mount Carmel was pushing her way towards the magazine. Adrian had to get to it before she did. If she saw the filthy pictures he would die of shame. People started wrestling with Adrian. Their damp bathing costumes rubbed against his belly. The girl from Mount Carmel was laughing softly, but Adrian couldn't see why. Everyone suddenly knelt down because a priest was saying mass near by. Adrian was the only one who couldn't kneel. He was flapping like a fish in the aisle of a church while the girl he loved was tearing pictures out of her *Argus* and wafting them towards him. They were pictures of naked boys lying on their backs rubbing suntan oil all over their bellies. The girl put up her hand to tell the priest what Adrian had done on the floor of the church.

Adrian woke up and lay very still. It was daylight outside—a cloudless Sunday morning. He remembered vague bits of advice that Brother Cyprian had given the boys of Form Four, and something that Cornthwaite had once said about wet dreams. In those days he had been so busy doing the real thing that he never once had an impure dream. He mopped up the mess inside his pyjamas. He was ashamed to realise he hadn't experienced all the facts of life in Form Four after all. But he went back to sleep pleased that nothing he had thought or done that night was sinful.

That same Sunday morning Adrian went to seven o'clock mass and walked boldly up to communion. He hoped his Earth Angel was somewhere in the church watching him. At the altar rails he knelt between two men—married men with their wives at their elbows. Adrian was proud to be with them. He belonged among them. He was a man at the peak of his sexual power whose seed burst out of him at night but whose soul was sinless because he was true to the woman he loved.

For days before he went back to school, Adrian wondered what he could say to his friends when they asked him his score in their competition. He couldn't simply hand in a blank score-card. The others would never believe he had gone for seven weeks without doing it. They would pester him all day to tell them his true score. Even if he made up a low score they would still be suspicious and ask him what went wrong.

Adrian's worst fear was that Cornthwaite or O'Mullane or Seskis would guess he had met a girl and fallen in love. They would think it a great joke to blackmail him. Either he paid some preposterous penalty or they would find out the girl's name and address and send her a list of all the film stars he had had affairs with.

In the end he decided to fill in his card as though he had taken the competition seriously and tried his best to win. He marked crosses in the blank squares for all the days he might have sinned if he had never met his Earth Angel. He was scrupulously honest. He left blank spaces around Christmas Day, when he would have been to confession. But he added extra crosses for the days of the heat wave, when he would have found it hard to get to sleep at night.

On the first morning of the new school-year the cards were handed round. The scores were O'Mullane, 53; Seskis, 50; Cornthwaite, 48; Sherd, 37.

The others all wanted to know what had happened to Adrian to make him score so poorly. He made up a weak story about getting sunburnt and not being able to lie properly in bed for a fortnight. He promised himself he would find some new friends. But he could not do it too suddenly. He was still frightened of blackmail.

That night Adrian went on searching through the Coroke trains for his Earth Angel. Two nights later he walked into a second-class non-smoking compartment of the 4.22 p.m. from Swindon and saw her. The face he had worshipped for nearly two months was half-hidden under a dome-shaped beige hat—his Earth Angel was absorbed in a book. If she loved literature they had something in common already. And it fitted in perfectly with the plan he had worked out for making himself known to her.

He stood a few feet from her. (Luckily there were no empty seats in the compartment.) Then he took out of his bag an anthology called *The Poet's Highway*. He had bought it only that morning. It was the set text for his English Literature course that year and it contained the most beautiful poem he had ever read—*La Belle Dame Sans Merci*, by John Keats.

When the train swung round a bend Adrian pretended to overbalance. With one hand on the luggage rack, he leaned over until the page with the poem was no more than a foot from his Earth Angel's face. He saw her look up as he swung towards her. He couldn't bring himself to meet her eyes, but he hoped she read the title of the poem.

For the next few minutes he stared at the poem and moved his lips to show that he was learning it by heart. Each time he practised reciting a stanza he stared out of the window, past the backyards and clothes-lines, as though he really could see a lake where no birds sang. Out of the corner of his eye he saw her watching him with some interest.

At the last station before Accrington he put his anthology away. He knew it was unusual for a boy to like poetry and he dreaded her thinking he was queer or unmanly. He pulled the *Sporting Globe* out of his bag and studied the tables of averages for the visiting South African cricketers. He twisted himself around and leaned back a little so she could see what he was reading and know he was well balanced.

For two weeks Adrian travelled in the girl's compartment. Every night he feasted his eyes on her. Sometimes she caught him at it, but usually he looked away just in time. His worst moment each night came when he opened the train door and looked for her in her usual corner. If she wasn't there it would have meant she had rejected his advances and moved to another compartment.

Some nights he was so frightened of not finding her that his bowels filled up with air. Then he had to stand in the open doorway for a few miles and break wind into the train's slipstream. His Earth Angel might have thought he was showing off—so many schoolboys hung out of doorways on moving trains to impress their girlfriends. But it was better than fouling the air that she breathed. In any case, she was still in the same compartment after two weeks, and he decided she must have been interested in him.

A wonderful change came over Adrian's life. For years he had searched for some great project or scheme to beat the boredom that he felt all day at school. In Form Four his journeys across America had helped a little. But it hadn't always been easy to keep the map of America in front of him—sometimes he had traced it with a wet finger on his desk-top or kept a small sketch of it hidden under his textbook. In Form Five his Earth Angel promised to do away with boredom forever. All day at school she watched him. Her pale, serene face stared down at him from a point two or three feet above his right shoulder.

With her watching him, everything he did at school became important. When he answered a question in class, she waited anxiously to see if he was correct. If he cracked a joke in the corridor and made some fellow laugh, she smiled too and admired his sense of humour. When he rearranged the pens and pencils on his desk-top or looked closely at his fingernails or the texture of his shirt-sleeves, she studied every move he made and tried to guess its significance. Even when he sat motionless in his seat she tried to decide whether he was tired or puzzled or just saving his energy for a burst of hard work.

She was learning a thousand little things about him—how his moods changed subtly from minute to minute, odd little habits he indulged in, the postures and gestures he preferred. For her benefit he deliberated over everything he did. Even in the playground he moved gravely and with dignity.

Of course she couldn't watch him every single moment of the day. Whenever he approached the toilet block she discreetly withdrew. He wasn't embarrassed himself—he felt he knew her well enough to have her a few feet behind him while he stood up manfully to the urinal wall. But she was much too shy herself, especially when she saw the crowd of strange boys heading for the toilet block with their hands at their flies.

It was hardly ever possible for her to watch Adrian in his own home. She hovered above him on his walk home from Accrington station and saw that he lived in a nearly-new cream-and-green weatherboard in a swampy street. (She was intrigued to see him choose a different path each night through the lakes and islands in his street—it was one of those teasing little habits that made his personality so fascinating.) But when he stepped over his front gate she melted away so she wouldn't have to see the dreary life he led with his family.

He was glad she would never see his bedroom furniture—the wobbly bed he had slept in since he was three years old, the mirror that had once been part of his grandparents' marble-topped washstand, and the cupboard that came originally from his parents' room and was always known as the glory box. He would have been ashamed to let her see the patched short trousers and the pair of his father's sandals that he wore around the house to save his school trousers and his only pair of shoes.

After tea when his mother made him wash the dishes, he was relieved to think his Earth Angel was safe in her carpeted lounge-room on the other side of Accrington, listening to her radiogram while he was up to his elbows in grey dishwater with yellow fatty bubbles clinging to the hairs on his wrists.

Later at night when he was in trouble with his parents, and his father said that when he had been a

153

warder he used to charge prisoners with an offence called dumb insolence for much less than Adrian was doing, he decided he would never even try to describe to his Earth Angel, even years later, how miserable he had been as a boy. And just before bed, when he stared into the bathroom mirror and pressed a hot washer against his face to ripen his pimples or held a mirror between his legs and tried to calculate how big his sexual organs would be when they were fully grown, he knew there were moments in a man's life that a woman could never share.

As soon as he was in bed he was reunited with her—not the girl who watched him all day at St Carthage's but the twenty-year-old woman who was already his fiancé. He spent a long time each night telling her his life story. She loved to hear about the year when they met on the Coroke train and he was so infatuated that he used to imagine her watching him all day at school.

While they were still only engaged, he didn't like to tell her he had thought of her in bed too. But she would hear even that story eventually.

Just out of Swindon, the Coroke train travelled along a viaduct between plantations of elms. On summer afternoons when the carriage doors were open, shreds of grass and leaves blew against the passengers, and the screech of cicadas drowned out their voices. The dust and noise made Adrian think of journeys across landscapes that were vast and inspiring but definitely not sensual.

Every day in February his Earth Angel was in the same corner seat. Sometimes she glanced up at him when he stepped into her carriage. When this happened he always looked politely away. He was going to introduce himself to her at the right time, but until then he had no right to force his attentions on her.

One afternoon on the Swindon station Adrian saw two fellows from his own class watching him from behind the men's toilet. He suspected they were spies sent by Cornthwaite and the others to find out who the girl was who had turned Sherd away from film stars.

Adrian edged along the platform before his Earth Angel's train pulled in. That night he got into a carriage well away from her own. He did the same for the next two nights, just to be safe. During his three days away from her he kept humming the song *If You Missed Me Half as Much as I Miss You*.

When he went back to her compartment again he thought she glanced at him a little more expressively than before. He decided to prove that he really was seriously interested in her and not just trifling with her affections.

He waited for a night when all the seats in the compartment were filled, and he had to stand. He walked over and stood above her seat. He took out an exercise book and pretended to read from it. He held it

155

so that the front cover was almost in front of her eyes. The writing on the cover was large and bold. He had spent half an hour in school that day going over and over the letters. It read:

Adrian Maurice Sherd (Age 16)

Form V

St Carthage's College, Swindon.

She looked at the book almost at once, but then she lowered her eyes. Adrian wanted her to stare at it and learn all she could about him. But he realised her natural feminine modesty would prevent her from seeming too eager to respond to his advances.

During the next few minutes she glanced at his writing twice more. He was still wondering how much she had read, when he saw her opening her own school-case. She took out an exercise book. She pretended to read a few lines from it. Then she held it in front of her with her own name facing him.

Adrian heard the blood roaring in his ears and wished he could kiss the gloved finger that held the name out naked and exposed for him to stare at. He read the delicate handwriting:

Denise McNamara

Form IV

Academy of Mount Carmel, Richmond.

When the train reached Accrington Adrian pretended to be in a hurry and dashed off into the crowd ahead of Denise. He did not want to look at her again until he had thought of a way to express the immense love and gratitude he felt for her.

That night in bed he turned to her and said her name softly.

'Denise.'

'Yes, Adrian?'

'Do you remember the afternoon in the Coroke train when you unfastened your case and took out an exercise book and held it in your dainty gloved hands so I could stare at your name?'

Adrian got used to calling her 'Denise' instead of 'Earth Angel'. Knowing her name made it much easier to talk to her in bed at night, although he still hadn't spoken to her on the train.

Each afternoon he stood or sat in her compartment and practised under his breath some of the ways he might start a conversation when the right time came.

'Excuse me, Denise. I hope you don't mind me presuming to talk to you like this.'

'Allow me to introduce myself. My name is Adrian Sherd, and yours, I believe, is Denise McNamara.'

Whenever he glanced at Denise, she was grave and patient and understanding—just as she was at night when he talked to her for hours about his hopes and plans and dreams. She wasn't anxious for him to babble some polite introduction. The bond between them did not depend on mere words.

157

Their affair was not all peaceful. One night a girl from Canterbury Ladies' College stood near Adrian on the Swindon station. She was one of the girls he used to see chatting to Eastern Hill boys on the trams. (Adrian wondered why she was waiting for a train to the outer suburbs when she should have lived deep in the shrubbery of a garden suburb.) If she got into his compartment and saw him looking at Denise and guessed that the girl from Mount Carmel was his girlfriend, the Canterbury girls and Eastern Hill boys would laugh for weeks over the story of the Catholic boy and girl who travelled home together but never spoke.

Adrian was ready to walk up to Denise and say the first thing that came into his head. But the Canterbury girl got into a first-class compartment, and he was free to go on courting Denise without being judged by non-Catholics who didn't understand.

Every day Adrian wrote the initials D. McN. on scraps of paper—and then scribbled them out so no one would know his girlfriend's name. It bothered him that he couldn't write her address or telephone number and enjoy the sight of them in private places like the back covers of his exercise books.

One night he stood in a public telephone box and searched through the directory for a McNamara who lived in Accrington. There were two—I.A. and K.J. Adrian knew how to tell Catholic names from non-Catholic. He guessed the K.J. stood for Kevin John and

158

decided that was Denise's father. Kevin's address was 24 Cumberland Road.

Adrian found Cumberland Road in a street directory in a newsagent's shop and memorised its location. Every night, walking down the ramp from the Accrington station a few paces behind Denise, he looked across the railway line in the direction of Cumberland Road. There was nothing to see except rows of white or cream weatherboard houses, but just knowing that her own house was somewhere among them made his stomach tighten.

He longed for just one glimpse of her home, and envied the people who could stroll freely past it every day while he had to keep well away. If Denise saw him in her street she would think he was much too forward in his wooing. The only way to see her house was to sneak down Cumberland Road late at night, perhaps in some sort of disguise.

On Saturday nights Adrian worried about Denise's safety. He hoped her parents kept her inside the house out of sight of the gangs of young fellows wandering the streets all over Melbourne. The newspapers called the young fellows bodgies, and every Monday the *Argus* had a story about a bodgie gang causing trouble. Bodgies didn't often rape (most gangs had girl members known as widgies) but Adrian knew a bodgie wouldn't be able to control himself if he met Denise alone on her way to buy the Saturday night newspaper for her father.

Adrian looked through the racks of pamphlets in the Swindon parish church. He bought one called *So Your Daughter is a Lady Now?* The picture on the cover showed a husband and wife with arms linked watching a young man with a bow-tie draping a stole over their daughter's shoulders. They were all Americans, and the girl was obviously going on a date. Denise hadn't been on a date of course (Adrian himself would be the first and only man to date her) but she was old enough to attract the attention of undesirables.

Adrian intended to warn her parents of their responsibilities. He sealed the pamphlet in an envelope addressed to Mr K. J. McNamara, 24 Cumberland Road, Accrington. He kept the envelope hidden in his schoolbag overnight. Next morning he could hardly believe he had planned to post it to Denise's father. He saw Mr McNamara opening the envelope and holding up the pamphlet and saying to his daughter, 'Got any idea who'd do an idiotic thing like this? Any young fellows been making calf's eyes at you lately?'

Denise looked at the young man in the bow-tie and thought at once of Adrian Sherd who stood devotedly beside her seat in the train each afternoon. She was so embarrassed that she decided to travel in another carriage for a few weeks until Sherd's ardour had cooled a little.

Adrian tore up the pamphlet and burned the pieces. On the back of the envelope he rearranged the letters

D-E-N-I-S-E M-C-N-A-M-A-R-A, hoping to find a secret message about his and Denise's future happiness. But all he could compose was nonsense:

SEND ME IN A CAR, MA
or SIN NEAR ME, ADAM C.
or AM I A CAD, MRS NENE?

He counted the letters in her name and took fourteen as his special number. Every morning at school he hung his cap and coat on the fourteenth peg from the end. Every Sunday in church he walked down the aisle counting the seats and sat in the fourteenth. He looked up the fourteenth verse of the fourteenth chapter of the fourteenth book of the Bible. It described Judah and the Israelites taking rich booty from captured cities. Adrian interpreted the text metaphorically. It meant that God was on his side and he would prosper in his courtship of Denise.

One night he wrote the names of all the main towns in Tasmania on scraps of paper and shuffled them together. The fourteenth name he turned up was TRIABUNNA. The quiet little fishing port on the east coast was destined to be the place where he and his wife would consummate their marriage.

The Tasmanian countryside was at its most beautiful in early autumn. In the days when dead elm leaves blew against the windows of the Coroke train, Adrian thought of the first days of his marriage.

Sherd and his wife spent their wedding night on a ship crossing Bass Strait. The new Mrs Sherd was still shy in her husband's presence. She went on chattering about the day's events until nearly midnight. Sherd knew she was worried about undressing in front of him. When she couldn't put off going to bed any longer he decided to make things easier for her. He took out a book and buried his face in it. He looked up at his wife once or twice, but only when she couldn't see him.

Sherd undressed quickly while his wife was kneeling with her face in her hands and saying her night prayers. Then he made her sit beside him on the bed. He kissed her gently and told her to forget all she might have heard from radio programs and films about the wedding night. He said he had never forgotten the story in the Bible about Tobias or someone who told his wife on their wedding night that they were going to pray to God instead of gratifying their passions.

Sherd said, 'The whole story of how we first met in Our Lady of Good Counsel's Church and got to know each other on the Coroke train and then learned to love each other over the years is a wonderful example of how God arranges the destinies of those who serve Him.

'I know you're tired, darling, after all you've been through today, but I want you to kneel down beside the bed with me and say one decade of the Rosary just like Tobias and his bride on their wedding night.

'We're doing this for two reasons—first to thank

God for bringing us together like this, and second (Adrian hung his head and sighed, and hoped she realised he had been through a lot before he met her) because I want to make reparation for some sins of mine long ago and prove to God and you that I married you for love and not lust.'

Sherd was surprised how easy it was to spend his wedding night like Tobias. While his wife dropped off to sleep beside him in her nightdress (should it have been a style recommended by the National Catholic Girls' Movement, or was it all right in the privacy of the marriage bed for a Catholic wife to dress a little like an American film star to help her overcome her nervousness?) he lay with his hands crossed on his chest and congratulated himself.

He remembered the year long before when his passions had been like wild beasts. Night after night he had grunted and slobbered over the suntanned bodies of American women. Nothing could stop him. Prayers, confession, the danger of hell, even the fear that he might ruin his health—they were all useless.

Then he had met Denise McNamara, and in all the seven years since then he had committed not one sin of impurity, even in thought. Of course, many times during those seven years he had looked forward to marrying Denise. But he had proved on his wedding night that his dreams of marriage were certainly not inspired by any carnal desire.

His only regret was that Denise herself would never know his story. He could hint to her that she had changed his life and saved him from misery. But in her innocence she could never imagine the filth she had rescued him from.

Sherd lay awake for a long time thinking over the wonderful story of his life. As the ship neared the pleasant island of Tasmania, his heart overflowed with happiness at the thought of the weeks ahead. His honeymoon was the last chapter of a strange story. And one day he would write that story in the form of an epic poem or a play in three acts or a novel. He would write it under a nom-de-plume so that he could tell the truth about himself without embarrassment. Even Denise would not know he was the author. But he would leave a copy in the house where she would see it and read it. She could not fail to be moved by it. They would sit down and discuss it together. And then the truth would slowly dawn on her.

At school Adrian kept away from Cornthwaite and his former friends. He thanked God that they all lived on the Frankston line and never came near his train at night. He could never have faced Denise again if she had seen him with them and imagined they were his friends. He saw them leering at her and heard O'Mullane scoffing at him (almost loud enough for Denise to hear), 'Christ on a crutch,

Sherd, you mean you gave up your American tarts for her?'

Adrian's new friends were some of the boys whose names he had once marked with golden rays on a sketch of the classroom. They were obviously in the state of grace. All of them lived in garden suburbs and travelled home on trams. They talked a lot about the Junction. (Adrian eventually discovered that this was Camberwell Junction but he was not much wiser, since he had never been there.) Every night at the Junction, girls from Padua Convent crowded onto the boys' trams. At St Carthage's, Adrian's friends squealed or waved their arms or pushed each other hard on the chest or staggered and reeled and did strange little dances whenever someone mentioned the Padua girls.

At first Adrian wondered if he had stumbled onto something shocking—a pact of lust between these fresh-faced boys and the Padua girls. Groups of them were meeting in a park somewhere in tree-shaded Camberwell and behaving like young pagans together. But when he had listened closely to his friends for a few weeks and learned to ignore their animal-noises and bird-squawks, he realised the most they ever did was to talk to some of the Padua girls on the crowded trams (although some of the more daring fellows did play tennis with the girls on Saturday mornings).

It puzzled Adrian that their only aim seemed to be to know as many Padua girls as possible. Sometimes they held frantic conversations that meant almost nothing but gave them the opportunity to blurt out dozens of Padua names.

'Helen told me Deidre couldn't play on Saturday because Carmel and Felicity called round with Felicity's mother to take them out in the car.'

'Yes, but Deidre told me she was upset to miss the doubles comp. and Barbara had to forfeit. She couldn't have Maureen or Clare for a partner.'

Adrian listened to them impatiently. He wished he could have told them he didn't have to babble to a tramload of giggling Padua girls because he had already chosen the pick of the Catholic girls on the Coroke line for his own.

Sometimes a fellow said, 'Tell us about your social life, Adrian.'

Adrian always parried the question. His friends would never have understood that he and Denise had no need for tennis and dances.

Sometimes Adrian's new friends seemed so innocent that he wondered if they had ever experienced an impure temptation. But one morning Barry Kellaway rolled his eyes and pretended to stagger and said, 'It's all right for you lazy baskets. You were snoring your heads off last night while Mother Nature was torturing me.'

Martin Dillon made eyes at Kellaway and sidled up to him and said, 'Did Mummy's little Barry mess his pyjamas in his sleep, eh?'

Damian Laity grabbed Kellaway from behind and twisted his arms and said, 'Tell us everything, Kaggs. Who were you holding in your arms when you woke up this morning?'

Adrian listened quietly. He knew Kellaway had had a wet dream. Over the next few weeks, every boy in the group had one and talked about it next day.

Their talk was very different from the stories that Cornthwaite and his friends used to bring to school. Adrian's former friends were reticent and modest about their adventures. Seskis would say simply, 'Rhonda Fleming nearly killed me last night.' Or O'Mullane would say, 'I saw a colossal tart on the train and when I got home I went into the woodshed and rubbed myself nearly raw.' The others would nod quietly as if to say, 'It could happen to anyone.'

Kellaway and Dillon and Laity were proud of their dreams and recounted them like adventure stories with themselves as heroes. It was all the more fun because nothing they did in dreams was sinful. (Adrian had his own wet dreams now, but he didn't enjoy them. They were confused struggles in landscapes suspiciously like America.)

Adrian's new friends looked forward to their dreams. Laity marked his in his pocket diary. He had calculated that he had a wet dream every twenty days or so. On the eighteenth or nineteenth day he would tell the others it was due any day. Kellaway and Dillon would say, 'Better not stand too close to Catherine or Beth in the tram this afternoon or you might end up married to them in bed tonight.' Adrian thought of himself and Denise in the Coroke train and was disgusted by the loose talk about the Padua girls.

If a fellow described a dream that was too unseemly he usually apologised at the end of his story. Kellaway said one morning, 'The tram was somewhere in East Camberwell. I kept praying, "Please, God, make the Padua girls get off before it's too late." But they kept crowding round me. The conductor asked me what was the matter and I told him to stand between me and the girls to hide what I was going to do. But then it happened. Some of the girls screamed. The conductor started wrestling with me. And I know you'll never forgive me for this, Dillon, but I reached out and tried to grab you know who. Yes, it was your one and only Marlene with the adorable legs. I just couldn't help myself.'

Some of the stories were lost on Adrian because the people or the places in them were known only to the Camberwell boys. But one morning he heard a story as sensational as any that Cornthwaite or his dirty friends had told.

It was the time of the Royal Tour of Australia. Every morning the *Argus* had full-colour pictures of the Royal couple, showing Her Majesty's frocks and hats in all their gorgeous detail. One Saturday the Royal car was due to pass only a few miles from Swindon. St Carthage's and every other school for miles around had a space reserved along the route. Nearly every boy from St Carthage's turned up early and waited for hours in the sun for the Queen and the Duke to drive past.

On the following Monday, Damian Laity gathered his friends together and told them solemnly that his dream had come a few days early and it was nothing to laugh about this time.

He said, 'It must have been all those hours I sat in the sun. I must have gone mad with sunstroke. I couldn't eat anything for tea except half a family brick of ice cream just before bed. All I can remember after that is waiting and waiting for Her car. When I saw it coming I turned into a raving lunatic. I ran out onto the road with only my singlet on and jumped up to the running board of the car. The kids from the public schools were all roaring and screaming at me. I think the Padua girls saw me too. I couldn't stop myself. I jumped into the back seat beside Her. She was wearing that beautiful lime-green shantung frock and the hat with white feathers. I tried to put my arms around Her. As soon as I touched Her elbow-length gloves it ended. Thank God I didn't do anything worse to Her with all those people watching. I lay awake for hours after it was over. I kept seeing the headlines in all the papers on Monday: MONSTER FROM CATHOLIC COLLEGE DISGRACES AUSTRALIA.

Mr and Mrs Adrian Sherd arrived at Triabunna in the early afternoon. They had been married exactly twenty-four hours. They unpacked their suitcases in a sunlit room on an upper floor of a hotel with every modern convenience. Then they strolled hand-in-hand along the beach-front.

The place was deserted. Sherd was glad there was no one around to overhear them when they stopped every few yards and he whispered, 'I love you, Denise,' and his wife answered, 'I love you too, Adrian.' He remembered a fellow at school named Cornthwaite who used to change his seat in a train to get a better view of a couple smooshing (as he called it) and to watch where the fellow put his hands.

On the way back to the hotel for tea, Sherd seriously considered waiting for another night to consummate the marriage. He could see his wife was in no hurry for it—she was quite content just to hold hands and hear her husband say he loved her.

Sherd felt the same way himself. He was experiencing the truth of something he had first discovered years before (when he lay awake at night thinking of a girl in a beige school uniform to save himself from a habit of sin)—that the joy of hearing a beautiful chaste woman say, 'I love you' was far more wonderful than rolling around naked with all the stars of Hollywood.

Later that night, when they were sitting together reading, Sherd reminded himself that his wife had grown up in the same pagan world as himself, that she must have learned from films and magazines what people expected newlyweds to get up to on their honeymoon, and that if he didn't introduce her to the physical side of marriage soon, she might start brooding over it or even suspect that he was not quite normal in mind or body.

When she was ready to undress for bed, he decided after all that now was the time to reveal the mysteries of the marriage bed. But he was determined that what he was about to do should be as different as possible from the purely animal things he had once dreamed of doing to American women. Denise must not have the least suspicion that he had ever been attracted to her purely for the physical gratification he might get from her.

He knelt down and closed his eyes to pray while she got into her nightdress. When she had said her own prayers and climbed into bed, he turned out the light and undressed himself. He did not want her to glimpse his organ before he had prepared her for it by a long speech.

Sherd lay down beside his wife and spoke. 'Denise, darling, no matter how carefully you were protected by your parents and the nuns at the Academy, you probably still stumbled on some of the secrets of human reproduction.

'Perhaps you had to go into a public lavatory once, and your eyes strayed up to the wall and you saw a drawing of a huge, thick, hideous monster of a thing and lay awake for weeks afterwards wondering whether men really had organs like that on their bodies and whether, if ever you were married, your husband would threaten you with one on your wedding night.

'Perhaps you borrowed a novel from a non-Catholic library without realising what it was about, and read a few pages about some American gangster with the morals of an alley-cat. You shut the book in disgust and returned it to the library, but you wondered for a long time afterwards how many men treated women as pretty playthings to be used for their pleasure.

'Perhaps you innocently looked into the practical notebook of a schoolfellow who was doing biology and saw her drawings of a dissected rabbit and noticed the little lump with the label, ERECTILE PENIS AND SHEATH and went away alarmed to think that male rabbits and therefore men, and your own future husband too, had something on them that could actually stretch and grow bigger.

'Perhaps you once spent a holiday on a farm and your parents were careless enough to let you see the bull running like a madman to climb on top of a cow. Or perhaps you were just shopping in Accrington one Saturday morning and there, right in front of your eyes, were two dogs in the gutter and one of them suddenly poked this long red sticky thing at the other one and forced it to submit.'

Adrian paused and sighed. He hoped Denise realised it was not his fault that she had had these rude shocks. If only it had been possible, he would have shielded her from all sight of male animals and broad-minded books and films. Then she could have learned the whole story from her husband.

He waited for her to speak. He was anxious to find out just how much she knew. Then she answered him, and he treasured for the rest of his life the words she said.

'Adrian, I understand how concerned you are for me, and I don't blame you for imagining that some of those dreadful things might have happened to me. But you needn't have been all that anxious.

'Oh, of course I was puzzled sometimes about things I read in the papers or heard non-Catholics whispering about. But don't forget I was a Child of Mary. (Didn't you ever go to eight o'clock mass on the third Sunday of the month and see the rows and rows of Children of Mary in our blue-and-white regalia and hope that your future wife was somewhere among them?) And whenever I did wonder a little about those things, I told myself they were none of my business. I knew if I ever got married I could learn all I had to know from the Pre-Cana Conferences for engaged couples. And if my vocation was to remain single, it was better for me to know as little as possible about that side of life anyway.'

When Sherd heard this he was so overjoyed that he kissed his wife and told her again and again what a rare treasure she was. He would almost have been content to lie there looking at her lovely face until he fell asleep. But he owed it to his wife to finish what he had begun explaining to her.

He said, 'Denise, my innocent angel Denise, now that I know how carefully you've guarded yourself all these years, it makes my task tonight so much easier.

'If you had in fact seen a dog or a bull chasing the female, or a foul drawing on a toilet wall, you probably would have thought people were no different from animals when they mated. I'm sorry to say there are plenty of men who do treat the whole thing as a kind of game for their own pleasure. But thank God you'll never come into contact with them. God Himself saw to it that your beauty and virtue attracted the sort of Catholic husband who understands the true purpose of sexual relations in marriage.

'I won't beat about the bush, Denise darling. In one sense, what I'm going to do to you tonight may seem no different from what a bull does to his cows or a Hollywood film director does to one of his starlets. (Denise looked startled and puzzled. He would have to explain this point to her later.) It's not a pretty thing to watch, I'm afraid, but it's the only way our poor fallen human natures can reproduce themselves. If it seems dirty or even ridiculous to you, I can only ask you to pray that you'll understand it better as time goes by.

'The trouble is that a man is cursed with a very powerful instinct to reproduce himself. One day when we've been married long enough to trust each other with our deepest secrets, I'll tell you a little about 1953. That was a year when I plumbed the depths of despair because (Sherd chose his words carefully) I could hardly find the strength to resist the male instinct to reproduce my species. And when you hear my story you'll realise what a mighty urge it is and why you'll have to excuse me for giving in to it about twice a week—at least until you find you're expecting a child.'

Sherd wanted to say much more, but he was anxious not to confuse his bride with too much information all at once. The moment he had waited for all his life had arrived.

He switched on the bedlamp, kissed his wife to calm her fears and rolled back the bedclothes. She was still in her nightdress, but fortunately she had closed her eyes and gone limp. He removed the nightdress as gently as he could and admired her nude body.

Her eyes were still closed. He wondered if she had swooned. But he said in any case the words he had memorised years before for just this occasion. (They came from a book that his mother had borrowed from the sixpenny lending library in Accrington. When his parents were out of the house he used to look through their library books. Most were respectable detective stories, but in one historical novel he had found a scene where a man surprised a young woman bathing nude in the village stream. Young Sherd had been so impressed by the man's words that he learned them to use on his honeymoon.)

Sherd said over his wife's body, 'Denise, it's almost a crime that such charms should ever be concealed beneath the garments that our society decrees as conventional. Let me feast on your treasures and praise them as they deserve.'

Before Sherd could praise his wife's charms separately, she opened her eyes briefly and looked shyly up at him and said, 'Please, darling, don't keep me in suspense too long.'

As gently and considerately as he could, Sherd lowered his body into position and engaged in sexual congress with her.

Afterwards he lay beside her with the blankets covering them both. He was ready to say, 'I'm sorry, Denise, but I did my best to warn you beforehand,' when she looked at him and said, 'Why, Adrian, I think it was somehow rather beautiful. Not that I don't appreciate all you said to prepare me for the worst, but really, I can't help being amazed at the wonderful way God designed our bodies so they complement each other in the act of generation.'

While she pulled on her nightdress in the darkness she said, 'And Adrian, if you feel a need for my body again in the next few days, please don't hesitate to ask me. After all, I did promise to honour and obey you. So if this act gives you all the pleasure I think it does, you're welcome to do it whenever you wish—within reason of course.'

The Tasmanian honeymoon of Mr and Mrs Adrian Sherd lasted for twelve days of a year in the early 1960s, but the thought of it sustained Adrian Sherd all through the autumn months of 1954. In all that time he never once confessed a sin of impurity in thought or deed.

Sometimes, while he knelt outside the confessional, Adrian arranged a debate between two of the many voices that started arguing whenever he tried to hear what his conscience had to say.

FIRST VOICE: Sherd is about to tell the priest that the worst sins he has committed in the past month are disobeying his parents and losing his temper with his young brothers. But in fact he lies awake every night dreaming of coition with a naked woman in a hotel room in Tasmania. I submit that these thoughts are mortal sins against the Ninth Commandment.

SECOND VOICE: In denying the claims of the previous speaker, I rest my case on three points.

1. When Sherd thinks about his marriage to Mrs Denise Sherd, née McNamara, he does not enjoy any sexual pleasure. True, he experiences a sort of exalted joy, but this is purely the result of his finding himself married at last to the young woman he has loved since his schooldays. We can see the truth of this, my first

177

point, if we examine Sherd's penis while he contemplates the happiness of his honeymoon. At no time does it seem aware of what is going on in his mind.

2. When, some time ago now, Sherd was unfortunately in the habit of thinking at night about the American outdoors and of lewd orgies with film personalities, he was enjoying something he knew to be quite imaginary. On the other hand, his thoughts of his marriage to Miss McNamara are thoughts of a future that he has every intention of bringing to pass. Far from indulging in idle dreams, when he thinks of his honeymoon in Tasmania he is making a serious effort to plan his life for the good of his immortal soul.

3. It goes without saying that in all his visits to America, Sherd never once married or proposed marriage to the women he consorted with. Mrs Sherd, however, is his wife. All the endearments he offers her are proper expressions of his conjugal love and, as such, are perfectly lawful.

Adrian Sherd as adjudicator awarded the debate to the Second Voice and was sure that any reasonable theologian would have done the same.

So long as Adrian was in love with a Catholic girl and in the state of grace, he wasn't ashamed to visit his Aunt Kathleen and talk about Catholic devotions.

One day when she said she had enrolled him as a Spiritual Associate of the Sisters of the Most Precious

Blood, he was genuinely interested to know what benefits this would bring him. In the days of his lust, the things his aunt did for him had been wasted, but now they earned valuable additions to his store of sanctifying grace.

Aunt Kathleen said, 'The names of all Associates are kept permanently in a casket beside the altar in the Mother House of the Sisters at Wollongong. Each day after their Divine Office, the Sisters recite a special prayer for all Associates. And best of all, they keep a lamp burning perpetually in their chapel for the intentions of you and me and all the other names in the casket.'

While his aunt was out of the room, Adrian leafed through her stacks of Catholic magazines, looking for other leagues or confraternities with special privileges for members. He puzzled over a magazine he had never seen before—*St Gerard's Monthly*, published by the Divine Zeal Fathers at their monastery in Bendigo.

The centre pages were full of photos with brief captions: *The Hosking Family of Birchip, Vic.; The McInerney Family of Elmore, Vic.; The Mullaly Family of Taree, N.S.W.* Each family consisted of husband and wife and at least four children. Four was the bare minimum. In some of the magazines Adrian found plenty of eights and nines and tens. The record seemed to belong to the Farrelly family of Texas, Queensland. There were sixteen people in the photo. Five or six were adults, but Adrian assumed that these were the oldest children. One of the women was holding a baby—she was probably the mother of the fourteen.

Adrian thought at first that the families were entrants in some kind of competition. But there was no mention of prizes. Apparently the only reward for a family was the pleasure of seeing themselves in the pages of *St Gerard's Monthly* and feeling superior to the Catholic families with less than four children.

The mothers were all what Adrian's father would have called well preserved. Some were even quite pretty. There were none with fat legs or large sagging breasts like Mrs De Kloover who led nine children into mass every Sunday at Our Lady of Good Counsel's.

It was this that interested Adrian most. He was planning to become the father of a Catholic family himself, and there were still a few things he wasn't sure about. One thing that worried him was whether he would still be attracted to his wife after she had borne him several children. The pictures in *St Gerard's Monthly* reassured him. Men like Mr McInerney and Mr Farrelly were apparently drawn to their wives long after the romantic excitement of the honeymoon had died away.

It would be possible for Denise to have at least ten children and still keep her youthful figure and complexion. Over the years she would probably develop a Catholic mother's face like some of those in the photos.

This was very different from the face of a non-Catholic mother of two or three children. The Catholic mother wore very little make-up—the non-Catholic plastered herself with powder and lipstick and sometimes even a little rouge. The Catholic's face was open, frank, quick to smile, but still as modest as a girl's in the presence of any man other than her husband. The non-Catholic's looked as though it concealed many a guilty secret.

The difference between the faces was probably the result of Catholic husbands' copulating with their wives quietly in the dark while their children were asleep in the surrounding rooms, whereas non-Catholics often did it in broad daylight in their lounge-rooms while their children were packed off to their aunts or grandparents for the weekend. Also, the Catholic men would have done it fairly quickly and without any antics that might have over-emphasised its place in the marriage, while the non-Catholics probably talked and joked about it and thought of ways to make it last longer.

As well as a Catholic face there was a Catholic figure—Catholic breasts with gentle curves and not enough prominence to attract unwanted admirers, and Catholic legs with ankles and calves neatly shaped to lead the eye away from the area above the knees. As the years brought her more children, Mrs Denise Sherd would develop these too.

It was only logical that there were also Catholic and non-Catholic *pudenda*. Although Adrian had got out of the habit of thinking of such things, he allowed himself to distinguish briefly between a modest shrinking Catholic kind and another kind that was somehow a little the worse for wear.

Each issue of *St Gerard's Monthly* had a column called *The Hand That Rules The World* by someone called Monica. Adrian read one of these columns.

'Recently on our holidays in Melbourne I boarded a tram with six of my seven. (Son No. 1 was elsewhere with Proud Father.) Most of my readers will be familiar with the cool stare of scrutiny which I had from Mrs Young Modern in the opposite seat with her pigeon pair.

'Of course I returned her gaze. After all, I had far more right to be critical, with six bonny young Australians to my credit.

'Well, it turned out that she was more interested in inspecting my children than their mother. Of course she was hoping to find a shoe unshined or a sock that needed darning. "Sorry to disappoint you, Mrs Two Only," I said under my breath, "but while you were gossiping at your bridge party or out in your precious car, I wasn't wasting *my* time."

'I had the satisfaction of seeing her face fall when she realised my six were at least as beautifully turned out as her two. If we had got on speaking terms I'm sure I would have had to answer the old question for

the hundredth time—Readers, are you tired of it, too?—
"How on earth do you manage?"'

There was much more, but Adrian paused to
think. He wished Denise could have read *The Hand
That Rules The World*. As the mother of a large family
she would have to be ready for all those stares and
questions from non-Catholics. Monica's columns were
full of arguments that Catholic mothers could turn to
when they were tempted to feel discontented with their
lot. For instance, she pointed out that bringing a new
soul into the world was infinitely more worthwhile than
acquiring a luxury such as a washing machine. (And
anyway, as she reminded her readers, a thorough boiling
in a good old-fashioned copper did a much better job
than a few twirls in a slick-looking machine.)

Adrian decided that after his marriage he would
send a subscription to the Divine Zeal Fathers so Denise
would get her *St Gerard's Monthly* regularly.

When his aunt found him reading the magazine
she took it politely from him and said, 'No harm done,
young man, but *St Gerard's Monthly* is really more suitable for parents only.' Adrian was angry to think there
might have been much more useful information in the
magazine that he hadn't found. He resented his spinster
aunt treating him like a child when he was seriously
concerned about the problems of Catholic parenthood.

One night towards the end of their honeymoon,
Sherd reminded his wife that the natural result of their

love for each other might well be a large family. He was about to list some of the problems this might bring, when she interrupted him.

'Darling, you don't seem to realise. Ever since I can remember, my mother got *St Gerard's Monthly*. It taught me what to expect from marriage and to accept whatever family God might send. And you might think this was silly of me, but after I fell in love with you, one of my favourite daydreams was opening up the centre pages of the *Monthly* and seeing a picture of the Sherd family from wherever we came from.'

While Sherd and his wife were still honeymooning in Tasmania, Adrian spent ten minutes each morning in the Swindon parish church searching among the racks of Australian Catholic Truth Society pamphlets. He was looking for one simple piece of information. When he found it he would know all that was necessary for his role as a Catholic husband.

Each day he borrowed two or three pamphlets and read them under the desk in the Christian Doctrine period. Next morning he returned them to the racks in the church and went on with his search. He read page after page advising husbands and wives to be courteous and considerate, to set a good example to each other, and to co-operate unselfishly in the upbringing of the children that God sent them. But he did not find the information he needed.

What he wanted to know was how often he should have carnal relations with his wife to be sure of fertilising her as soon as possible after the wedding. He believed there was a certain time each month when it was easy for a woman to conceive. If he (or his wife) could discover when this was, he could arrange to copulate with her on the correct date each month and so make it easier for God to bless them with children.

But the problem was to find when this important date occurred. Anyone could tell when a female dog or cat was on heat from the odd way it behaved, but it was unthinkable that Denise should have to get into a state like that to let him know she was ready to be impregnated. If women were no different from dogs or cats in this respect, the odds were that somewhere, at some time, he would have seen a woman on heat. But in all the years he had been watching women and girls on trains and trams he had never seen one who looked as if she was even thinking of sexual matters.

Adrian searched the pamphlet racks for a week and then gave up. But without the information he could not think realistically about his future. He decided to invent a game that would make his marriage to Denise seem true-to-life.

Each night when he got home from school he took two dice from his brothers' Ludo box. He shook the first and rolled it. An even number meant that Sherd (the husband) felt in the mood to suggest intercourse to his wife that night.

Before throwing the second of the dice he saw himself saying casually to Denise (they were still on their honeymoon, so the conversation could take place as they strolled back from the beach to their hotel) that it might be nice to give themselves to each other that night in bed. Then he rolled the die.

If it showed an even number, Denise would answer something like, 'Yes, darling, I'd be more than happy if you used your marriage rights tonight.' If it showed an odd number she said, 'If you don't mind, I'm not feeling strong enough for it. Perhaps some other time.' And she smiled warmly to show that she loved him as much as ever.

On a night when both dice came up with even numbers, Adrian would rest now and then from his homework and enjoy the quiet contentment that a husband felt when he knew his wife would willingly submit to him a few hours later. But it was almost as pleasant on the other nights to look forward to a half-hour in bed together sharing their inmost thoughts and looking forward to years more of such happiness in the future.

But throwing the dice was only part of the game. Assuming that a woman could conceive on one day of each month, there was one chance in thirty that an act of intercourse would be successful. Adrian chalked a

186

faint line around a section of thirty bricks on the outside of the lounge-room chimney. On one of the bricks near the centre of the marked area he put a faint X. Then he hid a tennis-ball in a geranium bush near the chimney.

Each morning after a night when the two dice had showed evens (and Mrs Sherd had yielded to her husband) Adrian walked quietly to the lounge-room chimney on his way back from the lavatory. He found the tennis-ball and wet it in the dew or under the garden tap. Then he took aim at the panel of bricks, closed his eyes tightly and tossed the ball.

He tossed it carelessly and with no deliberate effort to hit the brick marked X. When he heard the impact of the ball he opened his eyes and looked for the wet mark on the bricks. If this mark (or the greater part of it) lay within the perimeter of the brick marked X, then the conjugal act of the previous night between Mr and Mrs Sherd would have resulted in conception.

Adrian shook the dice each night until the honey-moon was over. On four of those nights a pair of even numbers came up, but in each case the mark of the tennis-ball was well wide of the lucky brick.

At the end of this time he was satisfied with the way the dice and the ball were working, except that things weren't happening fast enough. He wanted to share with his wife as soon as possible the joys of Catholic parenthood, but at the rate he was going it might take years—so many years, perhaps, that it might be time to marry Denise before he had discovered what marriage was really like.

He decided to throw the dice seven times each night. This meant he would experience a week of marriage every day of his life in Accrington. At that rate a year of marriage would take less than two months of 1954. By the end of Form Five he would have been married for nearly four years and fathered as many children. At that stage he would probably have to speed things up a little more. He would have to be careful not to get too close to the time (he could hardly bear to think about it) when Denise would begin to show signs of ageing. According to the pictures in *St Gerard's Monthly* she could produce at least a dozen children before this happened. But if he had a lucky run with the dice and ball they might have twelve children long before they were forty years old.

After the birth of each child beyond the fourth, he would have a special throw of three dice to decide his wife's health. If the number thirteen came up, she would be showing signs of varicose veins in her legs. He would send her to a Catholic doctor for a thorough check-up. If nothing could be done for her, he could alter the rules of the game so that he abstained unselfishly from time to time to give her a sporting chance.

Living through seven nights of marriage each night was not as interesting as he had expected. The high point of each week came each morning at the chimney.

Sometimes he had to toss the ball three or four times for a week when Denise had been unusually compliant.

At last, after eighteen weeks of marriage (eighteen days of Accrington time) he opened his eyes one morning at the chimney and saw a broad wet blotch in the middle of the brick that stood for conception. He had always thought he would be able to take such a thing calmly, but he found himself wanting to run and tell the news to someone—even his parents or brothers. All that day at school he wished he had a friend to share his secret.

Adrian went on throwing the dice for a few more nights. His wife couldn't be sure she had conceived until she saw a doctor. They were entitled to perform the act a few more times until then. But as soon as the doctor had pronounced her pregnant, Adrian put away the dice and spent his nights at Accrington living through the weeks when he and his wife spent their time before sleep holding hands and talking about their first child.

Much as he loved Denise, he found he was bored. It wasn't that he needed sexual gratification. He had always said, and he still maintained, that the touch of Denise's hand or the sight of her bare white shoulders was enough to satisfy all his physical wants. And it wasn't that he was running out of things to talk about. There were still hundreds of stories he wanted to tell her about his early years. The trouble was that he couldn't endure the long months of her pregnancy without the fun of seeing the dice and ball do their work.

The next day was Saturday at Accrington. Adrian knew what he had to do to make his future more inviting. He took the dice out into the shed in his backyard. He had a sheaf of pages from an exercise book to use as a calendar. There was enough space for all the years he wanted. He threw a die once to decide the sex of their first child. It was a girl. They named it Maureen Denise.

In the first week after the mother and child came home from hospital, nothing happened. Then the dice started rolling again. Adrian threw them thirty times and scored five acts of sexual union. He went outside and tossed the tennis ball five times without success. Then he went back to his calendar in the shed and crossed a month off his married life and rolled the dice again.

Adrian worked all day with the dice and ball. (He told his brothers he was playing a game of Test cricket, with the dice to score runs and the ball to dismiss batsmen.) By evening he had been married nearly nine years and was the father of five daughters and one son.

As soon as he was home from mass on the Sunday morning, he went out to the shed again. He was looking forward to throwing the ball at the chimney again, but he couldn't face another day with the dice. He decided on an easy solution. He would simply toss the ball ten times for each month. It seemed silly after so many years of marriage to be always asking his wife's permission before the act. In future she would have to submit to it ten times a month whether she liked it or not.

By midday the best part of his life was over. He had been married fifteen years and fathered eleven children—eight daughters and three sons. Their names and birthdays were all entered in his calendar.

Now that he had worked out a future for himself he was exhausted and a little disappointed. He was almost sorry he had cheated by speeding up events instead of using the dice and ball patiently and enjoying each year as it came. He knew what people meant when they said their life was slipping away from them.

He sat beside the chimney wondering what he could think about in bed that night. A simple solution occurred to him. He multiplied fifteen by twelve to obtain the number of months of his active sexual life. Then he went back to the shed and cut up small squares of paper. He numbered them from one to one hundred and eighty and put them all into a tobacco tin. Each night he would shake the tin and draw out a number. He drew out a number for that very night. It was forty-three. From his calendar he learned that in Month forty-three he was trying to father his fourth child.

That night (Accrington time) Adrian went to bed eager to meet the Denise who was already the mother of three young children. And the next day at school he wondered which of all the possible Denises would share his bed that night after he had consulted the numbers in the tobacco tin. She might have been a radiant young mother, fresh from breast-feeding her first child, or a mature woman like the mothers in *St Gerard's Monthly* with the curves of her body gently rounded by years of child-bearing and about her eyes the faintest shadows of weariness from caring for her eight or nine children all day.

On the last evening of their honeymoon, Sherd and his bride stood looking at the scene that had been called *Triabunna With Distant View of Maria Island* in the coloured booklet, *Tasmania, A Visitor's Guide*, on the bottom shelf of the bookcase in Sherd's boyhood home.

The newlyweds had to decide where to make their permanent home. Sherd wondered what was to stop them from settling among the low hills of Maria Island that were just then strangely bright in the last rays of the setting sun. If he could have been sure there was a Catholic church and school and a Catholic doctor on the island, he and his wife would have been happy for the rest of their lives on a small farm that looked across the water to Triabunna.

He only decided to return to Victoria for the sake of his wife. She was just a little homesick, and she said she preferred to live where she could visit her mother two or three times a year.

All that Adrian knew of Victoria was the western suburb of Melbourne where he had grown up and gone to primary school, Accrington and the few south-eastern suburbs that he crossed in the train to St Carthage's or explored on his bike at weekends, the landscape on either side of the railway line between Melbourne and Colac and a few miles of farmland around his uncle's property at Orford. None of these places seemed a fitting backdrop for the scenes of his married life—carrying a radiant Denise across the threshold of their first home, bringing her home from hospital with their first child and so on.

But Adrian knew of places in Victoria that were worthy settings for a great love story. They were landscapes so different from the suburbs of his childhood that even the trivial events of his married life would seem momentous, and Adrian, the husband, would forget all those Sundays when he had come home from mass with nothing to do but climb the solitary wattle tree in the backyard and look across rows of other backyards and wait for the six o'clock *Hit Parade* in the evening.

As a boy Adrian had travelled each January by train from Melbourne to his uncle's farm at Orford. On the morning of each journey he leaned against the dark green leather backrest and studied the photographs in the corners of his compartment.

The titles of the photographs were brief and sometimes curiously imprecise—*Erskine Falls, Lorne*; *In the Strzelecki Ranges*; *Road to Marysville*; *Walwa*; *Camperdown With Mount Leura*; *Near Hepburn*

Springs. In some of the pictures a solitary traveller, with arms folded, leaned against a tall treefern, or a motor-car empty of people stood motionless on an otherwise deserted gravel road leading towards a tiny archway where distant trees closed over against the daylight. Adrian knew from the waistcoats and moustaches of the travellers and the shapes of the cars and the brown hues of the sky and land that the photos had been taken years before. The be-whiskered men and the unseen people who had left their motor-cars standing on dusty roads might have died long since. But Adrian was sure, from their grave gestures and solemn faces and the way they had stationed themselves at unlikely spots in the forest or by the roadside, that these travellers of olden times had discovered the true meaning of the Victorian countryside.

Leaning back in his window seat at Spencer Street station while drab red suburban trains dragged crowds of clerks and shop assistants into Melbourne to work, Adrian wanted to leave the city forever and journey to the landscapes of the dim photographs. Somewhere among forests of mountain ash or damp treeferns or beside a foaming creek, he would search for the secret that lay behind the most beautiful scenery in Victoria.

But the Port Fairy train followed the same route each year and Adrian had to get out at Colac and travel with his uncle to the same bare paddocks near Orford.

Yet, as a married man at Triabunna, Tasmania, Adrian had still not forgotten the country of the photographs. He told his wife they would make their home in a valley beside a waterfall at Lorne or on a hillside overlooking Camperdown with Mount Leura, or, best of all, in the trees above a bend in the road near Hepburn Springs.

He would need a suitable job or profession. Farming was too hard—it would leave him too little time with his new wife. But there were men who drove up sometimes to his uncle's farm and strolled around the paddocks without soiling their hands. He would be one of them—a veterinary surgeon or an expert from the Department of Agriculture. Looking back, he saw he had always been destined for this sort of life. As a boy in Form Four he had often relieved his boredom by staring at pages in his General Science textbook with diagrams of dissected rabbits or pictures of soil erosion labelled *Before* and *After*.

Sherd took his bride to their new home on a timbered hillside near Hepburn Springs and bought a savage Queensland heeler dog to protect her while he was away in the daytime. On the first night after they had arranged their furniture and unpacked their wedding presents he sat down with her in the spacious lounge-room and looked thoughtful.

When she asked him what was the matter, he said, 'I was only thinking of the grave responsibility on my shoulders—to carry on where the nuns and priests left off and teach you the rest of the facts about marriage. Perhaps I should deal with one topic each night.

'Tonight I'll discuss a subject that probably made you shudder if ever you heard it mentioned when you were young and innocent—birth control. What I'm about to say is a summary of all I've read about birth control in Catholic pamphlets, and all I've been taught by priests and brothers.

'Any impartial observer would agree that the marriage act—that operation I've performed on you in the privacy of the marriage bed—must have a serious purpose quite apart from the fleeting pleasure associated with it. The purpose, as any rational person will agree, is the procreation of children. Now this purpose is a part of what philosophers and theologians call the Natural Law. And the Natural Law was designed by Almighty God to make the world run smoothly. It must be obvious, then, that any tampering with the Natural Law is likely to have disastrous consequences. (Can you imagine the consequences if someone interfered with the way the planets revolve around the sun?)

'Well, birth control violates the Natural Law by removing the purpose from the marriage act. (You may be wondering how this is done. Without going into the sordid details, I can tell you there's a certain little piece of slimy rubber that non-Catholic chemists sell for profit. Armed with this disgusting weapon, a man can enjoy the pleasure without the purpose and defy the Natural Law.)

196

'You won't be surprised to learn that this grave sin has grave consequences. It's a known fact that artificial birth control causes profound physical and mental disturbances. I've heard from a priest who knows all about these matters that many non-Catholic couples are so afraid of the psychological effects of birth control that they just will not practise it. So you see the Natural Law is not just something the Catholic Church made up.'

While Sherd paced up and down the lounge-room carpet, his wife reclined on the sofa and drank in every word he said. Behind her the huge windows framed a vista of a twilit forested valley more satisfying than any of the scenes that the young Adrian used to stare at in railway carriages, wondering what was the secret behind their beauty.

When the Sherds had first moved into their home near Hepburn Springs, they were so happy that they seemed to be enjoying a taste of heaven on earth. But looking through his lounge-room window after his discussion of birth control, Sherd realised that all they were enjoying was their rightful reward for following the Natural Law.

What he saw through his window was a valley where no sexual sin was ever committed. The Natural Law governed everything in sight. It caused the sky to glow and the treetops to tremble all over the forests near Hepburn Springs. It was at work too at Walwa, on the road to Marysville and in Camperdown with Mount Leura.

Sherd knew now what had drawn him to these scenes in the Port Fairy train years before. The mysterious secret beyond those lonely roads, the thing that travellers had abandoned their cars to search for, was the Natural Law.

He himself would never have to search for it again. He could see it in operation outside his lounge-room windows and even in the privacy of his own bedroom.

One night when the dice and the numbered tickets had transported Adrian to a night in the fourth month of his marriage when he would have liked to be intimate with his wife but she wasn't feeling up to it, he lay back with his hands behind his head and began to discuss with Denise the history of marriage down the ages.

He said, 'The union of Adam and Eve in the garden of Eden was not only the first marriage—it was the most perfect marriage in history, because it was God who introduced the young couple to each other and because the way they behaved in marriage was exactly as He had intended.

'You can imagine them meeting for the first time in some leafy clearing far more pleasant than any place we know of near Hepburn Springs. They were both naked—yes, stark naked, because Adam's reason was in full control over his passions and there was no need for Eve to practise the virtue of modesty. With their perfect understanding of what God wanted them to do, they would have agreed to live together there and then—there was no long courtship such as we had to observe. No doubt they went through some simple wedding ceremony, and surely it was God who officiated. What a wonderful start to married life!

'They had no need to go away for a honeymoon. There were scenic spots and secluded walks all round them already. What happened next? Well, we can deduce that their acts of sexual communion would have been the most perfect ever performed. They would have looked into each other's eyes one afternoon and understood it was time to co-operate with God in creating a new human life. As they lay down together Adam's body would have shown none of those signs of uncontrollable passion that you might have glimpsed on me some nights in bed. Of course, at the last moment, when it was time to deposit his seed in the receptacle designed for the purpose, his organ must have behaved more or less like mine, but whereas I (with my fallen human nature) tend to lose control of myself for a few moments, he would have lain there quite calmly with his reason fully operative. He may well have chatted to Eve about some gorgeous butterfly flitting above them or pointed out some inspiring view through the trees around them.

'They lived in such close contact with God and obeyed His Will so completely that in all probability it was He who reminded them now and then that it was high time they mated again. The Bible tells us that God came and walked with them in the cool of the evening. You can imagine Him politely suggesting it to them as the sun sinks below the treetops of Eden. They smile and say what a good idea it is and then lie down on the nearest grassy bank and do it without any fuss.

'Of course they wouldn't have been the least ashamed to have God beside them while they did it. And He wouldn't have been embarrassed either—after all, it was He who invented the idea of human reproduction. I can see Him strolling a little way off to look at a bird's nest or let a squirrel run down his arm. Occasionally He glances back at the young couple and smiles wisely to Himself.

'Just to remind you of the vast difference between our First Parents in their perfect state and ourselves with our fallen natures, I'd like you to imagine how we would have managed if we'd tried to live like Adam and Eve.

'Think of me getting into your compartment on the Coroke train for the first time. I haven't got a stitch of clothing on and neither have you. (We'll have to suppose the other passengers are naked too.) I look at your face to try to assess your character, but I'm such a slave to my passions that I let my gaze fall on your other charms below. Meanwhile you notice the way I'm looking at you, and you can't decide whether I'm thinking of you as a possible mate for life or just the object of my momentary lust. So you don't know whether to sit still and meet my eyes or fold your arms in front of you and cross your legs tightly.

'And when I put my schoolbag on the rack above your head and I lean on tiptoes over your seat and the most private parts of me are only a foot or so from your face, what do you do? If your human nature was as perfect as Eve's in Paradise, you would look calmly at my organs to satisfy yourself that at least I was a fully developed man capable of fathering children. But because you have a fallen nature you're too frightened or horrified to look at them dangling in front of your eyes, so you go on reading your library book.

'This example might seem far-fetched, but believe me, it's the way God intended us to court each other. It was the sin of our First Parents that made us shy with each other. If we hadn't been born with Original Sin on our souls, our whole courtship would have been simple and beautiful. Instead of waiting all those months just to speak to you, I would have walked hand-in-hand with you to your parents' place on the first night I met you. (Your home would have been a mossy nook with walls of some vivid flowering vine—Accrington before the Fall would have had a subtropical climate and vegetation.)

'We find your parents sitting happily together coaxing a spotted fawn to eat from their hands. They come

201

forward smiling to greet me—both naked, of course, but their bodies have no wrinkles or varicose veins or rolls of fat. I take no notice of your mother's body because I've seen thousands like it all over Melbourne. Your parents talk to me and soon understand what an ideal partner I'd be for their daughter. Next morning I come to take you away. There's no long-winded ceremony or speeches. They give us their blessing and we go off to find our own bower of blossoming foliage.

'It all seems so impossible and of course it is, because we live nowadays in a fallen world. And the worst result of our First Parents' sin is that a man can scarcely look at a woman now without his passions urging him to sin with her in thought or deed.

'I can see you're surprised to hear this, but you must remember that very few men have learned self-control the way I have. It's unpleasant to talk about, I know, but many men use their wives entirely for their own selfish pleasure.

'This sort of thing apparently began almost as soon as Adam and Eve's descendants started to populate the earth. The oldest cities in the world, Sumer and Akkad, had their walls covered with obscene drawings and carvings, so Brother Chrysostom told us once in his history class. The men of those cities must have had sexual thoughts all day long. The hot climate probably helped, but the main reason would have been that they had never heard of the Ten Commandments.

'You might have heard in your Christian Doctrine classes, Denise, that God gives every man a conscience, so that even a pagan in the days before Christ knew the difference between right and wrong. I'm afraid I find that hard to believe.

'One day I deliberately imagined myself growing up in Sumer or Akkad in those days. I discovered I would have had no conscience at all. I would have been a thorough pagan like all the others and enjoyed scribbling filth on the temple walls. (Don't be alarmed, darling. It's not the real me I'm talking about. The real Adrian Sherd is the one who's in bed beside you now.) I saw myself strolling along the terrace between the Hanging Gardens and the river. The sky was blue and cloudless. I was wearing sandals and a short tunic with nothing underneath. All the women walking past wore brief skirts and primitive brassieres.

'Well, as soon as a young woman took my fancy, a kind of raving madness came over me. (Remember it's only an experiment I'm describing.) No thought of conscience or right and wrong entered my head. I was very different from the young Catholic gentleman who courted you so politely and patiently in the Coroke train. I was as bold as brass with the pagan girl—asked her name and address and arranged to meet her that evening at one of the lonely oases beyond the city walls.

'I didn't wait to see what happened after that, but it wasn't hard to guess from the storm of temptations rising up inside me. From that day on, I knew that if I hadn't been lucky enough to be born a Catholic and learn the proper purpose of my instincts, I would have been some kind of beast. No girl in Sumer or Akkad would have been safe from me.

'But it wasn't just the pagans who couldn't control themselves. If you read your Old Testament you'll realise how far some of the Patriarchs were from being good Catholic husbands. Solomon had hundreds of wives and treated them like playthings to minister to his lust, David coveted another man's wife, and Abraham had a bond-woman to amuse himself with when he tired of his lawful wife.

'I have to confess that when I was much younger I sometimes felt like complaining to God that I was born in New Testament times instead of the centuries B.C. It didn't seem fair that those old fellows all pleased God and got to heaven after having all the women they wanted, while young Catholic chaps like me had to turn their eyes away from pictures of girls in bathers and only go to films for general exhibition.

'But after I met you and fell in love, I realised the men of the Old Testament were far worse off than me after all. They never knew the rare pleasures that I enjoyed in the years when I was wooing you. Solomon might have gazed all day at the hundreds of indecently clad wives sprawling on cushions in his luxurious palace, but he never knew the happiness of sitting in the Coroke train and waiting for one long soulful look from a girl who kept her beautiful body carefully concealed beneath a convent uniform. And no matter what pleasure he got from his women when he summoned them to his bedchamber, it could not have equalled my joy when I first kissed you on the day we became engaged and I knew I would one day possess a bride who had never even glanced immodestly at another man.'

A few weeks before the September holidays, Adrian's mother told him he deserved a rest from all his studies and homework. His uncle and aunt had agreed to have him at Orford for a week. If he behaved himself around the house he could go by himself on the train.

Adrian was anxious to let Denise know about his trip. When he went with his mother to book his seat at the Tourist Bureau he took away a coloured leaflet entitled *Spring Tours to the Grampians—Victoria's Garden of Wildflowers*. (The Grampians were a hundred miles from Orford, but there were no leaflets for any place nearer.) The following night on the Coroke train he stood near Denise and made sure she noticed him poring over the leaflet. She might have been surprised to think he was interested in wildflowers, but at least she would know what direction from Melbourne he was when she wanted to think of him during the holidays.

Adrian had a window-seat in the 8.25 a.m. to Warrnambool and Port Fairy. He left a few inches between himself and the window for Denise. He and she were not long back from their honeymoon, and the trip to Orford was to show her off to his relatives and let her see something of the Western District.

The pictures in the carriage were *Treeferns, Tarra Valley* and *Bulga Park, Yarram*. Adrian whispered to Denise that a moist valley in Gippsland would be the perfect spot for a weekend trip. She snuggled closer to him and squeezed his fingers. She understood that he was thinking of the kisses he would give her under the shady treeferns.

They looked into all the slum backyards between South Kensington and Newport and told each other how lucky they were to be able to live in a modern home with the bush right up to their windows. After Newport, when miles of grazing land came up to the windows for their inspection, they passed the time by imagining how they would like to live in this or that farmhouse, and giving each place a points score out of ten.

Adrian's uncle, Mr McAloon, met them at Colac station. Adrian left a space for his young wife in the back seat of his uncle's car. He watched her face closely all the way and enjoyed the surprises she got. She had no idea that Colac was such a busy town. She had never seen such green paddocks and rich red soil as she found on the farms near Orford. And she thought the view of rolling plains from the McAloons' house was nearly as exciting as all the mountain scenery in Tasmania (and gave Adrian's hand a squeeze when she mentioned the place where they had spent their honeymoon).

Two of Adrian's cousins, a boy and a girl, sat in the back seat with him. They had pale faces with freckles of all shades from fawn to deep chocolate. Adrian always found it hard to talk to them. The girl went to the little brick Catholic school at Orford and the boy to the Christian Brothers in Colac. He travelled to and from Colac each day in a truck driven by a Catholic neighbour of the McAloons.

Mr McAloon said to Adrian, 'I suppose you've read in the papers all about the school bus dispute.' (Adrian had never heard of it.) 'It's the same old story. Catholics have to pay taxes to support the secular education system, but when they ask for a few seats in the high school bus to Colac, all the non-Catholic bigots and wowsers for miles around are up in arms and writing to the Chief Inspectors in the Education Department in Melbourne.

'Of course all the top Inspectors and public servants are Masons, as you should know.' (He spoke as though Adrian and his parents should have done something about this years before.) 'Anyway, the result is that all the Catholics round here have banded together and organised a roster of cars and trucks to take the kids to secondary schools, and all the Catholic teachers in state schools have resigned from their union because of the anti-Catholic stand it took. We've got a long hard fight on our hands but we're not going to give up until we get elementary British justice for our children.'

After lunch Adrian showed his wife, Denise, around the farm. The freckle-faces weren't interested in going with him. They stayed on the back veranda and played Bobs and Disney Derby. Adrian pitied them. They mooned around the house all day and never knew what was missing from their lives. Two or three of them were old enough to have boyfriends or girlfriends. The miles of green dairy country should have inspired even the dullest freckle-face to fall in love with a face across the aisle in St Finbar's Church and then wait for months in suspense until the face turned round one day and showed by the faintest of smiles that there was some hope.

Adrian of course was much more advanced in his love affair than that, because he had so many proofs already that Denise returned his devotion. As he walked towards the farthest paddock he was already sharing with his wife the joy of looking back on the September holidays in 1954 when he walked alone across bare paddocks and wished his loved one had been with him.

That night Adrian found he had to share a bed with his oldest cousin, Gerard McAloon. Adrian kept his genitals carefully hidden while he undressed. Since meeting Denise he had rarely looked at them himself. They were no longer exclusively his, but the joint property of his wife and God and himself, to be used only in the marriage act on the nights when his wife agreed to it. He shuddered to think of the pale McAloon boy peering at things that were a secret between Denise and himself.

Next day Mr McAloon took Adrian and Gerard and two younger McAloon boys to visit a place called Mary's Mount. They drove to Colac and then south into the steep timbered hills of the Otway Ranges. Adrian's uncle talked all the way about the people of Mary's Mount.

'They're modern saints. Some of them are doctors and legal men and chaps with university degrees. They've given it all up to get back to the medieval idea of monasticism and living off the land. They bought nearly 600 acres of bush with only two cleared paddocks and they're turning it into a farm to supply them with all their needs. Except for books and clothes they share almost everything in common. They built their cottages and chapel with their own two hands. In a few years they'll be weaving their own clothes and tanning their own leather for sandals or shoes. It's the only sensible way to live.'

Mr McAloon aimed his words at Adrian. 'I don't know how much your father has told you about the world yet, young fellow. But if you're going to grow up a responsible Catholic layman it's time you realised this country has never been in worse danger. I don't know

209

how you city people survive with all those trashy books and films. And what about the spread of Communism?

'The only safe place to bring up a family nowadays is somewhere like Mary's Mount. You'll find in a few years there'll be thousands of Catholic families getting back to the land and cutting themselves off from the city altogether. If anything can save Australia the move back to the land can do it. Closer settlement. We haven't got much time left. The experts reckon by 1970 at the latest the whole of Asia will have gone Communist. We need a population of at least 30 to 40 million to defend ourselves. You can see what the Communists are doing right now in the jungles of Malaya. Well, people like the settlers at Mary's Mount are doing something about it.'

It was early afternoon, but the hills were so steep that the road between them was deep in shadow. Mr McAloon said, 'I think the time I admired them most was when the Bishop of Ballarat refused to give them one of his priests to live on the settlement as their chaplain. Well, some of the leading families fixed up some tarpaulins and made a sort of covered wagon and loaded some tents and blankets on pack-horses and started off walking and riding from Mary's Mount to Ballarat.

'I forget how many days it took them, but they got there and drove their wagon up the driveway of the Bishop's Palace and squatted right there on the lawn. Now don't get me wrong. They're fine folk. It's just that they're influenced by the customs of Catholic Europe.

They don't seem to care what ordinary Australians think of them. Some of the men wear their hair down over their collars, and one fellow who used to belong to the university has a bushy black beard. And I heard they had some home-made wine in their wagon and they started drinking the stuff on the Bishop's lawn and handing round pieces of rather ripe cheese on the end of a knife. And Doctor Ray D'Astoli (he's a talented man, Ray—gave up a wealthy practice in Melbourne to go back to the land), Ray D'Astoli rang the bell and said, "The Catholic farmers of Mary's Mount within this diocese are come to wait upon the pleasure of His Grace, the Bishop, and crave audience with him."

'Those were the very words he used. He's a wonderfully clever man, Ray. And the young priest who opened the door got all hot and bothered and didn't know how to answer him. And they say the Bishop himself peeped through the curtains upstairs and thought a tribe of gypsies had descended on him. In fact the police in Colac went down to the camping ground when they were passing through because someone actually rang up and said the gypsies or some escaped lunatics had come to town.'

Adrian said, 'And did they get their priest?'

'Unfortunately, no. It's a long story and some of it's not for young ears. (Mr McAloon glanced at his sons.) You'll see for yourself when we get to the Mount the single men and women have their own separate dormitories at least a hundred yards apart with all the married couples in between. But some people—even Catholics, I'm sorry to say—some people love to spread scandal and gossip whenever they see young men and women living up to ideals too high for themselves to match. More than that I'm not prepared to say. The Bishop didn't want one of his priests serving a community with even the faintest breath of scandal about it. And so Mary's Mount only has a mass in the chapel when a young priest comes down from Melbourne— he's a brother of one of the founders of the settlement.'

Mary's Mount was on the side of a hill so steep that the driveway for cars stopped half-way up. The McAloons and Adrian walked up a footpath with logs set into the slippery soil for steps. They passed small timber cottages that reminded Adrian of the illustrations in *Heidi*.

Mr McAloon stopped at a long building like a barn and asked a man was Brian O'Sullivan at home. The man led them inside. Mr McAloon whispered to Adrian, 'The single men's quarters—laid out like the dormitory of a Cistercian monastery—marvellous stuff.'

Ten little alcoves opened off a central passage. O'Sullivan came out of his alcove and took them inside. He and Mr McAloon sat on the bed—a camp stretcher covered with army blankets. Adrian and his cousins sat on stools cut from logs with globules of amber sap still stuck to their wounds.

O'Sullivan said, 'I spent the morning weeding potatoes, and now I've been reading St Thomas Aquinas.'

He held up a large volume entitled *Summa Theologica*. 'You know what we say up here at the Mount? "A man know's he's living well when he gets callouses of equal sizes on his knees and hands and backside." It means he's been kneeling in the chapel and working on the farm and reading in the library—all in equal proportions.' Mr McAloon laughed loudly.

When the men started talking about the potato crop, Adrian asked could he visit the chapel. The McAloon boys took him outside and further up the hillside. The chapel walls were of logs with the bark still on them. The seats inside were of unvarnished timber, but the altar and tabernacle were the real thing—polished wood draped with starched linen and coloured silk. And in the tiny sacristy Adrian opened the drawers of the cupboard and saw a coloured chasuble in each. While Adrian fingered the vestments, Gerard McAloon said he thought some clever women from the Mount had made them all with their own hands. There was supposed to be one lady who spent her whole time washing and ironing them and dusting the chapel and polishing the sacred vessels ready for the day when the community would have its own priest to say mass there every morning.

Adrian shut the drawers and stood still. Leaves were scraping against the chapel roof. A blue-green bull-ant wandered across the well-scrubbed floorboards. Specks of dust drifted in and out of a thin shaft of sunlight.

Denise was still beside him (although he had almost forgotten her in the excitement of visiting Mary's Mount). He led her out of the chapel and pointed out to her the beauty of it all—the cottages half-hidden among the trees, the rows of green potato plants in the rich red soil, the little sawmill with its heaps of pale-yellow sawdust—and whispered to her, 'How could we think of bringing up our children near Hepburn Springs when we could have them all here protected from the world with our own chapel on the property?'

Back in the single men's quarters, Mr O'Sullivan said, 'I tried my hand at baking bread yesterday. It's not too bad.' He gave them each a piece spread with soft butter from a billy-can. Adrian's piece tasted like a salted scone, but he finished it out of politeness.

On the way home Adrian asked his uncle whether the McAloon family might settle at Mary's Mount one day.

Mr McAloon said, 'Don't think I haven't given it a lot of thought. The only thing that stops me is I'd like to wait a bit longer and see what sort of farmers they turn out to be. Last year they lost a lot of money on potatoes through planting them at the wrong time. And they can't sell any milk or cream because they won't make their dairy conform to health standards. They should manage to be self-supporting in a few years, but they'll always need some ready cash to pay for the little extras they can't make themselves—like trucks and generators and machinery and rainwater tanks and cement and stuff.'

Adrian said, 'And books?'

'Yes, books too. But just quietly I think some of those university chaps ought to spend a bit more time dirtying their white hands with work and a bit less time with their books.'

At the top of a low hill near Colac Adrian looked back towards the Otways. From that distance he could see only gentle grey-blue slopes rising up from the cleared country. He was relieved to think that none of the people in Warrnambool trains or the cars that passed along the Prince's Highway would guess what was hidden beyond those timbered slopes. Even if the Malayan terrorists or the Chinese Communists invaded Victoria, the Catholic couples of Mary's Mount might still be safe and undiscovered in their shadowy gully.

Mr McAloon said, 'Now don't get me wrong. Those people ought to put us to shame. One day the rest of Australia will copy their way of life. But there's always got to be humble soldiers like yours truly to go on fighting Communism in the outside world. I could tell you about the Communists we're up against in the Labor Party, but that's a story in itself. You just wouldn't believe the terrific battle that's going on all round us right now.'

They left Colac behind and headed north towards Orford between tranquil green paddocks and through the long afternoon shadows of huge motionless cypresses.

Sherd and his wife spent several weeks planning their move from near Hepburn Springs to a Catholic rural co-operative called Our Lady of the Ranges, deep in the Otways. Denise was taking just two dresses, two sweaters, two sets of underclothes and her bathers. Her husband was taking one suit, one old pair of trousers with an old shirt and jumper to match, a pair of overalls and his swimming trunks.

They filled a small crate with all the books they would ever need—a Bible, the Catholic Encyclopedia, a History of the Church in twelve volumes, a bundle of Australian Catholic Truth Society pamphlets (mostly on purity and marriage to instruct their children in years to come) and some leaflets on farming published by the Department of Agriculture.

They were going to sell their house and furniture and pay the proceeds to the co-operative. They would draw a small living allowance if they needed it—Our Lady of the Ranges was a true community like a medieval monastery. (People often forgot that monks and nuns were practising the perfect form of Communism centuries before Karl Marx was ever heard of.)

One night just before they left for the Otways,

Mrs Sherd asked her husband to continue the talks he had begun a little while before on marriage through the ages.

Sherd propped a pillow under his head, arranged the lacy collar of his wife's nightgown into a pretty frame for her chin, and said, 'Like everything else, marriage changed a great deal after Our Lord came down to earth to teach. We know that He made marriage one of the seven sacraments of His new Church, but we don't know exactly when He did it. Some theologians think He instituted the sacrament of matrimony while He was a guest at the wedding feast at Cana. If so, then the lucky couple of Cana were the first man and wife to be properly married in the Catholic Church.

'This doesn't mean, of course, that all the couples who married in Old Testament times were not properly married. If their intentions were good and they were following their consciences to the best of their ability, then their marriages were probably valid. (It's the same with well-meaning non-Catholics today—many of their marriages are quite valid.)

'Anyway, the important thing is that Our Lord did make marriage a sacrament. And He taught his disciples quite a bit about it too. He said, "What God has joined together let no man put asunder," which of course makes all divorce impossible. And He said those beautiful words about the physical side of marriage. (I used to feel embarrassed whenever the priest read them out in the Sunday Gospel, but I suppose they were over your innocent head.) You know—the bit about a man leaving his father and mother and cleaving to his wife so they become one flesh.

'But the words I can never forget, the saddest words, I think, in the whole New Testament, are the ones He said when the Scribes and Pharisees told Him about the woman who had seven husbands on earth and asked Him which one would have her for his wife in heaven. And He told them there was no marrying or giving in marriage in heaven.

'They say everyone finds some stumbling-block in the Gospels—some teaching of Christ that doesn't make sense and has to be accepted on faith alone. Well, those words about marriage are my stumbling-block. I think they're cruel and unreasonable, I wish they weren't true, but because Christ Himself said them I believe in them.

'Bearing in mind what Our Lord Himself has said, let's be coldly realistic about the life we'll lead in heaven. After the end of the world and the Resurrection of the Dead and the General Judgement we'll all be given back our bodies. They'll be glorified bodies of course. So, beautiful and flawless as your body is now, (Sherd gently stroked the whiteness of his wife's throat) it will be a thousand times more perfect in those days. And let's be quite frank about it—none of us will be wearing clothes. Theologians believe we'll lose all our blemishes and moles and scars. I think myself we'll probably also be without the ugly hair under our arms and elsewhere on our bodies.

'There'll be millions of people around heaven, but eternity is a long long time and sooner or later you and I will meet up with each other again. Our glorified bodies will be based on those we had as young adults. So there we are, just as we were in the early years of our married life, meeting in some place even more beautiful than Tasmania. How will we feel towards each other?

'Well, because I'm in heaven and my soul is saved, it would be absurd to think of me having an impure temptation when I see you, even though you're stark naked and more beautiful than ever you were on earth. Besides, I would have got used to seeing beautiful young women naked all over the lawns every day in heaven (including, I suppose, a few film stars who repented on their deathbeds). In fact, if Our Lord was right about heaven (and He should have known, because all the time He was on earth His Divine Nature was enjoying Itself in Heaven, and as God the Son He helped to create the place anyway) you and I won't feel any more affection towards each other than we feel towards any of the millions of other men and women of all colours in heaven—because otherwise we'd start to fall in love again and want to get married.

'But the unfortunate thing is, we can't help remembering all our lives together on earth. So when I look at your perfect body and all its most striking features

I actually recall how excited they used to make me, although I don't feel the slightest excitement any more.

'When I look at your firm young breasts I probably admire them for the part they played in God's plan for us by catching my eye some nights as you slipped into your nightgown and prompting me to ask you to yield to me in bed. Or else I simply praise them for the wonderful job they did each time you brought another child into the world—swelling to a prodigious size before the great day and then pouring out gallons of nourishing milk through the conspicuous nipples during the weeks when your infant pressed its hungry mouth against them.

'And when I happen to glance at your supple white thighs and my eye quite naturally travels up them and rests for a moment on the intimate place enclosed between them, I suppose all I do is praise God for designing your body so that a part of it could accommodate my seed and afterwards perform its noble task of propelling another new creature into the world.

'And that, I'm afraid, is all that will happen between us in heaven. I still think we'll be allowed to stroll now and then through pleasant groves that remind us of Tasmania or Hepburn Springs or the Otways. And because those places once meant so much to us, we surely wouldn't be breaking the laws of heaven if we held hands now and then or even exchanged an innocent friendly kiss.

'If we feel like it we can both dive into a crystal-clear stream and swim around naked. You can even lie floating on your back all afternoon if you like and I won't be the least bit interested. I won't even have to be on guard against strangers finding our secluded spot. If a whole tribe of men and women saints suddenly appears beside our stream and stands looking down on us, we'll just wave to them and go on swimming.

'In fact our little outing will probably end with some handsome young man wading out to you and looking down on you with nothing but friendship in his eyes and telling you the story of how he was martyred fighting the Saracens in the siege of Acre. You and he will stroll off hand-in-hand, with you looking up into his eyes and telling him how you were married to a chap in the twentieth century and all about your children. I'll watch you go, knowing I mightn't run into you again for years, but I won't be at all concerned.

'Well, that's what the Gospel teaches us anyway. I still think it's hard that couples like us who love each other so passionately must be no more than good friends in heaven. Perhaps the trouble is that my love for you is far greater than God expects of a husband. After all, He only requires people to be attracted to each other so they'll marry and ensure a constant supply of new souls to do His Will on earth and glorify Him in heaven. If you and I have the largest possible number of children and turn them out good Catholics, that should

221

be a sufficient reward in itself. We've got no right to expect that we'll enjoy for all eternity the emotional and physical pleasures of being in love.

'If you look at the history of the Church you won't find any saints who got to heaven simply because of their love for a wife or husband. The people honoured by the Church as saints are those who never yielded to their emotions or passions. And I don't mean just priests and brothers and nuns. Only today I was looking through my Daily Missal at the notes on some of the saints who were ordinary lay people like you and me.'

Sherd picked up the missal from beside his bed and read from it.

'"St Praxedes consecrated her virginity to God and distributed all her wealth to the poor.

'"St Susanne, a holy virgin of high lineage, refused to marry the son of Diocletian and was beheaded after grievous torments.

'"St Frances of Rome was the type of a perfect spouse and, after her husband's death, of a perfect religious in the house of Oblates which she founded.

'"St Cecilia, of an illustrious Roman family, converted her husband Valerianus and her brother-in-law Tiburtius, preserved her virginity and was beheaded.

'"St Henry, Duke of Bavaria and Emperor of Germany, used his power to extend the kingdom of God. By agreement with his wife he preserved virginity in marriage."

'These are the people we're supposed to model ourselves on. There's no record of any man who was canonised because he had an extraordinary love for his wife and gave up every other happiness to serve her as I've done for you.

'When the saints I've mentioned got to heaven you can be sure they didn't moon around looking for their lost loved ones. St Henry would have smiled politely whenever he passed his wife on some heavenly avenue. He might not have seen her for months, but he didn't miss her because he had learned on earth that there are things more important than conjugal love.

'I've never mentioned this to you before, and I hope it doesn't dismay you, but I think I envy the people who haven't been baptised. At least they have a chance of meeting their wives or husbands again in limbo and continuing their great love affairs. Limbo, as you know, is a place of perfect natural happiness. It seems reasonable to suppose that the greatest natural happiness of all will be permitted there. In fact, when all bodies have been resurrected after the General Judgement, there might be nothing to prevent a man and his wife in limbo from enjoying also some of the purely physical pleasures they once enjoyed in this life.'

Early in the third term Adrian's class went on a retreat at the monastery of the Pauline Fathers. For three days and nights the boys lived at the monastery and observed some of its rules. They kept the Great Silence from evening prayers until after mass next morning; they ate their meals in the refectory while a lay brother read aloud the life-stories of great saints; and they walked in the garden for a half-hour of meditation after breakfast.

The monastery was in a garden suburb a few miles from Swindon. Adrian arrived in a bus after dark. Next morning he stood at his upstairs window and looked across the huge lawns to the tall front fence and couldn't work out the direction of Swindon or Accrington. He knew the name of the street and the suburb where he was. But it was a part of Melbourne he had never visited before. He might have walked for miles from the front gate of the monastery before he came to some tramline or railway station that could give him his bearings.

All the time Adrian was at the monastery he enjoyed feeling cut off from the world. He was hidden for a few days in one of the best suburbs of Melbourne for the purpose of looking into his soul and making sure he was on the right path.

Before the retreat, the brother in charge of Adrian's class had suggested that each boy should take some spiritual reading. He said there would be free periods during the retreat when the best thing a boy could do was to read and chew over the sort of things he didn't usually have time to read because of the pressure of his studies.

Adrian arrived at the monastery with three Australian Catholic Truth Society pamphlets and a *Reader's Digest* in the bottom of his bag. The pamphlets were called *Purity: The Difficult Virtue*; *Now You're Engaged*; and *Marriage Is Not Easy*. The *Reader's Digest* had an article entitled, *Physical Pleasure—What Should a Wife Expect?* Whenever the retreat program allowed free time, he went to his room and read.

On the last evening of the retreat, the priest in charge called the boys into the monastery parlour and invited them to start a discussion on some problem facing a Catholic young man in the modern world. The priest said he would act as chairman and perhaps give a short summing-up at the end.

The boys seemed embarrassed about talking in front of a strange priest, but at last John Cody stood up and said they ought to discuss the moral problems of boys and girls mixing together. The priest said it was an excellent topic and told Cody to start the ball rolling.

Adrian was glad he had taken a seat on the very edge of the boys and almost out of sight of the priest. He was angry with the priest for letting the boys choose such a frivolous topic.

The boys in his class talked for hours at school about girls they met on trams or at dances. They said such and such a girl was adorable or gorgeous or luscious or cute, but no boy ever dared to claim one of them was his girlfriend. Adrian knew that all these

225

fellows dreamed of was to walk some girl home from tennis on Saturday or fetch her a paper-cup of lemonade at the learn-to-dance class and stand beside her while she sipped it.

Adrian was sure none of his classmates ever lay awake for hours at night planning seriously his whole future with the young woman he loved. They wasted their time on tennis and dances and parties, and yet they were ready to discuss in all seriousness (in a retreat house, too) the moral problems of their childish games.

Adrian was spared all the petty troubles of teenagers because he had found quite early in life a young woman worthy to be his wife. At the first sign of any temptation against purity with any female he happened to see in the street, he only had to think of Denise McNamara and the danger was over. But his danger was far less than other fellows' anyway—knowing that Denise returned his affection, he didn't have to worry about dances and parties and company-keeping and goodnight kisses and all the rigmarole of modern courtship.

He looked out of the window into the dusk. The fence around the monastery was hidden in shadow. From where he sat he could see no sign of any street or even a neighbouring rooftop. If he could have kept his eyes on the dark shapes of trees and shrubbery and shut out the affected voices of his classmates as they stood up by turns and had their say and sneaked a look at the priest to see if they were saying anything heretical, he could have imagined himself in a forested landscape— the sort of place he preferred when he wanted to talk seriously to Denise.

A boy was saying, 'Although we're all students, and the main duties of our station in life are to obey our teachers and pass our exams, just the same we have to live in the world outside. You know what I mean—we go to dances and mix with the opposite sex. Some of us might even attend parties where the girls' parents don't come to collect them afterwards. So we're expected to walk the girls home to their front doors. Now the problem I'd like to hear discussed is this business of the goodnight kiss. You take this girl home and get to the front door and she says, "Thanks for everything." And then what do you do? I mean do you kiss her or just leave her standing there? I'd like to hear some other fellows' opinions on this.'

Adrian was very anxious to be alone with Denise. Only a few hours before, in the recreation period after lunch, he had found information in his pamphlets and his *Reader's Digest* that he had to share with her.

There was no time to fuss over which month or year of their marriage they were meeting in. He led her straight out through the french windows on to the deserted veranda. She sat on the stone parapet and leaned back prettily against the ivy-covered pillar. They both stared into the sombre forest.

Sherd said, 'I know the *Reader's Digest* is a non-Catholic magazine, but a lot of the things it says are quite useful if you're careful to see that they're not about faith or morals and they don't contradict the Church's teachings.

'Only today I found something in a *Digest* article that you ought to think about carefully. It seems that one of the causes of so much boredom in marriages these days is the wife always waiting till her husband asks her whether they can be intimate. This might shock you (I was a little surprised myself when I read it) but there's no reason why the woman shouldn't ask the husband sometimes whether he feels inclined to perform the act.

'From my own point of view, I wouldn't think any less of you if you whispered to me in bed now and then that you wouldn't say no if I asked you.

'And just to prove that all this isn't just some idea dreamed up by sensual Americans—I've read in an A.C.T.S. pamphlet that each partner in a marriage founded on Christian charity learns to anticipate the moods and inclinations of the other. Which means for our purposes that you could make an effort sometimes to watch my moods and learn to tell when I'm likely to approach you. Then you can take some of the responsibility off my shoulders by asking me before I have to ask you.'

This was one of the most difficult conversations that Sherd had ever had with Denise, and he thought it best to leave her alone for a few minutes while the full meaning of it sank in. He turned back to the parlour of the retreat house.

Barry Kellaway stood up and said, 'Wait a minute. Doesn't it make all the difference whether the girl's a Catholic or not? I mean, if she's a good Catholic she'll naturally be very careful what happens when she's alone with a chap outside her front door.

'If she thinks it's the time and the place for a quick little goodnight kiss, the chap can do it quickly and she'll make sure none of them puts themselves in any moral danger. And if she's not a Catholic, then the chap ought to examine his conscience because he could easily be going into an occasion of sin whenever he takes her home on her own.'

Kellaway sat down and looked at the priest in the corner.

The priest said, 'For argument's sake we'll assume we're talking about Catholic young people. It's hard enough to make rules for ourselves without trying to sort out non-Catholics' consciences for them. But I do agree that there's no reason whatsoever for boys of your age to be hanging around front doorsteps with non-Catholic girls.'

Adrian went back to Denise and took her hand. He was a little afraid he might have spoken too frankly to her or given her too much new information at once. But her smile told him she was grateful for all the trouble he was taking to explain the whole range of Catholic teaching on marriage and the latest findings from America.

He said to her, 'It's interesting to note that both the A.C.T.S. pamphlets and the *Reader's Digest* think it's most important for each partner to make the act of love enjoyable for the other.

'The pamphlets don't use those words exactly, but they do point out that either partner would commit a mortal sin if he or she executed the sexual act for no other reason than his or her selfish enjoyment.

'I think we both ought to examine our consciences to see if we're doing all we can for each other in this matter. And perhaps in future you'll do your best to make the act more enjoyable for me, while I make sure you're perfectly comfortable with a nice soft pillow under your head and treat you gently and not get carried away with selfish lust.'

Denise stared into the twilight. All the talk about intimacy had put Sherd in the mood for it, and he hoped Denise would soon notice he was a little more agitated than usual and guess the reason for it.

Just then Alan McDowell stood up behind him and said, 'No matter whether the girl's a Catholic or not, she must have seen some modern films and realised it's the custom nowadays for young people to have a quick goodnight kiss at the front door after a night together. If you don't do it you could be making a fool of yourself and next time you see her she won't be so easy to get on with.'

McDowell kept his eyes away from the priest, but several boys looked round as though they expected the priest to break in and explain how wrong McDowell was. The priest only pressed his lips tightly together and made notes on a slip of paper.

McDowell kept talking: 'I reckon it all depends what sort of kiss you give her and how long it takes. (The room was suddenly very quiet.) If it's just a quick little one where you just brush your faces together it's probably no worse than a venial sin. But if it's one of those other sorts you sometimes see in films where they take a long time to finish (someone blew his nose with a peculiar sound that might have disguised a snigger) well I think they're probably dangerous and they ought to be forbidden for Catholics.'

Adrian didn't bother to listen any more. It digusted him to think of big, lumpish Alan McDowell trying out different sorts of kisses on girls he had no intention of proposing marriage to.

Sherd put his hand gently on Denise's knee and said, 'I found something else very interesting in the *Reader's Digest*. You know, for many years people have thought it was only the man who was supposed to get some pleasure from the marriage act. The woman was expected to be a good wife and put up with whatever her husband did to her and get her happiness from the romantic love they shared.

'Well, just lately these scientists and doctors in America have discovered that if a woman tries hard enough and learns not to be frightened, and the man doesn't hurry too much, she might be able to get a sort of pleasure almost equal to her husband's.'

On the veranda it was almost too dark to see what Denise thought of this. Sherd wondered whether she would say she didn't need any more pleasure than she already got from seeing him happy and rested after the act, or whether she would smile shyly and say she would try to be more relaxed next time and see if the *Reader's Digest* was right.

But before Denise could speak, Bernard Negri said, 'It's all right for Alan to concentrate on what sort of goodnight kiss you're going to give a girl, but I think the most important thing for a Catholic boy to worry about is where the kiss takes place. I mean we've been taught all our lives not to go into an occasion of sin. I think I heard once that if you deliberately go into an occasion of sin that you know full well will probably cause you to sin, you've already committed a mortal sin as serious as the one you thought you were probably going to commit anyway.

'Well, as I was saying, it depends where you are when the kiss takes place. If you're standing on her front veranda with the front light on and you know her parents are sitting up inside waiting for her, there's probably no danger in it. But if you're at one of these parties where the parents go away and leave the young people on their own and somebody turns the lights off, isn't there a grave danger that you'll be tempted to do something worse than kissing?'

Adrian congratulated himself for having avoided all the tangled moral problems of company-keeping. He kissed Denise tenderly on the forehead and said, 'So much for the pleasures of marriage. To speak of more serious matters—even many good Catholics are not aware of all the graces and spiritual benefits they're entitled to get from marriage. Luckily for us, I've always read everything I could find on the subject. And buried away in an A.C.T.S. pamphlet today I found a wonderful bit of news.

'The author (a priest, of course) says marriage is a sacrament that goes on providing grace for the marriage partners all their lives. Year after year they can draw on this bottomless reservoir of grace to increase their own sanctity and earn for themselves a higher place in heaven. How? Well, believe it or not, every act of sexual intimacy between the partners (provided it's performed with the right motives and isn't sinful for some other reason) actually earns them an extra amount of grace.

'That's something to think about some night when you're just about to say you're too tired for it. If you can make a special effort to oblige me, you'll enjoy a spiritual reward.'

It was now completely dark on the veranda. Sherd couldn't see his wife's face, but she squeezed his fingers to show she was quietly thrilled by what he had told her.

Inside, the boys had finished their discussion and the priest was walking out from his corner into the middle of the room to sum up.

The priest said, 'You'll notice I kept right out of the discussion, boys. It's very important in a job like mine to hear the views of people like yourselves who have to live in the world, and let you explain your attitudes without any fear of having your heads bitten off by a priest for contradicting the Church's teachings.

'By and large, most of you seem to have a fairly sound idea of where a young Catholic man stands when he's dealing with the opposite sex. But I think the whole discussion went wrong somehow when you got onto this business of the goodnight kiss. (He looked at the notes in his hand.) Now I don't want to single out any one boy for what he said, but one of you seemed to think that just because, "it's the custom nowadays" or "everybody's doing it" or "you see it in all the latest films", then a Catholic has to be in it and go along with the mob for fear they'll laugh at him or think he's old-fashioned.

'If any boy still thinks after all his years at a Catholic secondary school that he's going to decide what to do in life by what the rest of the world is doing, he'd better use the time remaining in this retreat to sit down and ask himself some very serious questions. Or, better still, he'd better make an appointment to see me or one of the other priests for a man-to-man chat.'

The priest paused and looked at his notes. The boys all knew it was childish and unfair to look at Alan McDowell just then, but most of them sneaked a look, even so. McDowell was pale and still, but otherwise he was taking it fairly well.

The priest said, 'Perhaps this is the time to go over very briefly the few facts a Catholic has to know about this whole matter of mixed company-keeping.'

While he talked, the priest looked hard at one boy after another. Adrian was sure the priest was annoyed with the boys. He hoped the priest had noticed how he himself kept aloof from the childish discussion. Perhaps the priest would even realise from the look on Adrian's face that he was far beyond the stage of kissing on doorsteps and already deep into the Church's teachings on married life.

The priest was saying, 'It's quite simple, really. The basic rules cover all possible situations that you're likely to come up against. To commit a mortal sin you have to fulfil three simple conditions. There must be grave matter, full knowledge and full consent.

Now there's no need to explain about knowledge and consent. All of you are sane rational creatures and you all possess free will. You know what it means to know fully what you're doing. And you know what it means to consent to something fully with your will.

These things are clearcut. The third condition—grave matter—might not be so clear in your minds, but the Church's rules are very simple.

'The pleasures of the body are for married people alone. At your age anything you do with a girl that gives rise to physical pleasure is sufficient material for a mortal sin. With regard to the bosom, the breasts of a girl—those are grave matter at all times. And you shouldn't have to be told that her private places are absolutely out of bounds.

'But of course you can commit a mortal sin with any part of a girl's body. I can readily imagine the circumstances when a young fellow would sin over a girl's hands or arms, the exposed skin around her neck, even her feet or her bare toes.

'It's no use saying afterwards, "But I only intended to give her an innocent kiss." The Church is older and wiser than any of you. Listen to her advice.'

While the boys followed the priest into the chapel for evening prayers, Adrian looked at their solemn faces and pitied them. They could do no more than look at the faces and forearms, and perhaps the ankles and calves, of all the girls they met until they finally married. How could they face such a bleak future without the thought of someone like Denise to inspire and console them?

Sherd's daily life at Our Lady of the Ranges left him plenty of time for thinking. Thrusting his potato-fork

236

into the clotted red soil and lifting out the ponderous tubers, swollen with nourishment, or perched on a hand-made stool in the milking-shed, resting his head against the glossy flank of a Jersey cow and squirting her warm creamy milk so that it rang against the silvery metal of the bucket or lost itself with a rich satisfying sound in the fatty bubbles all over the surface, he looked back on his youth or pondered over the problems of the modern world.

He often remembered the year before he met Denise—the year when he became a slave of lust and couldn't sleep at night until he had seduced some film star. When he looked back on that year from the peace of the Otways (where he and his wife went to mass and communion every morning and confession every fortnight—although they had only a few petty faults to confess) he squirmed with shame. It was the episode in his life that still disturbed him.

Sometimes, to make himself more humble and less self-satisfied, he deliberately paused just before making love to his wife and thought, 'If I were to do to this angelic creature beneath me what I once did to those bold-faced film stars; if I grabbed those parts of her that I used to handle and slobber over on their bodies; if I did everything slowly to prolong the act and tire her as I tired them; or if I lost control of myself at the last moment and said to her the crazy things I used to blurt out to them—.' But he could never imagine what she would do—the very idea was preposterous.

He often tried to work out why he had turned, in that year, from a normal Catholic boy in a decent household to a sex-crazed satyr rampaging across America. Thinking it over in the quiet valleys of the Otways he was inclined to blame American films.

Not that he had ever seen his favourite film stars on the screen. It was not as simple as that. Adrian Sherd the schoolboy never saw more than five or six films a year. Half of those were Walt Disney films and the rest were chosen by his mother because they were classified 'For General Exhibition' and recommended for children.

Adrian's mother used to say before he went to one of these films, 'There's bound to be a bit of love and romance and that sort of rot. But just put up with it and wait for the adventure parts.'

From the distance of the Otways, Sherd suspected that these supposedly harmless films might have started him on his year-long orgy of lust. Meditating on a leafy hillside, he watched them again and blended their complex plots into one.

An American man arrives in a strange town near a jungle or a desert or an enemy country that he must soon venture into. He looks across a hotel lobby crowded with foreign faces and finds himself staring into the eyes of a beautiful American woman aged about twenty-five. He falls in love with her at once, but he knows from the cold way she meets his eyes that others before him have fallen for her and been repulsed.

The man goes to hire the native porters for his expedition or to rendezvous with an army officer or a master spy who will give him his final instructions. When he returns to the hotel, he finds the woman sitting alone at a table in the dining room. Because he is leaving next day on a mission that may well cost him his life, the man is keyed-up to an extraordinary pitch of bravery. He sits down at the table without being asked, and even starts a conversation with the woman.

He soon learns that she is single. (If she had been married, the romantic interest of the plot would have ended there and then—the man would have apologised for bothering her and left the table.) She has never allowed a man to do anything more than hold her hand or give her a friendly goodnight kiss. (This becomes apparent when the man's eyes glance downwards at the inch or so of cleavage above the neckline of her evening frock. She catches him at it and gives him a long severe look that makes him glance away and fiddle with his glass from embarrassment.) She is visiting remote parts of the world to recover from a broken heart. (She is understandably vague when she talks about her past, but the most likely interpretation of her pauses and broken sentences is that she fell in love with a man in her home town in America but found her love was not returned.) Finally, she has no steady boyfriend just at present. (She says quite explicitly, 'There's been no one else since—I don't think there ever can be.' The man at the table understands from this that he is free to become her suitor.)

The man and woman dance together in the hotel ballroom, then walk out to the marble balcony. He tells her a little about the journey that he must begin next morning. A stranger leaps out of the shadows and throws a knife at the man. The man dodges the knife and shields the woman with his body. He is so anxious to protect her that the mysterious stranger escapes. However, the man is well rewarded when the woman leans on him and clutches the lapels of his coat. He does not hide his pleasure at having her so close to him. And it makes it clear to her that she has awakened his strongest instinct—the urge to protect a beautiful helpless woman at a moment of danger.

Because she is now frightened of the foreigners in the hotel, the woman asks the man to her room for a drink. While he fills her glass and hands it to her, he looks her over. Her hair is so neatly done and her lipstick and make-up are so carefully applied that she would obviously not welcome any man who tried to kiss or embrace her and disturb it. Her dress is securely fastened across her breasts. (It has not slipped a fraction of an inch during the whole time that Adrian has been watching it.) The dress is such a tight fit that no man could hope to loosen it even a little without her noticing what he was trying to do. Below her breasts the cloth is as taut and forbidding as a suit of armour—and there are no fastenings visible on it that a man could try to interfere with. Even the furniture in the room is designed to keep a man at a distance. She sits with her arm outflung along the back of a thickly padded couch that makes her look as regal and unapproachable as a queen.

Nevertheless, the man does dare to kiss her once before he says goodbye and leaves her room for the night. He does it in a restrained polite way, pressing his lips against hers for no more than half a minute and holding her so that no other parts of their bodies come into contact.

The man starts on his journey next day. He has many worries on his mind, but when he looks back for the last time at the town where the young woman is waiting, he is obviously hoping she will be true to him until he returns to continue his wooing.

Soon afterwards, the woman learns how perilous the man's journey is and prepares to set out after him. When she explains this to a girlfriend, the girlfriend teases her and accuses her of getting too serious about a man who is only an adventurer. The young woman denies this, but with a dreamy look in her eyes that suggests she really is falling in love. She appears to have known from the way the man kissed her that he was in love with her, and now her own heart is beginning to melt.

For a long time after this the film shows only the troubles of the man on his journey. The woman is captured on her way to join him. It seems as though they will never meet again and have the chance to declare their love for each other. But in the end, the man (helped by loyal natives or friendly foreigners) outwits his enemies and approaches the place where the woman has been kept captive.

The very last scene between the couple has to be watched closely to reveal its full meaning. First, the man notices that the top buttons of the woman's blouse have come undone during her struggles with her captors. She is still tied to a post with her hands behind her back. She is at his mercy. If he were only interested in her body he could lean forward for a moment and peep down the front of her gaping blouse or even slip his hand inside it or do much worse to her. But he does not even pause to consider these possibilities. He rips away the ropes that bind her and takes her tenderly in his arms.

This time she lets him kiss her more than once. She knows from the gentlemanly way he has rescued her that he really is in love with her. And in the excitement of being rescued she sees no harm in allowing him a few extra kisses, especially since the leader of the native porters or the foreign peasants is standing only a few yards off and grinning at them.

The film ends before the man actually proposes marriage. But anyone can see from the more relaxed way they behave towards each other that the man is only waiting for the right moment to ask her and that he knows already what her answer will be. And the woman seems to know what is in his mind and to be only waiting for the chance to say 'yes'.

Looking back at such films from the pure air of the Otways, Sherd understood how they had contributed to his year of sin. The films had introduced him to a kind of woman he never came across in Australia—the attractive young woman in her twenties who had no boyfriend but travelled around waiting for the right man to fall in love with her and begin courting her. Because her heart had been broken in the past, she was fairly reserved with a new suitor. She only let him kiss her after he had given some proof of his devotion, and she would have slapped his face if he had tried to touch her improperly.

Adrian had never seen one woman of this kind in Accrington or anywhere in Melbourne. Yet he learned from films that thousands of them sat waiting at hotel tables from Maine to California—and even in foreign cities. If Adrian had had a girlfriend of his own at the time, he could have rejoiced to see films showing other people achieving the same kind of happiness that he himself enjoyed. But those were the days before he had met Denise. When the films were over he went home to his lonely bed and envied the men who met these young women on their travels.

What happened next was only too familiar to the man Sherd. He remembered it and did penance for it every day. In the heat of his lust he had invented a sequence of events that was a travesty of the films that inspired them. Like the male stars of the films, he had met eligible young women. But instead of courting them patiently and waiting for some sign of encouragement before he kept exclusive company with them or ventured to kiss them, he had undressed them and defiled them only hours after their first meeting. It was all so absurd compared with what really happened in films.

After years in the peaceful Catholic community of Our Lady of the Ranges, Sherd could see clearly all the faults of modern life in Australia. He knew there was something very wrong with a society that made it so hard for young men to meet young women with a view to marriage.

A young man growing up at Our Lady of the Ranges was free to choose a girlfriend from one of the families he mixed with every day. Their affection for each other grew steadily over the years. A smile from her at morning mass or a few words as they met on a rustic pathway would inspire him to work like a Trojan all morning in the potato paddocks or bend over his books of theology and church history all afternoon in the library. The years passed quickly until the fellow was old enough to call on her parents and ask for the young woman's hand. From then until the day of the wedding, the young couple would sit together by the riverbank on Sunday afternoons, within sight of their elders but far enough away to talk privately together.

As more and more people left the cities and settled in co-operative rural communities, there would be fewer young women in any country who had to spend hours doing their hair and putting make-up on their faces and then sitting alone at hotel tables waiting for the right man to turn up. And of course there would be fewer single men walking past those tables and noticing the women sitting there. But best of all there would be fewer young men who had to spend years of their lives as solitary sex maniacs because they could only watch those single men and women meeting in films and never get the chance to do the same thing in real life.

During a House football match one Wednesday, it rained so hard that the brother who was umpire sent the boys to shelter under trees. Adrian Sherd and his team-mates crouched under the dripping branches and looked for a break in the weather. The sky was unnaturally dark. Someone started talking about the end of the world.

The boys of Adrian's class often discussed this topic when no brother was around. One or two of them had tried to bring up the subject in Christian Doctrine periods, but their teacher had always ended the discussion before it got interesting. The brother would agree that the world was going to end some day, but he insisted that no one—not even the most learned theologian or the holiest saint—knew whether it would happen tomorrow or a thousand years from now. The brother

245

would allow that parts of the *Apocalypse* described the last days of the world and the signs of the coming end, but he said it was a risky business trying to look for these signs in the present day. All a Catholic boy had to do was to live each day of his life as though it was *his* last day on earth, and leave it to God to work out His plans for bringing the world to an end.

A boy looked out at the sodden football ground and said, 'We know He won't destroy the world again by water or send a terrible deluge again because in the Old Testament He showed Noah the sign of the rainbow when the flood had gone down.'

Another boy said, 'It can't happen yet because the prophet Elias hasn't come back to earth. And there was someone else in the Old Testament who didn't die properly either. Elias went up body and soul in a fiery chariot, and the Church teaches that he has to come back to earth again and die properly. I've heard he'll come back when the Church is really in trouble and lead us in battle against our enemies.'

All the boys around Adrian joined in the discussion.

'The Antichrist is going to be the Church's worst enemy. But he hasn't come yet, and the world can't end until he does.'

'Will Elias know he's Elias when he comes back? Or will he grow up thinking he's just an ordinary Catholic schoolboy? He could even be one of us now.'

'He'd have to be a Hebrew, though, wouldn't he?'

'Wouldn't he more likely come back the way he went up? I don't mean in a fiery chariot, but roughly the same age.'

'His body is somewhere in heaven right now. Seems creepy to think about it.'

'That's nothing. Our Lady's body is there too according to the dogma of the Assumption.'

'But what about the Antichrist? He won't call himself that, will he?'

'I used to think Stalin was him, the way he persecuted Catholics. But he's dead now and the Church is still going strong. Anyway, isn't the Church supposed to be defeated or nearly die out just before the end of the world? That's not happening now, is it?'

'There are four hundred million Catholics all over the world.'

'Our Lord said, "Behold I am with you all days even to the consummation of the world." The Church can never be defeated.'

Stan Seskis joined in and said, 'Listen. My old man's a nong most of the time. But he's right when he talks about Communism. You droobs don't realise what the Communists are doing in Australia right now. When my father heard the Russians were coming into our country during the war he packed everything into a little leather bag and my mother carried me and my little brother in her arms and we got for our lives. After the war we sneaked across the border of Germany into the West. We had to cross a ploughed paddock and I was bawling the whole time because my shoe fell off and I couldn't go back to get it. That's all I can remember—I lost my shoe. I wonder what the Reds did with it if they ever found it. But my father knows what Communism means because he's lived with it.'

Seskis kept talking. No one wanted to interrupt him. 'And you know all this Petrov business and all the facts about Russian spies in Australia? Well, my old man's known all about it for years. He knows the names of dozens of Communist spies in all the unions and the Labor Party and if it hadn't been for him and his anti-Communist mates, the Commoes would have taken over Australia already. When I was a kid and we had all those strikes in Australia and grass was growing on all the train-tracks and tramlines for months, well my father came home one night and told us the Communists were just about ready to overthrow the government. He said it could happen any day, only this time they weren't going to drive him out of his homeland a second time—he was going to stay and fight. And if you saw the list of Communists in his secret notebook (they're all written in code) you'd be amazed how many enemies we've got all round us.'

Another fellow said, 'That Bishop from China who spoke to all the senior forms that day—the one with the white beard who wrote Chinese words on the blackboard and showed us his chopsticks—didn't he say the Chinese Communists had a plan to come down through the islands to Australia? That's why these terrorists are fighting in Malaya right now.'

Someone else said, 'But the Bishop told us there were millions of secret Catholics all over China—all the people the Columban Fathers had converted for fifty years. And if they get the chance they'll rebel against the government and kick the Communists back where they came from.'

Adrian Sherd said, 'I was reading in a *Reader's Digest* the other day how the greatest allies the West has are the millions of Russians and Poles and Czechs and so on who hate Communism. They're waiting for the chance to rise up if only we could encourage them.'

'Well, why doesn't America just send an army in? The Russian people wouldn't fight for Communism, would they?'

'But the Russians have got the hydrogen bomb. There was a story in the *Argus* one day about a foreign power dropping a hydrogen bomb on Melbourne. (They meant the Russians, of course.) Well, this old bushman from the Dargo High Plains rode his horse down to Gippsland once a year and caught the train to Melbourne. Only this year he wondered why everything was so quiet and the trees all looked as though a bush-fire had passed through. And about fifty miles from Melbourne he started to notice all these dead bodies.

249

Well, he headed back to the bush, but the whole of Melbourne was wiped out.'

'But why would the Russians pick on Melbourne anyway? Wouldn't they bomb New York or Washington first?'

'You know Theresa Neumann. She's a living saint in Germany. She's still alive today in a village called Konnersreuth. For thirty years now she's never eaten any food or drunk any water. The only thing that keeps her alive is her holy communion every morning. And every Thursday night she starts to suffer all the wounds and pains that Our Lord suffered in His Passion. And by Friday afternoon her face is covered with blood as if she had a crown of thorns pressing into her forehead, and all the marks of the stigmata appear on her hands and feet. The cleverest Protestant doctors in Europe have studied her for years and no one can explain how it happens. My mother wrote away to Germany once and got back a bundle of holy cards from Theresa Neumann's own village. All the prayers were in German but my cousin translated some of them. And there was this little leaflet with the whole story of the Miraculous Stigmata of Theresa Neumann.

'Anyway, Theresa Neumann has made some prophecies, and the worst one I can remember is that priests will be hanging from lamp-posts in Melbourne in 1970.'

No one spoke for a while. All round the tree where they crouched, the raindrops made little holes like bomb craters in the mud. On the far side of the deserted football field, a ragged file of boys stumbled and ran towards the pavilion. Further still, on the other side of the creek, was a long grey paling fence that marked the end of all the backyards in some street of a suburb that Adrian Sherd had never entered. (He guessed it was Woodstock or Luton or even the edge of Camberwell.) The back porches were swept by rain and the doors and windows were all shut.

A boy said, 'What's the percentage of Catholics in Australia, anyway?'

Adrian answered, 'Only about twenty-five per cent,' and looked at the rows of locked non-Catholic houses on the hills around them.

A man came towards them with a black oilskin cape hiding his face. It was a brother to tell them the football matches had all been abandoned and they'd better get for their lives back to the pavilion.

The football pavilion had timber nailed over the windows where the glass should have been. The sky was so dark that the boys inside could barely recognise each other. Some of them went on talking about prophecies while they changed into their school uniforms.

A boy said, 'There was an old Irish monk centuries ago. His name was Malachy, I think. He made all these prophecies about the popes who were going to come after his lifetime. He said a few words about each pope like "Great Builder" or "Defender of the Faith" or

"Destroyer of Heresies", and so far they've all turned out true. He called Pius the Twelfth "Very Saintly Shepherd" or something, and it's true he's one of the holiest of all the popes.

'Well, the scariest thing is—there's only five or six popes left on Malachy's list. So if he's right, the end of the world could happen before the year 2000. Because the Catholic Church has to last until the end of time, and if there's no more popes that's the end of everything.'

A fellow said, 'But the Antichrist still has to appear. He's probably alive now—a young man growing up in Russia or China and planning to destroy the Church.'

They all joined in again.

'Antichrist will have to beat Elias first.'

'Who wins in the end anyway? Does the *Apocalypse* say whether the Catholics or Communists win the last battle?'

'Our Lady told the children at Fatima that if enough people all over the world offered up prayers and penance, she would make sure Russia was converted and there'd be no Third World War after all.'

Adrian Sherd said, 'We won't have to fight the Russians on our own. I read a *Reader's Digest* article about Turkey, and the Turks have always hated the Russians, even before they turned Communist. And they're ready to fight them again if the Russians start anything. The end of the article was this big Turkish soldier looking across the frontier and saying, "One Turk has always been as good as three Russians in battle."'

'What about the secret message that Our Lady of Fatima gave to the children in a sealed envelope and told them not to open it for twenty years? And didn't Francesca give it to the Pope and when he opened the first part of it a few years ago he fainted? And Francesca is a nun now, and her hair's turned white because she knows the first part of the message too. When are they going to open the second and third parts?'

'I'm not sure, but the nuns told us at primary school that when the Pope was seriously ill a few years ago he had a vision of Our Lord that he wouldn't tell anyone about. But people in the Vatican think Our Lord must have told him something about the future and what will happen to the Church and he's hardly ever smiled or laughed since.'

'If only Our Lord or Our Lady would appear to the Russians and show them a cross in the sky to frighten them or convert them or make them leave us alone.'

'Even if they appeared in Australia to tell us how many years we've got before the end of the world! If it's only going to be a few years we all ought to study for the priesthood instead of going to work or getting married.'

'Did anyone read in the paper last year about that woman who drowned her two little kids in the bath and tried to gas herself because she didn't want to be alive when the Communists took over the world? They put her in the looney bin but one of my mother's friends knew her well and she said she could understand how any woman with young kids would do a thing like that nowadays.'

Adrian and the little group around him were the last to leave the pavilion. They walked across the playing fields in pouring rain to the East Swindon tram terminus. No one talked any more about the end of the world.

In the tram back to Swindon, Adrian stood near the door because his clothes were too wet to sit in. He stared at the enormous houses along the tramline and wondered, as he always did, who else beside doctors and dentists and solicitors could be wealthy enough to live in such places. In all his life he had never been inside the front gate of any house like them. But instead of envying the people inside (as he usually did), he almost pitied them.

While hundreds of millions of Chinese and Russians were preparing for a Third World War, the people of Melbourne's garden suburbs were going about their business as though there was nothing to worry about. They were thinking of wall-to-wall carpets and radio-grams and washing machines while saints and prophets and the *Reader's Digest* foresaw at least a terrible war and perhaps the last days of the world.

Even if they went to church, the garden suburbs people only sang Protestant hymns or listened to long sermons about Hospital Sunday or gambling or being converted in your heart. Their sons went to Eastern Hill Grammar and enjoyed themselves at parties or looked forward to years at the University and careers in the professions, while Adrian prayed to God every night to put off the end for a little longer so he could enjoy a few years of happiness as the husband of Denise McNamara.

But it wasn't unfair that thoughtful Catholics had such worries while non-Catholics enjoyed themselves in their spacious homes. It was far better to look at the future realistically than to live for the pleasure of the moment. Adrian and his classmates had been brought up to think deeply about the things that really mattered. Their Catholic education had trained them to use their reason—to probe beneath the shallow surface that Protestants and atheists never questioned. And if the price that Catholic intellectuals had to pay was to worry about the terrible times ahead—well, at least they would have the last laugh one day when the Communists took over the garden suburbs or the armies of Elias and Antichrist drew up for battle on the outskirts of Melbourne.

Adrian hoped that all these prosperous doctors and solicitors and their spoilt sons and daughters would have time before the end to apologise to the Catholics and admit they were right after all. Of course the fools would spend all eternity blaming themselves for their folly anyway, but it would be very satisfying to have some big golden-haired Eastern Hill fellow come up to the boy he hadn't even noticed on the trams years before and say, 'For God's sake, why didn't you Catholics tell us what was coming?'

The answer to the fellow's question, of course, was that he wouldn't have listened anyway. All over Australia, Catholics like Stan Seskis's father were trying to warn people about Communists in the unions, but how many listened to them? Only forty years before, Our Lady of Fatima had worked one of the most spectacular miracles of all time—the sun had danced and spun around and floated down towards the earth in front of 60,000 witnesses—but how many people were doing what Our Lady had asked, and praying and offering up penance so that Russia would be converted?

Even while the non-Catholics of Melbourne were sitting in front of their electric fires and their wives were fiddling with their expensive pressure cookers, a holy woman in Germany was still alive after fasting for twenty-five years—but who listened to her prophecies or took notice of her visions?

The tram climbed the last hill towards the Swindon Town Hall. Adrian looked back at the miles of dark-red roofs and grey-green treetops and the mass of rain-clouds above them. He knew it was wrong to gloat over the fate of thousands of people who had never deliberately done him harm. But he whispered into the breeze blowing past the tram that they were all doomed. And he saw the end of the world like grey rain bearing down on suburb after suburb—Oglethorpe by its winding creek, Glen Iris on its far hills, yes, and even Camberwell, the leafiest of them all—and the people in their last agony crying out that if only they could have had a Catholic secondary education they might have seen it coming.

Early in the third term, the boys of St Carthage's started practising for the House Sports Meeting. Adrian Sherd decided to train for the B Grade 880 yards. Three nights each week he got out of Denise's compartment at Caulfield and went to the racecourse to run. On those nights he always let his bag dangle open in the train so Denise would see his sandshoes and running singlet and realise he wasn't deserting her for some frivolous reason.

He thought of her all the time he trained. In his last year at St Carthage's, after he had started to talk to her on the train, she would tell a white lie to her teachers and turn up at the Swindon Cricket Ground to see him run in the A Grade 880. Meanwhile he improved his stamina by hissing her name under his breath as he ran.

One night three other boys agreed to run a trial 880 yards with him at the racecourse. Adrian dropped out well behind them in the early part of the race. His breath came easily and he barely whispered Denise's name. With about 300 yards to go, he began his run. The effort to reach the others made him puff. He hissed the beloved name fiercely and didn't care who heard him.

The other runners were stronger than Adrian had expected. In a last desperate effort to catch them he fixed her face, pale and anxious, a little to one side of the winning-post and punished his weary body savagely for her sake. A few yards short of the finish he caught and passed one of his rivals, but the other two were already crossing the line.

When the runners all stopped and looked at each other, Adrian suddenly heard the strange noise he had been making. It was always hard to fit the word 'Denise' into the rhythm of his breathing, and in the strain of the last hundred yards it had changed to a meaningless gasp, 'Nees-A! Nees-A' that was no help at all to him.

That night, for the first time since he had met Denise, he wondered if her influence over him might be weakening. A few nights later Sherd and his wife were climbing down towards a lonely riverbank in the Otways. It was Sunday afternoon and they wanted to be alone for a few hours away from the people of Our Lady of the Ranges. They were surprised to hear squeals coming from the river. They got to the little beach in time to see a naked man and two naked women dash out of the water and sprint towards a big beach umbrella and a heap of towels and clothes.

One of the women was a tall leggy brunette, and the other was a blonde with ample curves. Each of them kept an arm across her breasts and a hand between her thighs as she ran, so that Adrian was not forced to shield his eyes from them. But he flung himself in front of his wife to save her from seeing the man's big hairy organ flopping up and down.

Sherd took his wife to the far end of the beach, but he kept thinking of the man and the two women. More than once he was tempted to stroll over and start a friendly conversation with them. He tried to convince himself there would be no harm in it, since the women would almost certainly be fully dressed. But when he remembered he was a married man with a beautiful young wife beside him, he came to his senses and admitted he was experiencing an impure temptation.

The boy Adrian Sherd was as shocked as the man when he realised how close he had come to turning his back on his wife and going into an occasion of sin. A few months before, the thrill of chatting to his wife in her bathers would have been so powerful that he could have kept his back turned all day on a beach full of naked film stars.

He realised that the married life of the Sherds was becoming too remote from the daily life of the young Adrian Sherd. Mrs Denise Sherd was a wonderful wife, but perhaps a boy in Form Five needed someone nearer his own age.

Adrian decided to act. On the very next night, he lay down in bed as usual, but instead of reaching out a hand to stroke the long black hair and the pale shoulder of his wife, he leaned across the compartment in the Coroke train and said to Denise McNamara, 'Excuse me, but I've been meaning to speak to you for some time.'

He wasn't brave enough to look her in the eyes as he spoke. He watched her hands and was encouraged to see her fiddling with her gloves and exposing the creamy-white skin of her wrists. When she answered him, her voice was just as gentle and sincere as he used to dream it might be when he sat opposite her in the train and waited for them both to grow older so he could talk to her and begin his long patient wooing.

They called each other 'Denise' and 'Adrian' without formally introducing themselves—although they were both too shy to mention the day when they showed each other their names on exercise books. There was so much to talk about—the subjects they studied at school, the sports they played, the radio programs they listened to at night, the things they did at weekends. When Denise said she liked going to the pictures when she got the chance, Adrian knew she was inviting him to ask her to the pictures in Accrington some day when they knew each other better.

Adrian got more pleasure from hearing the school-girl Denise talk about her likes and dislikes and hobbies than he had once got from imagining her as his wife.

He chatted to her every night for nearly two months. The only bother he had was that sometimes when he stood near her in the train of an afternoon, he almost forgot himself and blurted out the story he was saving for their conversation that night.

When it was almost December, Adrian decided to speed up events so he would be deeply involved with her before they had to part for the long summer holidays. One night in bed he asked her quietly would she care to go to the pictures with him on the following Saturday night. It was much easier than he had expected. She even blushed a little as she answered, proving that this was the first time any young man had asked her out. She told him she would ask her parents, and the next day it was all arranged.

On the Saturday night Adrian and Denise sat together in one of the special buses that took crowds of young couples from outlying suburbs into Accrington to the Plaza or the Lyric.

During the first picture Adrian leaned his upper arm against Denise's shoulder and was pleased to see she did not draw away from him. At interval he gently grasped her elbow when she was jostled by the crowds around the ice-cream counter.

The main picture had a lot of kissing and romance. Adrian was not interested in the plot. He was planning for the moment when he would reach out boldly and take Denise's hand. It was lying naked and limp and

261

easily within his reach, just above her knee. He couldn't approach it where it was—Denise might see his hand coming and think for an instant he was going to touch her on the thigh. But at last she lifted it onto the armrest between them, which he had left unoccupied for that very purpose. He still had to wait until there was no kissing on the screen. (He reasoned that if he reached for her hand at a moment when a man and woman were pressed together in the film, Denise might think he was planning to court her with kisses and hugs like a man from Hollywood.)

At last, when a band was playing a song with only a suggestion of romance in its words, he rested his hand on hers. The white hand did not move. He lifted it up with all the tenderness that his five fingers could express and laid it between his palms (keeping it as far away as possible from his own thighs and lap). Still it did not even twitch or tauten. He saw from the corner of his eye that Denise was watching the film as if nothing had happened to her hand.

He knew it was only modesty that made her hand so limp. She must have suspected he was deeply in love with her, but she would have to be absolutely certain of it before she could yield any part of her body to him. He kept her hand in his and tried to convince himself that his dream really had come true at last, that he was actually sitting beside Denise McNamara and caressing her hand. And then he had a powerful erection.

It was the biggest and strongest that he had ever had in a public place—almost certainly more fierce than the monster that had appeared for no reason one morning in Form Three and lasted all through a Latin period. It made a conspicuous mound in his trousers as it tried to stand upright and flex itself.

Adrian's first thought was that he must keep the thing hidden from Denise. He lifted her hand back onto the armrest, gave it a farewell pat, and left it there. Then he slid his left hand (the hand farther from Denise) into his trousers pocket and slowly eased the huge thing until it lay pointing along the inside edge of his thigh. It was uncomfortable and restless in its new position, but at least it no longer made a threatening lump in his trousers. He thanked God that Denise kept her eyes on the screen while all this was going on.

Adrian gave up trying to follow the film and prepared for the moment when the lights came on and he had to stand up and walk outside with Denise beside him. He concentrated on the most frightening thoughts—losing his trousers on the way back from the communion rails at mass; letting off a thunderous fart as he walked past the microphone to receive his prize on the stage of Swindon Town Hall at St Carthage's Speech Night; vomiting all over his examination answers just before the supervisor came to collect them in the crowded Exhibition Building. But he could not make his erection go down.

When the film finally ended Adrian kept his left hand in his pocket to hold the thing down. He had to walk very slowly, but he pretended to yawn a lot so Denise would think he was tired. In the bus he had some trouble getting Denise to sit on his right side, away from the battle going on in his trousers.

Denise invited him to her house for a cup of tea. Adrian limped towards her front gate, trying to look down at himself in the light from a street lamp to see how much was visible.

He prayed that her parents would be in bed, but they were in the lounge-room listening to *Geoff Carmichael's Supper Club* on the radio. Of course Adrian had to take his hand out of his pocket to be introduced to them. He was sure Mrs McNamara didn't notice anything unusual. (She looked to be in her forties, so she probably hadn't seen anything like it for years.) But Denise's father looked him up and down quickly before shaking hands. Adrian was sure the father of a girl as beautiful and innocent as Denise would be always alert for signs that her purity was threatened. If Mr McNamara had noticed the least sign of movement in Adrian's trousers he would be too polite to say anything about it with his wife and daughter in the room, but he would tell his daughter afterwards that she was forbidden to associate with that young Sherd fellow any more.

The parents soon left the young people alone in the dining room. Denise leaned forward across the table to talk to Adrian about the film. He said to himself (slowly and distinctly, so the message would travel down his nerves into his groin) that he was looking into the eyes of the most chaste and modest and beautiful girl in the world. But instead of dying of shame, the thing in his trousers reared up as if he had promised it some filthy pleasure.

For the rest of his time in the dining room, Adrian let his erection do what it liked out of sight under the table while he took a pure delight in looking at Denise's pink ear-lobes, the white hollow at the base of her throat, and the faultless symmetry of her face.

When it was time to go, he walked behind her to the front door. Then he dodged quickly past her and said goodnight over his shoulder. He had never intended to kiss her after their first outing together. He wanted to emphasise that it was not physical gratification he was looking for when he went out with her. It was just as well—he shuddered to think what might have happened if he had stood with his body close to hers and no free hand to keep in his pocket.

By the time he had closed the McNamaras' front gate his erection had shrivelled up and promised to cause no more trouble that night. But Adrian was already planning how to outwit it when he next went out with Denise.

After school a few days later, Adrian took a tram from Swindon into the city and went to a shop he had learned about from advertisements in the *Sporting Globe*. In the window he saw wheelchairs, artificial legs, bedpans, braces for injured backs, strange thick stockings, and things he supposed were trusses. He asked the man at the counter for an athletic support and hoped he looked like a footballer or bike rider who needed one for a genuine reason. The man came towards him with a tape-measure. Adrian shrank back. He couldn't believe he had to take out his privates in the shop and have them measured. But the man only pulled the tape-measure around Adrian's waist and went to some drawers behind the counter. Adrian would have asked for a size smaller than his fitting but he was afraid the man would think he was some kind of pervert who tortured his organ before he masturbated.

That night Adrian wore the jock strap to bed under his pyjamas. Before he lay down, he pressed his penis flat against his testicles and pulled the belt of the jock strap as high as it would reach around his waist. Purely as a part of his experiment, he teased his organ by poking it with his fingers. It swelled a little, but the elastic easily held it down. Adrian was satisfied it would give him no trouble that night, no matter how long he held Denise's hand, or even if she responded by squeezing his.

A little later he was chatting to her again in the Saturday night picture bus to Accrington. Everything was peaceful between his legs because he knew he wouldn't be reaching for her hand until they had settled down in the theatre and the lights had gone out. Suddenly the young woman in the seat in front of them leaned her head on the shoulder of the young man beside her and shifted her body until it pressed against his. Adrian shifted an inch or so away from Denise to show her he didn't approve of couples making an exhibition of themselves in public. Denise sat very still. He supposed she was as irritated as he was by the couple. But then she placed her hand calmly and deliberately on the seat between them, with the fingers neatly arranged as though she meant him to place his own hand over them.

Before he had time to consider whether Denise was actually inviting him to hold her hand and whether he ought to take it so early in the evening, there was trouble in his jock strap. His member was straining against its bonds and arching itself into a shape like a banana. He clasped Denise's hand quickly to distract her attention.

He held Denise's hand all through both films. He avoided giving it any unusual signs of affection such as squeezing it or stroking it, and he was glad to find that it lay quietly under his the whole time. Some time after interval his penis seemed to concede defeat and lie down peacefully.

As the film ended Adrian was looking forward to talking with Denise on the bus and in her dining room. He was half-way to the bus stop before he realised he had underestimated the enemy in his jock strap. While he had been watching the second film it had eased itself into a new position. (He might even have helped it unwittingly when he shifted his legs around.) Now it was pointing ever so slightly upwards and stretching just enough to keep itself there. Whenever it chose—in the bus, or in McNamaras' lounge-room in front of Denise's parents, or more likely on the front veranda when he tried to kiss her goodnight, it could draw itself up to its full height and stand out like a broomstick against the front of his trousers and make a mockery of his courtship.

Adrian stood for a minute in the middle of his darkened bedroom. He took a few steps forward and then reached down once more to check what was happening beneath his pyjamas. His enemy had consolidated its position still further.

Adrian realised he could never escape from the danger of mortal sin. He would always be at the mercy of his own penis. He took off his jock strap and hid it in his wardrobe. Then he put on his pyjamas and climbed into bed.

There was just one more thing to do before he went to sleep. He walked up the path to McNamaras' house and knocked on the front door. Denise herself opened it. She was not his wife or his fiancée or even the young woman he had twice taken to the pictures. She was a sixteen-year-old schoolgirl in the tunic and blouse and jacket of the Academy of Mount Carmel.

She hesitated to ask him inside because her parents were both out and she was alone in the house. He stepped past her and strode into the lounge-room. She closed the front door and stood in front of him. She had never looked more beautiful and pathetic. She said something like, 'I always thought it would end like this,' or 'It was impossible from the start.' But he was not really listening.

He gripped both her wrists with one hand. With his free hand he tore at her clothing. Something, perhaps the memory of all she had once meant to him, made him hesitate to undress her completely. He simply exposed the charms that he would never enjoy and stared at them for a long, solemn moment. Then he released her.

She stumbled backwards and fell among the cushions on the couch. She lay there, fumbling with her clothes to cover herself. The last thing Adrian saw before he turned and walked out of the house forever was the emblem on the pocket of her jacket, the snowcapped holy mountain of Carmel with a circle of stars above it, falling back into place over her naked left breast.

After his jock strap had let him down, Adrian still caught his usual Coroke train, but he got into the rear carriage, well away from the Mount Carmel girl's carriage and he only travelled as far as Caulfield. He was training every night at the racecourse for the House Sports. He wore his new jock strap whenever he trained, and found it improved his running.

One morning instead of the usual Christian Doctrine period, Adrian's class had a priest to speak to them.

The priest was a stranger. He put his hands in his pockets, leaned back against the brother's desk and said, 'My name is Father Kevin Parris and my job is to visit secondary schools to give advice to any young chaps like yourselves who want to find out about the work of the secular priest.

'You all know the difference of course between a secular priest like myself and a religious priest—a member of a religious order—who takes a vow of obedience to the head of his order. I think it's fair to say that the secular priests are the backbone of the Church. Not even the most ancient of the religious orders can trace its history back as far as we can. The first priests that Christ ordained were secular priests. I'm talking of course about the Apostles—the very first Catholic clergy. And the work that Christ sent them out to do is the same work that the secular priests of the Melbourne Archdiocese are doing today.

'You boys know without being told what that work is. Maybe a few of you live in parishes that have been entrusted to some order or other, but the great majority of you were baptised by a secular priest, you made your first confession to a secular priest, and you received your first communion from a secular priest. Those of you who marry in later life will probably receive that sacrament in the presence of a secular priest. And when you come to die, please God you'll receive the last sacrament from one of us too.

'Of course there's a thousand and one other tasks we perform as well. You might compare us to the rucks and rovers in a football team. We have a roving commission to go wherever we're needed and do the heavy work. And boys, just like any other football team, the priests of your Archdiocese need a steady stream of recruits.

'You might be interested in a few facts and figures about vocations to the priesthood here in Melbourne. I was ordained myself in 1944—that's ten years ago now. At the ceremony in St Pat's Cathedral there were seventeen of us ordained for this Archdiocese. Now in those days, seventeen new priests were barely enough to meet the demands of the Archdiocese. I remember the Archbishop telling us all that we were only going to fill the gaps left by deaths and serious illness among the priests of Melbourne.

'Well, that was 1944. Now I don't have to tell you how Melbourne has grown in the last few years. Think of all the new suburbs stretching for miles out towards Frankston and Coroke and Dandenong where there were only farms and market gardens a few years back. And all those suburbs need Catholic churches and schools for the families growing up there. Then think of the thousands of New Australians who've come to this country since the war—most of them from Catholic countries. All these people need priests to serve them.

'And what do we find? This year, 1954, we had twenty-three ordinations. That's just six more than in 1944. You can see we're not really keeping up with the demand for priests. It's been calculated that we need a minimum of fifty to sixty ordinations each year until 1960 just to properly staff the parishes we've already got and keep some of our overworked priests from cracking up under the strain. Our team is up against it. We've got our nineteenth and twentieth men on the field and we're fighting overwhelming odds. The coach is crying out for new recruits. And this brings me to the point of my little talk to you.

'Theologians tell us that God always provides enough vocations for the needs of His Church in every age. In others words, this year all over Melbourne God has planted the seeds of a vocation in the hearts of enough young men to meet the needs of our Arch-diocese. But God only calls—He never compels. So if we find next year an insufficient number of candidates entering our seminary, we can only conclude that a great many young men have deliberately turned their backs on a call from God.

'And now I'm going to speak bluntly. Bearing in mind the needs of our Archdiocese at present, I would say that each of the major Catholic colleges (and this

272

includes St Carthage's of course), that each of them should have at least ten boys in the matriculation class this year who've been called by God to be priests in the Archdiocese of Melbourne. Next year most of you chaps will be in matric and the same will apply to you. Which means there could well be ten of you listening to me now who've already been called, or will soon be called by God, to serve Him as priests.

'To have a vocation to the priesthood, a boy needs three things—good health, the right level of intelligence, and the right intention. Good health means an average constitution strong enough to stand up to a lifetime of hard work—you all look to me as if you've got that. As for intelligence, any boy who can pass the matric exam (including a pass in Latin) will have the intelligence to cope with the studies for the priesthood. Health and intelligence are fairly easy to judge. The third sign of a vocation is the one you have to be really sure of.

'A boy who has a right intention will first of all be of good moral character. Now this doesn't mean he has to be a saint or a goody-goody. He'll be a good average Catholic boy who's keen on football and sport and works hard at his studies and doesn't join in smutty conversations. Of course he'll have temptations like we all do. But he'll have learnt how to beat them with the help of prayer and the sacraments. And as for the right intention, well, it could be the desire to win souls for God—to give up your whole life to do His work.

'An example of a wrong intention would be, for instance, to want to be a priest as a way of advancing yourself in the eyes of the world. But thank God in these days it's very rare for anyone to offer himself for the priesthood for reasons like that.

'And that's really all there is to it. If you have good health, the right level of intelligence, and a right intention, you've almost certainly got a vocation to the priesthood. The trouble is, too many young fellows think they have to get a special sign from heaven. They expect an angel to tap them on the shoulder and say, "Come on, son, God wants you for a priest!" Or perhaps they think they'll have a vision some morning after mass, and see Our Lord or Our Lady herself beckoning to them. Nonsense! All the priests I know have been thoroughly normal young chaps like yourselves who realised one day that they had all the signs of a vocation. Then they prayed and thought about it and talked it over with a priest and that was that.

'Sometimes a fellow can realise he's got a vocation in funny ways. One of our outstanding young priests always maintains he got his vocation at a dance. It seems he was standing in a corner watching all the happy young people enjoying themselves around him when he suddenly realised that all this was not for him. God was calling him all right, and compared with the life of a priest, all the pleasures of the world seemed worthless.

'Some men say they knew from the time they were small boys that they had a vocation. Others never realise it until they're grown men—sometimes years after they've left school. The idea that God is calling you can grow on you slowly or it can hit you like a flash of lightning. There may be someone in this room right now who has never before asked himself this simple question, "Is God calling me to be a priest in the Archdiocese of Melbourne?" If any one of you is in this position, it might be a good time now when you're approaching your last year of school, and wondering what you're going to do with your life—it's a good time to ask yourself seriously and honestly, "Is God calling me?"

'Boys, would you each take a pencil and a piece of paper and write down something for me. For the sake of privacy I must ask you all to write something. If you can say in all honesty that you definitely don't have a vocation to the priesthood, just write "God bless you, Father," or something like that on your paper and don't put your name. If you're at all interested in the priesthood, just sign your name and write the word "Interested".

'Those who are interested can have a chat with me in the brothers' front parlour some time today. I'm not a salesman, remember. No priest would ever dare to put pressure on a boy in such a serious business as this. If you care to have a chat with me I'll arrange to send you some literature and leave you my phone number if you want any further advice from time to time.

'Now would every boy write on his paper and fold it up small and pass it to the front, please.'

Adrian wrote, 'Definitely interested—Adrian Sherd'. He folded his paper and passed it forward. Then he sat back and told himself he had just taken the most dramatic step of his life. But then he remembered you couldn't make a decision as important as this without a lot of prayer and thought. Yet the young man at the dance had decided in a flash that he would give it all up. (Some of the girls in their ballerina frocks would have been almost as beautiful as Denise McNamara.) And now that man was an outstanding young priest and the girls were all happily married to other chaps.

Soon after lunch a message came for a certain boy to see Father Parris in the brothers' parlour. The whole class watched him get up from his seat and go. They were not surprised—he was quiet and solemn and he objected to hearing dirty jokes.

Adrian waited for his turn to visit the priest. He was worried about Seskis and Cornthwaite and O'Mullane seeing him leave the class. He saw them putting up their hands and saying, 'Please, Brother, Sherd can't talk to the vocations priest—last year in Form Four he committed nearly two hundred mortal sins.'

Father Sherd stepped up to the pulpit to begin his first sermon in his new parish. He saw the three of them grinning up at him from the back seats. They were ready to heckle him with shouts of 'What about Jayne and Marilyn?' They had already sent an anonymous letter about him to the Archbishop.

But God would keep their lips sealed. He would never allow one of His own priests to be reproached in public for sins that had been forgiven years before. And how could Seskis and the others speak out without revealing their own guilty secrets?

When it was Adrian's turn to leave the classroom, he stood up boldly and strode to the door and silently offered up his embarrassment as an act of reparation to God for the sins of his past life.

Adrian said to the priest, 'My story is probably unusual, Father. When I was at primary school I served as an altar boy for years and developed a great love for the mass and the sacraments and often wondered whether I might have a vocation to the priesthood. But I'm sorry to say a few years ago I fell among bad companions and had a bit of trouble with sins of impurity—not with girls, fortunately, but on my own—mostly thoughts, but sometimes, I'm sorry to say, impure actions.

'Luckily I never gave up trying to fight against these sins and I'm happy to say that now for a long time I've led a normal life in the state of grace. I've thought a lot lately about the life of a priest, and I'll certainly be praying about it before it's time to make up my mind next year about entering the seminary. But I sometimes wonder if my past sins would mean that I couldn't possibly have a vocation.'

Adrian was surprised at how calmly the priest heard him out. Father Parris said, 'Take my advice and forget all about whatever you might have done years ago. You know your sins have all been forgiven in the sacrament of penance. What counts now is the sort of fellow you are now. Keep on praying to God and Our Lady and you'll soon find out what's expected of you.

'Now, let's have your name and address and I'll send you a booklet about the life our young fellows lead in the diocesan seminary. Have a good look at it and just go on quietly with your studies and have a chat to your parish priest from time to time. And next year, if you're still interested, we can talk about your applying to enter the seminary.'

The priest looked at his watch and consulted a list of names in front of him. He said, 'Now would you ask John Toohey to see me when you get back to your room?'

When Adrian left school that afternoon he knew he could catch Denise McNamara's train if he strolled down Swindon Road to the station. But he walked into the Swindon church and knelt in one of the back seats.

He saw how the last few troubled years of his life were really part of a wonderful pattern that could only have been worked out by God Himself.

First came the year of his American nonsense—it

revolted him now, but its purpose had been to show him that sinners were never happy. Then came Denise's year. God had arranged for him to meet Denise because at that time the influence of a pure young woman was the only thing that could have rescued him. Now, Denise had served her purpose. The terrible scene in her lounge-room only a few nights before had proved that she no longer had the power to keep his lust in check. It was God's way of warning him not to rely on a mere woman to save his soul.

Now, after a year without sin, Adrian was the equal of those average Catholic boys of good moral character that the priest had talked about. The next part of the pattern was becoming clear. He was almost certain he had a vocation to the priesthood. Like the young man on the dance floor he had sampled the joys of mixing with the opposite sex and found them shallow and unsatisfying.

He still had a year to wait before he could enter the seminary. He would devise a scheme of meditations on his future as a priest to sustain him through his year of waiting.

Adrian knelt and prayed until he knew he had missed Denise's train. Then he left the church and hurried to the station. He decided to visit the church each afternoon until the end of the year to spare himself and Denise the embarrassment of meeting again after it was all over between them. She would be puzzled for a while, but a girl so beautiful would soon attract other admirers. And one day, eight years later, she would open the *Advocate* and see pages of pictures of the newly ordained priests and realise what had been on his mind when he stopped seeing her on the Coroke train years before, and forgive him.

In the last weeks of the school year Adrian had to spend most of his time preparing for his Leaving Certificate exams. But every night before he began his studies he allowed himself to consider his future as a priest.

A booklet called *The Priest* came in the post to Adrian from Father Parris. It was made up of articles written by young priests of the Melbourne Archdiocese. Adrian was especially interested in the articles describing life at the diocesan seminary. This was the life he himself would lead for seven years after he had left school.

The seminary was surrounded by quiet farmland a few miles beyond the western suburbs of Melbourne. The students were safe from all the distractions of the city. Instead of reading about the Cold War and the bodgie gangs in the *Argus*, they got up before six each morning and went to mass. They had hours of lectures each day. They called their teachers 'professors'. It was like a university except that the seminary courses were longer and harder. And instead of the descriptive sciences such as physics and chemistry, the seminarians studied the Queen of Sciences—theology. Adrian wondered how he could wait a whole year before he threw himself into the life of the seminary.

Several articles in the booklet were written by young priests describing their experiences in their first parishes. They could hardly express in words the joy and excitement of their first masses and the satisfaction they got from preaching sermons and administering the sacraments.

Father Sherd stepped into the pulpit. He kept his voice deceptively mild while he introduced himself. His congregation edged forward in their seats and hoped their new curate would not be overcome by nervousness during his first sermon. Then he let them have it.

He was sorry to have to speak so sternly on the occasion of his first sermon, but they were lax. While the Catholics of Russia and China were risking their lives to practise their religion, the Faith was growing steadily weaker in the suburbs of Melbourne. Too many of that very congregation were neglecting the sacraments. They sat back in their seats at communion time each Sunday, unable to visit the altar rails because their souls were marked by sin.

He delivered a short sharp attack against the more common sins. He went through the Commandments in order. He tried not to place too much emphasis on the Sixth and Ninth, but he knew from a certain tension among his listeners that impurity was their weakness.

He ended by stressing the value of confession. He was ready, he said, to wear himself out in the confessional if the lukewarm of the parish would only come regularly to have their sins forgiven. He hoped to see double the usual crowds at confession next Saturday.

On the following Saturday Father Sherd settled himself in the dark confessional. A fellow confessed impure thoughts about the young women he worked with and occasional impure actions by himself. Father Sherd advised him to keep his eyes on his own desk at work and to take up a hobby to occupy himself in his spare time at home.

The fellow said, 'What hobby did *you* take up to cure yourself of the habit, Sherd?' It was O'Mullane grinning through the grille of the confessional.

What could the young priest do? Make O'Mullane confess the additional sin of sacrilege for showing such disrespect to a priest? Tell him the true story of how a good Catholic girl had once rescued Sherd from impurity, and then bind O'Mullane under pain of mortal sin never to mention it outside the confessional? The best course was probably to slam the wooden screen in O'Mullane's face and turn to the penitent on the other side, and later that evening apply to the Archbishop of Melbourne for a transfer on urgent compassionate grounds to some obscure parish far from Swindon and Accrington and anyone who might have known him as a misguided young man.

The Archbishop was reasonable. He did not ask what were the 'circumstances of a very personal nature' that Father Sherd referred to in his application. Sherd was sent to a distant outer suburb where the parishioners were nearly all young marrieds.

His first sermon in his new church was on the sacrament of matrimony. He knew he was peculiarly well qualified to extol the blessings of a pure Catholic marriage after his affair with Denise McNamara before he entered the seminary. He preached so frankly about the spiritual and moral problems of the bedroom that many of the upturned faces registered amazement at a celibate priest's knowing such things.

On the following Saturday at confession a young wife murmured to him that her husband was making excessive and unreasonable demands on her body and offering as his only excuse that he could not resist her charms. Through a narrow gap in the fingers that he held to his brow, Sherd saw that it was Her. Denise was a young matron, still radiantly beautiful, and troubled by the worst possible affliction that could befall a Catholic wife.

The young confessor was in difficulties again. It was his moral duty to support the oppressed wife, to provide her with arguments that would dissuade her husband when he was too ardent. But how could he, Sherd, blame any man for losing his head over Denise—least of all the poor wretch who had to watch her for hours each night moving about the kitchen in her negligee, who saw the cluster of jars and tubes of her intimate toiletries every time he opened the bathroom cupboard, and who passed a few feet from her unmentionables, filled to roundness by the wind, on Monday's clothes line?

Father Sherd petitioned the Archbishop for a second transfer and was appointed to the Cathedral itself, to an administrative position. There, in a quiet ivy-covered building in the shadow of the great spire of Saint Patrick's, he was at the spiritual nerve-centre of Melbourne.

In carpeted conference rooms behind locked doors he sat with a select group and saw the Archbishop rapping his cane against wall diagrams showing the financial health of the Archdiocese. (Within the boundaries of each parish a bar graph in vivid red stood for the School Building Fund overdraft. Some graphs in the outer suburbs towered like church spires themselves. Others in older parishes were a more respectable size.) He was present when charts were unrolled showing the comparative strength of the Faith in hundreds of parishes. (The usual indicator was the number of communion breads consecrated each week—expressed as a percentage of the population of the parish.)

Weeks before the end of the football season he knew the likely premiers in the A Grade Young Catholic Worker competition. He saw in writing the actual value (calculated for insurance purposes) of all the chalices and sacred vessels and furnishings and devotional bric-a-brac in the Cathedral. He was among the first to know when a lady in Sandringham claimed to have been favoured with a series of visions of Our Lady, or when two non-Catholic doctors in Essendon testified that they could find no natural explanation for the disappearance of a man's tumor and the man himself swore he had been cured by the miraculous intervention of a saint.

It was no surprise when Father Sherd was appointed private Chaplain to the Archbishop himself. The Chaplain's duties included the hearing of His Grace's weekly confession. But Sherd soon grew used to keeping a straight face no matter what secrets were poured into his ear.

And even on the night when the Archbishop confessed the news of his elevation to the College of Cardinals, Father Sherd's first words were to warn him that a Cardinal's hat would not fit onto a swelled head.

In the fullness of time when word reached Melbourne that Pope Pius the Twelfth had gone at last to meet his Maker, Father Sherd went quietly to his room and began to pack his suitcase. Of course the Cardinal-Archbishop of Melbourne would be taking his Chaplain to Rome for the election.

In the Holy City Sherd stayed quietly in the background while the movie cameras whirred and the journalists shouted their absurd questions. But in his apartment in the wings of a Renaissance Palace, on the night before the College of Cardinals was immured, he did not shrink from his task.

His Grace drew up a chair beside him. (They had come to dispense with formalities during confessions.)

'Father, as my Chaplain you should know that the European and American votes are equally divided between three candidates. Australia and the missionary countries will almost certainly tip the scales. It's a terrible responsibility.'

Sherd kept all trace of human curiosity from his voice. 'And who are the favourites, so to speak?'

The Archbishop sounded old and tired. 'Dell 'Ollio of Ferrara, Ruggieri of Padua and Basile, the local chap. I can't separate them.' His voice quavered. 'Help me, Father.'

Sherd looked pointedly away until the Archbishop had composed himself. Then he asked calmly, 'What do they have to recommend them?'

So His Grace outlined their careers, their stated policies, their reputations for sanctity, all the while waiting for some hint from his confessor in a matter that would affect the future of Christendom.

Sherd was in no hurry to offer any decision. He closed his eyes and thought of Melbourne far away. It was nearly midnight—Eastern Standard Time. Darkness lay all over the great sprawling suburbs from the idly slapping waves of Port Phillip Bay to the moist leafy hillsides of the Dandenong Ranges. But under the night sky with its fiercely blazing Southern Cross, the city was not at peace.

In thousands of back bedrooms and sleepouts and detached bungalows, young Catholic men lay in the age-old posture of the solitary sinner—resting easily on the left side; the right hand free for its frictional work and the left hand poised with a crumpled handkerchief at the ready. Elsewhere in the same suburbs, their chaste white bodies enclosed in voluminous nightgowns or fleecy pyjamas, were the young Catholic women who could have inspired the passionate young men to reform their wasted lives if only they had met and understood each other.

And Melbourne was not the Masturbation Capital of the World, as Adrian Sherd had once imagined. It was likely that the same problem occurred in every civilised country on earth. The Catholic clergy should have been more aware of it. Not only parish priests but bishops and the most eminent theologians should have been devising a policy for bringing together the wretched self-abusers and the girls who might have saved them. The sheer number of mortal sins committed each day by those desperate young men was sufficient justification for His Holiness himself to issue some instruction in the matter.

And there slumped at Sherd's side and waiting for his advice, was the Cardinal who might have the casting vote for the election of the new pope. It was within Sherd's power to ensure that the next supreme pontiff was the man with the best plan for relieving the torment of thousands of Catholic boys all over the world.

But all this was mere dreaming. It was surely absurd to expect a candidate for the papacy, the highest office on earth, to announce to the College of Cardinals that he was seeking election on a policy of abolishing masturbation.

Adrian Sherd knew he had to be realistic about his future. It would be all too easy to dream of the priesthood just as he had once dreamed of a sex life in America or a married life near Hepburn Springs. As a young man with a religious vocation he should have drawn a lesson from his unhappy past. He had spent too much time in unreal conjectures, in devising whole years of a future that would never eventuate. On his visits to America he had wasted the better part of his adult years pursuing carnal pleasure. His projected marriage to Denise had brought him to the threshold of middle age. His dreams had spanned a lifetime. He had spent a lifetime on clouds. Now was the time to think of his real future.

Father Sherd was a humble parish priest. On a typical Saturday night he drew back the screen and shifted wearily to hear the next confession. It was a young man's voice. 'Bless me, Father, for I have sinned.

It is one month since my last confession and I accuse myself of committing a sin of impurity by myself nineteen times. This is all I can remember, Father, and I am very sorry for all my sins.'

Sherd first praised the poor fellow for making a clean breast of such a total. (From memory, he himself had never confessed more than a dozen at one go.) Then he gave his usual advice.

'Son, as soon as you can, find a good Catholic girl and make her the object of your dreams. And when you're tempted to commit this disgusting sin, ask yourself what she would think if she could see you.'

Father Sherd handed down a moderately severe penance and absolved the young fellow. Then he shifted in his seat for perhaps the hundredth time that evening and pulled back the screen on his other side.

'Bless me, Father...' It was a girl, a young woman almost. And in a convent uniform. Father Sherd could not quite distinguish the emblem on her breast pocket—it might have been a flaming torch, the entwined letters B.V.M. or even the sacred mountain peak of Carmel. Her voice was soft and earnest.

'Father, I haven't come to confess anything tonight. I just want your advice. For a few weeks now, I've noticed this fellow staring at me on the afternoon train. I'm sure he wants to talk to me or ask me to go out with him or something. He wears the uniform of a Catholic college, but he has a rather odd look in his eyes.'

Sherd answered her without hesitating. 'Don't do anything to encourage the fellow. Sit modestly and keep your eyes on the book you're reading. If he happens to meet your eye, just lower your gaze or look out of the window. He won't get much encouragement from staring at your profile. I'm not saying there's any harm in the fellow, but there's no reason to sell yourself cheaply to the first young hobbledehoy who ogles you on a train.'

When confessions were finished, Father Sherd walked slowly along the path towards the presbytery. He looked up at the heavens. The glow from the city lights obscured the stars across much of the sky. It was Saturday night and thousands of young people were out enjoying themselves. He thought of the two he had tried to advise in confession. He trusted they would sleep a little more peacefully that night and not be troubled by impossible dreams.

Text Classics

textclassics.com.au

The Scarecrow
Ronald Hugh Morrieson
introduced by Craig Sherborne

The Dig Tree
Sarah Murgatroyd
introduced by Geoffrey Blainey

A Lifetime on Clouds
Gerald Murnane
introduced by Andy Griffiths

The Plains
Gerald Murnane
introduced by Wayne Macauley

The Odd Angry Shot
William Nagle
introduced by Paul Ham

Life and Adventures 1776–1801
John Nicol
introduced by Tim Flannery

Death in Brunswick
Boyd Oxlade
introduced by Shane Maloney

Swords and Crowns and Rings
Ruth Park
introduced by Alice Pung

The Watcher in the Garden
Joan Phipson
introduced by Margo Lanagan

Maurice Guest
Henry Handel Richardson
introduced by Carmen Callil

The Getting of Wisdom
Henry Handel Richardson
introduced by Germaine Greer

The Fortunes of Richard Mahony
Henry Handel Richardson
introduced by Peter Craven

Rose Boys
Peter Rose
introduced by Brian Matthews

Hills End
Ivan Southall
introduced by Jacqueline Harvey Malouse

Ash Road
Ivan Southall
introduced by Maurice Saxby

Lillipilly Hill
Eleanor Spence
introduced by Ursula Dubosarsky

The Women in Black
Madeleine St John
introduced by Bruce Beresford

The Essence of the Thing
Madeleine St John
introduced by Helen Trinca

Jonah
Louis Stone
introduced by Frank Moorhouse

An Iron Rose
Peter Temple
introduced by Les Carlyon

1788
Watkin Tench
introduced by Tim Flannery

The House that Was Eureka
Nadia Wheatley
introduced by Toni Jordan

Happy Valley
Patrick White
introduced by Peter Craven

I Own the Racecourse!
Patricia Wrightson
introduced by Kate Constable

textclassics.com.au